The Long Road Home

Home to Collingsworth
Book 4

by

Kimberly Rae Jordan

THREESTRAND
PRESS
A CORD OF THREE STRANDS IS NOT EASILY BROKEN.

A man, a woman & their God.
Three Strand Press publishes Christian Romance stories that intertwine love, faith and family.
Always clean. Always heartwarming. Always uplifting.

This is a work of fiction. The situations, characters, names, and places are products of the author's imagination, or are used fictitiously. Any resemblance to locales, events, actual persons (living or dead) is entirely coincidental.

Chapter One

CAMILLA Collingsworth propped her feet up on the end of the wooden picnic table and wiggled her freshly-painted toes. She recapped the nail polish bottle, dropped it into the grass, and then picked up her drink from the cup-holder of the lawn chair she sat in. Swirling the liquid so the ice cubes clinked the edge of the glass, she wished it held more than just lemonade.

She took a sip and grimaced. Lemonade. Iced tea. Soda. Water. That's all they drank around here. It had been almost a month, and she was dying for something with a little more kick. Hard lemonade, Long Island iced tea, or even soda with a shot of rum would do. Of course, the hard stuff straight up would be fine, too. Anything to ease the boredom and give her a break from the barrage of memories she couldn't escape. These had been the longest three weeks of her life.

Reclining more into the chair, Cami listened to the sounds of nature and realized that she missed the hum of engines and blare of horns that made up the backdrop of her New York City life. One more week—just one—then she could get her money and kiss this place goodbye. For good. It was bad enough that the big hulking monstrosity to her left, otherwise known as Collingsworth Manor, held no good memories, but she'd had to endure watching three of her sisters find love, happiness, and purpose in their lives while she still struggled to find a good reason to get up each day.

She straightened a little when someone emerged from the front corner of the manor. Lifting a hand to shade her eyes, Cami smiled as she recognized the lanky figure. He wore his usual attire of faded blue jeans, heavy work boots and a T-shirt. His curly, light brown hair fringed the edge of the ball cap he always wore. It was a mystery to her why the guy intrigued her, but there was no denying that he did.

"Hey, Josh!" she called as the tall man took long strides toward his trailer.

Josh Moyer paused and waved. "Hello, Cami." But then he continued on without any further conversation.

That was nothing new, but it still rankled Cami to no end. She had never met a man so immune to her charms. Married or not, most men responded on a verbal level at the very least. She never crossed the line with the married ones—she did have *some* standards—but Josh didn't even bat an eye at her flirtatious remarks. And she was willing to bet half her inheritance it had nothing to do with the ring on his finger. That would almost have made it more acceptable. She didn't know exactly what the ring represented, but it wasn't a marriage. She'd bet the other half of her inheritance on that.

He and his cousin, Lance had been at the manor for three straight weeks. If there was a wife in the picture, there would have been some sign of her by now. A man his age, at the very least, would have booked a room at a local hotel for some conjugal time. But no woman had showed up to claim him, and it seemed he wasn't making trips to see anyone either. She'd find it easier to believe the ring was for a purity pledge or that he'd taken a vow of celibacy. But a wife? No way.

It didn't really matter. Only one week remained of the wretched deal Gran had cooked up, and then she would be free. Free to be Cameron Collins instead of Camilla

Collingsworth. Free to continue her pursuit of a music career. Free of a family who looked at her with judgment and condemnation in their eyes. It couldn't come soon enough.

The rumble of an engine drew her gaze to the gap between the manor and the garage. She recognized the SUV as Dean's, which meant that Laurel and Violet were back from visiting their mother. With a frown, she watched as the two women and their significant others climbed from the vehicle and headed her way. Matt slipped his arm around Laurel's waist, while Dean and Violet held hands as they walked to where she sat.

The streak of jealousy caught her off-guard...and made no sense. She didn't want to be tied to a man or, worse yet, this place. Why would she be jealous of them?

"So how was dear old Mom?" Cami asked as they joined her at the picnic table. Though she and her oldest sister, Jessa, didn't agree on much, they did share a reluctance to visit the woman who had given birth to—but then abandoned—them.

"Cami," Violet said, her brows drawn together. "Don't talk like that."

Cami took another sip of her drink. "Okay, fine. How is our mother doing today?"

"The same as our last visit," Laurel said with a sigh as she settled on the bench of the picnic table. "From what everyone says, they don't expect any significant changes in her condition."

She knew this was not the outcome Violet had hoped for when she'd begun her search for Elizabeth Collingsworth. But life wasn't life without a few disappointments. That was one lesson Cami had learned early on.

"So, she doesn't know you're there?" Cami asked.

"I think she knows we're there," Violet replied. "It's just that she doesn't know who *we* are. And there is no explaining, because the beating apparently caused severe head trauma and memory problems, both short- and long-term."

"Hey, Josh," Matt said.

Cami glanced away from Violet and saw that the man who had so recently occupied her thoughts had joined them.

He lifted the ball cap from his head and ran a hand through his light brown curls before replacing it. His dark blue gaze went to Violet. "How did your visit go?"

"I was just telling Cami that Mama doesn't know who we are and likely never will."

"I'm sorry to hear that," Josh said, his expression sympathetic. "I'll continue to pray for you as you spend time with her."

Pray? Of all the useless things, Cami thought, but knew enough to keep that opinion to herself. She went to church each Sunday with the family because they expected her to, and it was only an hour of her time that served to prevent more conflict. But praying was something she didn't waste time on. How often had she prayed and had her prayers answered? Never.

She looked at Josh as he continued to converse with the group and wondered if he really believed that stuff the way the others did. And what in the world made him so serious? The man rarely smiled. Not that he appeared angry. Just...serious. Cami hated to admit that he intrigued her like no man had before, and it was more than him not responding to her flirting. There was just *something* different about him.

"Where is Jessa?" Violet asked.

Cami grinned. "Probably down by the lake making out with Lance."

"Cami." This time it was Laurel speaking in a warning tone.

"Oh, come on. You expect me to believe that you guys don't have a little fun?" Cami jerked her feet from the table and straightened in her seat.

"Well, we do," Matt said, a teasing lilt to his voice as he winked at Laurel. "But we have the piece of paper that says we're allowed to."

Cami sighed. "Fine. They had a bit of a discussion about something to do with the renovations, and the next thing I know they were heading toward the lake. So they either wanted to fight or make up in private."

Laurel looked at Josh. "Problems?"

He shook his head. "Not really; just a slight difference of opinion on the type of tub that should go in a couple of the bathrooms." Surprisingly, a small smile lifted the corners of his mouth. "I think Jessa won."

"Jessa is going to win every difference of opinion," Cami said. "Lance seems willing to do just about anything for her."

"And so he should," Violet commented with a grin. "They've got a lot of time to make up."

Not wanting to get into a sappy love fest, Cami asked, "What's on the menu for supper?"

"I think Lance said he'd barbeque," Matt replied.

Josh nodded. "He and Jessa went in to town earlier and bought food."

"Lily is picking up Rose, so they'll be home soon," Laurel said. "And I think Will planned to be back from Sylvia's for supper, as well."

"Looks like they've settled whatever they needed to," Matt commented with a nod in the direction of the lake.

Cami turned and saw Lance and Jessa walking across the large backyard. They had their arms around each other, so obviously Matt was right. Cami sighed. Being around all this lovey-dovey stuff was starting to wear on her.

One more week. One more week. It had become her mantra.

As the others talked, Cami tried to come up with a way to get to town later. She figured her best bet would be Lily. Though the younger girl couldn't go into a bar because she was still under-age, she would probably be willing to drive her. And getting a ride back to the manor shouldn't be too much trouble.

Cami watched Josh as he stood talking to Lance. The cousins, aside from build and attire, couldn't look more different. Lance appeared to be about an inch or so taller than his cousin, but they both had muscled builds that seemed to be more from the work they did than visiting a gym. Lance's hair was dark and cut short while Josh's lighter curls touched the collar of his shirt. Oh, and that dratted ring. And, by the look of things, it wouldn't be long until Lance was sporting one himself.

She didn't know why the ring on Josh's hand bothered her so much. It wasn't like she was looking for any kind of relationship at the moment. Particularly with someone who lived in or around Collingsworth. It was just a mystery, and with nothing else to do in this quiet hick town, it gave her something to think about. She had one more week to get to the bottom of that mystery, and she planned to have it figured out before she shook the dust of Collingsworth from her feet.

After helping Lance with the meat, Josh Moyer sat down at the table inside the trailer they shared and let out a sigh. He twisted the ring on his finger as he stared out the window to the trees that brushed against the back side of the trailer, which had become his temporary home for the duration of the renovations at Collingsworth Manor.

Lance slid into the booth across from him. "What's up, bro?"

Drawing his gaze from the window, Josh looked down at his hands and then slowly pulled the ring from his finger. He put it down in the middle of the table and looked up to find

Lance watching him, his dark gaze intent.

His cousin's eyebrows raised a fraction. "What's going on?"

Josh took a deep breath. "I always told myself that when I started to feel an attraction to a woman, I'd take it off. It's disrespectful to Emma to continue to wear it when my thoughts have moved in another direction, even if it's not serious."

"Please," Lance said. "Please don't tell me it's Cami."

"It's a couple of different things. Part of it is her, yes. But it's also Matt and Laurel. Dean and Violet." He smiled at Lance. "You and Jessa. As I've seen you guys fall in love, I find myself at a place I never thought I'd be. Wanting to move forward."

Lance scowled. "And you want to do that with Cami?"

"No. I will admit she's hard to ignore and stirs things in me that I haven't felt in a long time, but I know there's no future there. Faith issue aside, I'm pretty sure she doesn't really want anything to do with me. I think she sees me as a challenge. But just the fact that seeing you guys together is making me think about a relationship tells me maybe it's time to seriously consider moving forward."

"Well, I'm happy to hear that. I can tell you from recent experience that finding the right person is amazing. I will certainly join you in praying for that woman to come your way."

"Thank you." Josh was surprised by how right it felt to remove the thin gold band. He'd worn it since he was nineteen, but it was time to move on. Emma was part of a tragic past and, while he wished it had ended differently for them, he was fairly certain that had she lived, divorce would have followed shortly after all that had transpired around that time.

Josh hoped God would bless him with a relationship like Lance had with Jessa, although he still wondered if he was worthy of such love. He'd failed miserably once already. Perhaps God wouldn't want to give him a second chance at something so precious, even if it was something he now wanted.

Cami managed to corner Lily shortly after she got back with Rose.

"Are you going in to town tonight?"

Lily nodded. "I'm going to see a movie with Nate."

"Can I hitch a ride?"

Lily's eyes widened briefly. "Where to?"

Cami debated lying, but she knew her sister would guess where she was going anyway. "To the bar."

Lily frowned. "Jessa and Violet won't like that."

Trying to rein in her irritation, Cami asked, "How old am I?"

"Twenty-five."

"Exactly. Last time I checked that meant I was an adult. I know Jessa and Violet won't like it, but I've been stuck out here since the day I arrived. Frankly, I need a break. You must understand that."

Lily hesitated and then nodded. "Okay. I'm heading out around eight. We're catching the late show."

"Perfect. I'll be ready then."

Having figured out her plan, Cami felt more energized than she had since arriving at the manor. Anticipation of what the evening might hold distracted her throughout the meal, and most of the conversation didn't even register. She helped clean up afterwards and then slipped into the trailer with Lily to get ready. The others stayed outside visiting, which suited Cami just fine.

When they stepped out of the trailer to leave, Cami felt all eyes on her and Lily. She had chosen a more demure outfit of skinny white jeans and a black sleeveless button-up top that she'd knotted at her waist. Of course, her definition of demure and that of her sisters was a bit different.

"Where are you going?" Jessa asked, shielding her eyes with one hand as she looked up at them.

Lily glanced at Cami and then said, "Heading to town for a movie."

Jessa picked her phone up and looked at the display. "This late?"

"The late show starts at 8:45."

"Don't be too late. We have church in the morning," Jessa reminded them.

With nods, they left the group and headed for the driveway.

"Thanks," Cami said once they were out of earshot.

"Just don't get into trouble or Jessa will never let me drive the car again," Lily cautioned as she opened her door and slid behind the wheel.

"I won't."

When Cami stepped into the darkened interior of the bar a few short minutes later, she felt immediately at ease. This was her world. Now, if she could just make a deal with someone to get some free drinks.

Josh heard the sound of an emotional exchange going on outside the trailer. He left his computer and opened the door to see what had happened. The globe-shaped patio lights that Lance had strung up gave off enough illumination that he could see the group standing together around the slender figure of the youngest Collingsworth.

"What do you mean she's still in town, Lily?" Jessa demanded.

"I'm sorry, Jessa," Lily said, her voice tight. "I thought she was coming home with me after I dropped her off."

"Dropped her off where?" Agitation was clear in the oldest Collingsworth sister's voice. "Where is she?"

"At the bar. I dropped her off there before we went to the movie. When we went back to pick her up, she wasn't waiting. Nate went in since I couldn't, and she told him to go home."

"So you just left her?"

"She said she'd find a way home. I didn't know what else to do," Lily said with a sob. "I didn't know she was going to stay."

"Did Nate say how she was?" Violet asked.

"He said she was at the bar drinking," Lily told them.

"With her clothes on?" Dean asked.

Josh glanced at Dean in surprise. Clearly something had happened in the past to cause this level of alarm over a trip to the bar.

He looked back in time to see Lily shrug. The young girl stood in front of her older sisters with hunched shoulders, and arms crossed tightly over her middle. "Nate didn't say."

Violet let out a long breath. "I thought she was doing so well, but I guess it was too much to expect her to stay out of trouble the entire time she was here."

"Guess I'd better go see what she's up to," Dean said, his tone resigned.

"Remember, no special favors for her this time," Jessa said, her words clipped.

"Why don't I go get her?" As soon as the words were out, Josh wished he could take them back. Everyone turned to look at him in surprise.

"Really?" Lance asked. "I'm not sure that's a good idea."

"I'm probably the least likely to upset things further by going into the bar after her."

Jessa shook her head in clear exasperation. “Well, be prepared for anything. Last time, she made quite a spectacle of herself, and the bar called in law enforcement. Thankfully, Dean bailed her out.”

Josh glanced at Dean, and the sheriff nodded. “Alcohol seems to do a number on the girl.”

“I’ll get my keys and see what I can do.” Josh turned without looking at his cousin. After their earlier conversation, this probably called into doubt his comment about not including Cami in his future, but he couldn’t seem to help the concern he felt for her.

Lily gave him directions to the place she’d left Cami and, within fifteen minutes, he’d found a parking spot and was headed into the drinking establishment. Once inside the darkened interior, it took him a minute to orient himself. He could hear a woman’s husky singing, accompanied by a piano. For a small-town bar, they seemed to have some quality entertainment. He knew something about singers with talent, and whoever was singing definitely had some.

His gaze skimmed the people sitting on the bar stools and then moved on to the tables, hoping to spot the blond curls of the woman he’d come to rescue. When he didn’t see her, Josh wondered if Lily had given him the wrong directions or, worse yet, maybe Cami had left with someone else already.

As the song ended, Josh moved a little further into the bar but paused when he heard the singer speak into the microphone. “This is for all you folks out there who are looking for love.”

He swung around to stare at the woman seated at the piano. Stunned, Josh stood for a long moment watching as Cami played and sang her way through the romantic ballad.

He was jostled from behind by a patron and moved to the bar counter in search of a seat.

“What can I get you?” the bartender asked as he settled on a stool nearest the wall.

"Coke," Josh said.

"Just Coke? Nothing in it?"

"Just Coke. I'm the designated driver," Josh told him. Because, whether she liked it or not, he was going to be Cami's sober ride home.

When the man returned with his drink, Josh nodded toward Cami and said, "She's good."

"She's great," the man replied. "Strange, though, I'm pretty sure she's one of the Collingsworth sisters. But she came in and asked if she could do a couple of sets in exchange for free drinks. She's been very good for business tonight."

Josh could only imagine, but he was happy to see that she still wore the outfit she'd left the manor in earlier. Whatever had happened before, it didn't seem to be repeating itself. Mind you, the evening was still young.

For now, he wouldn't interrupt her because he heard in her voice and saw in the way she played that her music had been cooped up for too long. Josh understood that. He'd felt it himself. And he thought he understood her need to be in a place like this. So he would let her have her time, and when she finished this set and came for another drink, he'd somehow talk her into returning to the manor. Hopefully, without causing a scene.

She must have only been at the start of her set when he arrived because she continued to perform for almost half an hour. With each song, his respect for her talent grew. Cami sang recent popular songs as well as tunes from decades ago, all flawlessly from memory. While waiting for her big break, she certainly wasn't just sitting around. He found himself humming along with her on some of the songs. While he had never performed secular music, he had listened to plenty over the years. Some songs he liked better than others, but none of it came from his memory the way it did from hers.

He watched as a couple of people approached her and, he assumed, requested songs. She seemed to be able to fulfill the requests without any trouble. People left tips in the glass on the edge of the piano, though she seemed unaware of them. Without a doubt, this girl was lost in her own world of music. He wondered if her family had any idea about her talent.

Finally, she came to the end of her set. When the last haunting strains of the song drifted away, Cami lifted her hands from the piano and rested them in her lap. As people clapped, she nodded her acknowledgement and then got up. After picking up her glass, she made her way in his direction.

Josh didn't move from his seat, waiting to see when she'd notice him.

Chapter Two

CAMI tucked the tip jar in the crick of her elbow and alternately flexed and fisted her hands to stretch them out after the workout she'd just given them. It had been a while since she'd sung and played to the extent she had tonight. At most, she usually did one set a night, but it had been over a month since she'd last performed, and she hadn't wanted to stop. It was her escape, her retreat from all the emotion and confusion she felt out at the manor.

She took a deep breath and let it out as she approached the bar. Time for a few of the free drinks they'd promised her. Her steps faltered when her gaze landed on the man sitting on a barstool close to the wall at the very end of the long counter. At first she was sure her eyes were deceiving her, but as she got closer, she realized it was indeed Josh.

He'd changed clothes at some point and now wore a white, button-up, heavy cotton shirt which was rolled up to his elbows. His hair was no longer confined by his ball cap and fell in wavy curls over his ears. He leaned back against the wall beside his seat, his booted heels hooked onto the lower rungs of the barstool. The darkness of the bar prevented her from seeing his expression too clearly, but she imagined it held the same censure her sisters' would have.

She thought about ignoring him, but it was a pretty fair guess that he wasn't going to go away if she did. The bartender met her at the bar as she slid onto a barstool next to Josh.

"Want a job?" the man asked as she set her tip jar down. "You're the best entertainment we've had in here in...forever."

"Sorry. One time appearance." Cami smiled at him. "I do appreciate the opportunity, though." She gave him her drink order then turned to Josh. "Well, I knew they'd likely send someone after me, but you're just about the last person I expected to see. Figured I'd be seeing the sheriff again."

Josh shrugged. "I wasn't doing anything else, so I volunteered to give you a ride back to the manor."

The bartender set her drink down, and Cami picked it right up to take a few sips. The moisture felt good on her throat and almost immediately the warmth of the alcohol began to spread through her body. "Did they warn you about the last time I went drinking in Collingsworth?"

Josh stared at her then said, "They did mention something about Dean having to come after you, but I didn't stick around for the details."

"Well, you can tell my big sisters that I kept my clothes on this time," Cami said, well aware that she was trying to shock the man.

Apparently he didn't shock easily because he nodded and said, "I'll be sure to pass that along to them."

Cami noticed that he had a drink sitting on the bar as well, but she was pretty sure it didn't contain any alcohol. "So, when was the last time you darkened the door of a bar?"

Josh cocked his head. "This would be the first."

Cami's eyes widened. "Been leading a bit of a sheltered life there, preacher man?"

One of Josh's eyebrows lifted. "By choice. I've had no reason to go to a bar before tonight."

"Were you here long?" Cami asked, unable to keep from wondering what he might have thought of her performance.

"About half an hour. You're a very talented musician."

Cami felt a rush of warmth that had nothing to do with the alcoholic drink she continued to sip. "Why, thank you."

"I believe in giving credit where credit is due. You play beautifully. Your voice is distinct, and you use it well. Do you take voice or piano lessons?"

As Cami listened to his words, she realized that he hadn't, as yet, made her feel guilty for coming to the bar or worse yet, having a drink. "I took some piano lessons after I moved to New York." She swirled the liquid in her glass. "Gran wouldn't pay for me to take them here. I think she realized that I'd inherited a love, and perhaps talent, for music from Elizabeth. To her that was not a good thing. She didn't encourage anything related to music."

"Denying a musical talent is a sad thing," Josh commented.

Cami nodded. "I couldn't afford many lessons. Thankfully, I found a roommate who had an electric piano. She let me use it as often as I wanted. From that point on, I basically taught myself."

The bartender returned to offer her a refill which she took. As she sipped the fresh drink, she looked at Josh. "Aren't you supposed to be dragging me out of here and taking me home?"

He shrugged. "Maybe, but I think you needed this. It will probably be beneficial for everyone if you are able to unwind the way you need to."

"You seem to be very intuitive for a man." Cami wasn't at all sure how she felt about this man "getting" her so well. "Your wife must be a very lucky woman."

Josh's gaze dropped briefly at her comment. "My wife is

dead. And even when she was alive, I'm pretty sure 'lucky' wasn't a word she used to describe herself in relation to our marriage."

Cami felt his words like a kick to the stomach. She had figured out there was no current wife, but she hadn't imagined he was a widower. He was too young for that. Her gaze dropped down to the hand he had wrapped around his glass. Even in the dimly lit interior she could see that the ring he'd worn since she'd known him was gone.

"My condolences for your loss," she said without looking at him again.

Oh no. This is not good. Not good at all. If he had interpreted her flirtations as wanting something serious, things were going to get awkward in a hurry. Sitting in a bar with him, chatting over drinks...it all smacked a little too much of a date. He seemed like a nice guy and all, but Cami knew without a doubt that she wasn't the right woman for him, and he was the last thing she would want in a guy—if she were actually looking for one.

The flirting had been in fun. A way to kill time and alleviate her boredom. It wasn't supposed to have been anything but a little entertainment. Surely he knew that. Any one of the family could tell him she was bad news, not at all serious relationship material for a guy who prayed and read his Bible.

Suddenly she needed to get away from him. Any urge to flirt that may have been there earlier had taken flight and wouldn't be coming back. Cami would make sure of that.

She took a final sip of her drink and then pushed it away before gathering up the bills from the tip jar. "I guess we'd better go. Jessa is no doubt thinking that sending you after me was a bad idea, since it's taken you so long to get back."

The bartender came over to ask if she needed a refill, but she declined and once again thanked him for the opportunity to perform.

"Any time," the man said and held his hand out.

Cami gave it a shake. “I’ll keep that in mind.”

Acutely aware of Josh following her, Cami wove her way around tables to the exit. The heat of the day had given way to a cool evening, and it felt good on her warm skin. As she waited for Josh to lead the way to where he had parked, she buttoned one more button on her shirt and tugged at the knot so that it opened and allowed the fabric to fall below the waist of her jeans. Everything she’d done to tease and flirt with Josh felt wrong now. And she was afraid her outfit might send him a message she hadn’t planned on. It was all just good fun until someone decided to take their wedding ring off.

This next week needed to go by fast.

Josh sensed the immediate change in Cami when he mentioned that Emma had passed away. And he hadn’t missed the way her gaze had gone to his hand…the one that no longer had the ring on it.

As he opened the door of his truck for her, the musky scent of the perfume she wore teased his senses, and his gut tightened. Josh thought back to his conversation with Lance. He’d told him that it hadn’t been about Cami when he’d taken the ring off, but after tonight he wasn’t so sure. Initially, he’d thought they had nothing in common, but watching her perform, he’d seen a whole new side to her and with it came the realization that they had one very big love in common. Music.

Surprisingly, she was more subdued than he’d ever seen her. He wasn’t dumb nor was he naïve. He knew that her flirtations over the past three weeks had been a game. Because of the ring he wore, she may have made the assumption that he was married and seen him as safe. That had all changed as they sat on a couple of barstools, and he had the feeling that now she was trying to regroup.

The ride back to the manor was quiet, and Josh would have paid a pretty penny to know what was going through her head. He wasn't under any delusions that there was a future for him and Cami. However, he also couldn't deny that, while she had been just an attractive distraction earlier, the last hour had turned her into a fascinating young woman. That was a bit more dangerous. Hopefully the knowledge that she planned to hit the road as soon as her month was up would help to keep his interest in check.

This woman wasn't for him, but that didn't mean that he couldn't try to help her. He sensed in her a conflicted spirit, and it had been clear from day one that she didn't share the faith of her family. As he'd done for the past three weeks, Josh would pray for her and for the opportunity to encourage her if he could. But that would be all he could—or would—do when it came to pursuing any kind of relationship with Cami Collingsworth.

"Thank you," Cami said when he pulled to a stop in front of the manor. Without waiting for him to shut off the engine, she opened her door and hopped out. She headed in the direction of the trailers, where the figures of her sisters and their men were illuminated by the strings of white lights. Sadly, she hadn't had enough alcohol to burn the edge off her agitation, and the last thing she wanted was to be lectured by her sisters.

"Cami." Jessa stood up as she approached.

Cami held up her hand and shook her head before heading to the trailer. Trying not to break her neck in the heels she wore, she stomped to the door and jerked it open. Once inside, she pulled off her shoes and took them to her bed. If there was ever a time she wanted privacy, it was then. Instead, she dropped down on her bed and looked straight into the accusing gaze of her youngest sister.

She sighed. "Listen, Lily, I'm sorry."

"You got me into trouble. Big trouble," Lily said, her voice tight with anger. "Why did you do that?"

"I just needed to get away. You know what it's like here, but you get to leave. You have a car. A boyfriend. Friends. You come and go as you like. I've been stuck out here since I arrived." Cami took a deep breath. "I needed a break."

Lily frowned. "But you shouldn't have lied to me. You didn't tell me you weren't going to come home with me."

"I know. But I figured if I told you that you wouldn't agree to take me." Cami was starting to feel bad about a whole bunch of stuff from the evening, but this was her biggest regret. "Listen, I'll talk to Jessa and tell her it wasn't your fault. You shouldn't be punished."

Lily flopped down on her stomach, her head on her pillow facing Cami. "I know it sucks to be around here sometimes. I just wish you'd been honest with me."

"Well, I won't do this again. In a week, you won't have to worry about me anymore."

"Are you really leaving?" Lily asked.

"Yes. Gran's will stipulated a month, and that's all I'm here for. This is not where my life is." Cami picked up her makeup case from where she'd dropped it on her bed earlier. "I have to get back to New York."

"Just so you know," Lily said as Cami stood to go to the bathroom. "I worry about you more when you're not here than when you are."

The young girl's words pierced Cami's heart. She bent to place a kiss on her head. "Don't worry about me, sugar. I know how to take care of myself. And I'll be back to visit. I have a feeling there's going to be at least one wedding in the near future. Plus, I need to meet my new niece or nephew at some point."

Lily turned her head to face the wall and didn't say anything more, so Cami took her things into the small bathroom. She pulled her hair back into a scrunchy and cleaned off all the makeup she'd so carefully applied earlier that evening. As she wiped the last of it from her face, Cami stared into the mirror. It was a rare thing for her to be without make-up. Even during the mess of the renovations, she made herself up every day.

The woman who stared back at her from the mirror was a stranger. Without the makeup, her face held an innocence that certainly wasn't a true reflection of who she was. It had been many years since 'innocent' had been an accurate description of her. Which was why, more than anything else, she knew that she was in no way the right woman for Josh.

"I still can't believe you got her out of there without a hassle," Jessa said. "It was taking you so long we thought we'd need to send Dean after you both."

"When I got there she was still fully-clothed and doing something she clearly loved." Josh shrugged. "I saw no reason to drag her out."

"You didn't think maybe she shouldn't be in a bar?" Laurel asked.

"Like I said, if she'd been making a spectacle of herself in a bad way, I would have stepped in." Josh was beginning to understand the constraints Cami felt whenever she was with her family. "Do you realize how talented she is?"

"We know she loves music," Violet said.

"People can love music and not be able to carry a tune in a bucket," Josh pointed out. "Cami loves music, yes, but she also *lives* music." He pulled his phone from the holder on his belt and swiped through the screens to bring up the video he'd taken earlier. "You can't see her too well, but that's your sister playing the piano *and* singing."

He handed it to Jessa, who happened to be seated closest to him. She took it and bent her head to look at the screen. Laurel and Violet got up to join her and, even though it wasn't a quality video, Josh knew there was no denying the level of talent their younger sister had.

"*That's* Cami?" Violet asked as she glanced at him and

then back at the video.

"Yes. That's what I saw when I walked into the bar tonight. And that's why I didn't rush to get her home. I think she needed to be there doing that tonight."

No one said anything more while the video played. When it ended, Jessa started it over. After the second time through, she handed the phone back to Josh.

"I don't think any of us realized," Jessa said, her voice subdued. "I remember her begging Gran to get a piano and let her take lessons. Gran absolutely refused. She wouldn't let her participate in choir at the church or school, either."

"I think she was terrified of Cami turning out like Mama," Violet added.

"And in the process, she likely crushed her spirit," Josh said. "With someone like Cami, music isn't just a way to entertain, it's a necessity."

"Is that how it is for you, Josh?" Lance asked.

Josh hesitated. "Yes, it was very much like that."

"Was?" This time it was Jessa who asked, and Josh wondered how much, if anything, Lance had shared with her.

"There was a time that I lived for my music. However, ever since my public music ministry failed, I have prayed daily that God would remove the desire to sing from me." Josh didn't want to talk about his music, though. "I think Cami is trying very hard to find her way in an industry that eats people up and spits them out. And she's doing it all without the support of her family."

"That's a little harsh, Josh," Matt said. There was no anger in the man's voice, but clearly he wasn't going to let the words pass without defending his wife.

"I'm saying that their grandmother made sure no one knew how truly talented Cami is or encouraged her to pursue her dreams."

"He's right," Jessa said. "I think Gran was so scared to

have a repeat of what happened with Elizabeth that she clamped down hard on Cami. Maybe harder than she would have if she'd expressed an interest in anything but music."

Josh wasn't so sure about continuing the discussion on Cami without her there. He just wanted them to understand a bit more about their sister. "Anyway, that's why I stayed at the bar and let her finish her set. I'm pretty sure that her need to be there had less to do with alcohol than it did music."

"She was still mad when she got here, though," Jessa pointed out.

"She misunderstood something," Josh said. "But I'm pretty sure her days of flirting with me are over. So it's probably just as well that I didn't correct things."

Josh could sense their curiosity, but he wasn't about to go into more detail. Instead, he braced his hands on his knees and stood. "I think I'm going to call it a night. See you all in the morning."

He could hear the murmurings of conversation as he left the circle of chairs, and he didn't doubt that some of it was about him and Cami. Let them wonder. Goodness knows, he was.

As he sat in front of his laptop again, he quickly read through his email and answered the one from his mom and dad. His older sister had also sent one, but he'd reply to her later. Shutting down his email program, he opened his browser to a search site. His fingers hovered over the keys briefly before typing in "Cami Collingsworth." He frowned when nothing came up. If she really was pursuing a career in music, she'd have some sort of Internet presence. But there was absolutely nothing.

Staring at the screen, he remembered how Cami was always eager to distance herself from the Collingsworth family. It was entirely possible that she used a different name when it came to her music career. In which case, he had no idea what to search for. And New York City was a pretty large place to try to pinpoint which bars or lounges she might be performing in, especially when he didn't have a name.

With a sigh, Josh closed the laptop. He leaned back in the booth, stretching his legs out under the table. If someone had told him that he'd come to see Cami as something other than a shallow flirt, he wouldn't have believed them. However, tonight had given him a better understanding as to how she'd become the person he'd seen over the past few weeks. The big question was...what, if anything, was he going to do with that insight?

Cami breathed a sigh of relief when the last of her sisters left the trailer. She threw off her covers and made a beeline for the bathroom. She'd had zero interest—less than zero interest, actually—in going to church with the family that morning. And she no longer cared about the argument it might cause. When Lily had poked her earlier, she'd just mumbled for her to leave her alone. No one else had bothered her after that.

After coming out of the bathroom, Cami retrieved her laptop from under her bunk and sat down at the table to fire it up. While it booted, she got herself some yogurt, toast, and a cup of coffee. Yesterday the silence hadn't sat well with her, but right then, it was golden.

She checked her social media pages and then her email. Before leaving New York City, she'd set up a new email address and given it to close friends. She hesitated for a second but then logged into her original one. She winced when she saw the barrage of emails. All from the same person. All with the same subject line.

Where are you??!!??

Cami didn't bother to read them, but as she scrolled through them, her throat tightened. As she got further down the list, the subject lines began to change.

How could you leave without telling me??!!

She felt a chill creep up her spine as she read the most recent ones. *I will find you!!*

Maybe it was time to put New York in her rearview mirror and head for the west coast instead. Though she had plenty of contacts in New York, they hadn't gotten her any big breaks. She'd miss her friends there, but Albert Smythe was making it very difficult to return to the city that had been her home for the past six years. Thankfully, she'd never told him her real name.

They'd met about a year ago at a lounge where she was a regular at the mic. At first she'd been flattered. He was an attractive man who clearly had some money. Every time she performed, he'd been her biggest tipper. He'd always made sure to give her his tip directly. She realized now it was so that she would know just how much he was giving her. They'd even gone out a couple of times, but then things had started to take a creepy turn when he began to show up at every single gig. And he watched her with an intimidating fierceness that had scared off more than one male fan.

In the two weeks before she'd come to Collingsworth, the calls had started. Day and night he called her. If she didn't answer, he'd leave her ranting voice mails and then send a bunch of texts for good measure. She'd had to deactivate some of her social media and lock down the rest as tightly as she could. It had been a pain because she'd been starting to build a following on her social media platforms. But when he started to write weird messages on her public page, she'd had no choice but to shut it down. Even if she blocked one account, he'd show up on another.

Before leaving New York, she'd put all of her things into storage and sublet her apartment in anticipation of moving to a new place upon her return. One he wouldn't know about. Her friends had encouraged her to go to the police, but in doing so, she'd have had to reveal her true identity to the man who stalked her since he would no doubt have lawyers who would fight her in court. It would be easier to just leave and start over again on the west coast with a new stage name. At least money wouldn't be an issue. If she were wise with her inheritance, it would last her quite a while. Thankfully, she'd already learned how to live on a frugal budget in an expensive city.

Cami logged out of the stalker-filled email account and back into her new one. She sent an email to her best friend telling her of her decision to head to California instead of going back to New York. Hopefully, Janey would be willing to help get her stuff shipped out once she'd found a place to stay. And she'd happily fly her out if she wanted to relocate as well. It would be nice to have a friend in a new place. The only person she didn't want to know where she'd gone was Albert.

Closing her laptop, Cami went to get dressed. Afterwards, taking her phone and headphones with her, she walked across the backyard to the path leading to the lake. She sat down on the heavy wooden swing, tucking one leg underneath her. With her other foot, she set the swing in motion as she put her headphones on and started her favorite playlist.

Chapter Three

JOSH was helping Lance put up chairs when Lily appeared out of the trailer she shared with her older sisters.

"Cami's not there," she said, her brow furrowed.

"She's not?" Jessa asked from where she, Laurel and Violet were unpacking the meal they'd picked up from a restaurant in town. "Did you check in the bathroom?"

"Yes. It's empty."

"Well, give her a call," Violet said. "I'm sure she's around. All the cars are here, so it's not like she drove off somewhere."

Josh kept an eye on the young girl as she pulled her phone out and placed the call. He heard the murmur of her conversation and when her gaze went toward the lake, he realized that was probably where Cami had taken off to.

Lily lowered her phone. "She's down by the lake. She'll be right here."

"I didn't think she'd gone too far," Violet said with a smile for her young sister.

"I just wasn't sure...after last night," Lily explained. "I was mad at her, and she was mad, too."

Laurel went over to Lily and slipped an arm around her shoulders. "Cami's here for at least another week. Don't worry about that. She's a big girl. She can take care of herself. Plus, we're going to fight, but we'll get past it."

"I wish she wouldn't leave," Lily said.

"We each have our own path," Jessa told her. "Cami's is taking her away from us right now, but that doesn't mean she won't come back. Maybe just to visit. Maybe to stay. Only time will tell."

Josh tried to watch the path from the lake without being too conspicuous. It wasn't long before Cami appeared in the break in the trees and began to walk across the grass toward them. As she got closer, Josh could see she wore shorts that showed off her long, tanned legs and a T-shirt that fit her curves. While not the most revealing outfit he'd seen her in, it still drew his attention to places it shouldn't go. The sunglasses she wore hid her expression, but she didn't even glance his way as she joined the group.

Lily sidled up beside her and slipped an arm around Cami's waist. Cami looked down at her and pulled the girl close. Apparently, whatever had transpired between them the night before was now forgiven.

Jessa asked Will to say grace for the meal and then they began to fill up their plates and find seats. The meal unfolded not unlike meals had over the past few weeks. Conversation swirled around him as he ate, which was also pretty normal. It wasn't that he didn't want to interact with these people. They had welcomed him without reservation when he and Lance had shown up. He was just a little leery of letting people get too close. Usually, once they found out about his past, there was a subtle shift in their attitude toward him.

Cami also didn't enter into the conversation much unless comments were directed right at her. She didn't look in his direction at all, and when they'd finished eating, she helped clean up and then retreated to the trailer.

He told himself it was for the best that she ignored him. Seeing her at the bar had changed his perspective, and that wasn't necessarily a good thing. Of all the women to grab his attention, Cami Collingsworth was one who spelled trouble with a capital 'T'.

"No, I don't want to go," Cami said as she settled onto the small couch in the trailer.

"Are you going to see her before you leave?" Violet asked. "I would think you'd at least be curious."

Cami shook her head. "Not really. And if she won't even know who I am, what's the sense in going?"

"She's our mother," Violet said. "You at least owe her one visit."

Cami lifted a brow at her older sister. "I do? Not sure why. She may have given birth to me, but she was never my mother. At least not to my recollection."

"Still," Violet began.

"Leave her alone," Jessa said before she could continue. "We all have our reasons for whether we want to see Elizabeth or not. I understand why you and Laurel want to see her. You need to accept that Cami and I don't feel the same way."

Cami was surprised by Jessa's defense of her decision. She figured that at some point Jessa would cave and go see the woman. Cami would most likely be the last woman standing, but it wouldn't really matter since she wouldn't be around much longer to face the pressure Violet liked to place on her about it.

Violet crossed her arms and frowned. "I just don't want you guys to regret not seeing her if something should happen."

"That will be our regret to deal with if it should come to

that," Jessa said. "I love you, but you need to stop constantly asking about this. If, or when, it gets to the point that I want to see Elizabeth, I'll let you know."

"Ditto," Cami said. "I'm not saying never. Just not now. And if I don't see her before something happens, I'll deal with it then."

Violet didn't look happy, but gave them a quick nod before leaving the trailer.

Cami headed for her bunk, but before she got there, Jessa said, "Do you want to talk about what happened between you and Josh at the bar last night?"

Cami swung back around. "No."

Jessa tilted her head, and for a second Cami thought she was going to push. It was what she expected from her, but to her surprise, Jessa nodded. "Okay. But if you need to talk, I'm willing to listen."

"Thanks," Cami said, though inwardly she added *not in a million years*. She appreciated that Jessa was making an effort to build a relationship with her, but Josh was not a subject she was going to talk about with anyone. And really, there wasn't much to talk about because she had no idea how to explain what had happened at the bar. All she knew was that she needed to keep her distance from him over the next week.

Where every other man looked at her body, Josh had looked into her eyes and seen her soul. It had shaken her more than she was willing to admit to anyone.

At her bunk, Cami pulled out her laptop and sat down with it. If she was going to go directly to California instead of returning to New York, she needed to make some arrangements and look for a place to stay. Planning would give her the focus she needed and distract her from all the stuff she didn't want to think about.

Josh stepped out of the trailer with his hair still damp

from his shower. He hadn't had time to take one before supper since he'd been talking with a few of the workers before they left for the day. It felt good to be free of the dirt and grime.

"Want to take a walk through?" Lance said when he spotted him.

At Josh's nod, his cousin stood and joined him. Matt had left the night before to get back to his job in Minneapolis. He had given his two weeks' notice when he'd gone back to work the previous Monday, so had one more week to go. Josh missed having the other man around on the job site and suspected that Lance felt the same way. They worked well together as a team, and he looked forward to not just this job, but future jobs with Matt.

After the loss of work because of the skeleton discovery, things had gotten back on track, though they were still behind a few days. Neither of them was too worried out about it. Delays happened and stressing out too much about them usually resulted in more interruptions. Of course, the weeks ahead were the ones that involved the things that could cause longer delays. The arrival of the custom ordered products always brought a higher level of stress because any mistakes with those items could grind things to a halt.

The manor renovation was one of their largest projects, and Josh was actually surprised that on the renovation side of things, they'd had relatively few issues. The problems that were cropping up were not connected to the project. What they'd hoped would be a straightforward investigation into the facts surrounding the death of Scott Lewis had turned more complicated as Sylvia was investigated to determine exactly what she knew of the incident. And he'd heard them talking about a possible wrongful death suit being brought by Scott Lewis's family.

The Collingsworth lawyer and the private investigator Violet had hired had been out at the manor several times in the past couple of weeks. Included with the letter that Jonathan had left had been pictures of Elizabeth

Collingsworth following her beating, as well as medical records documenting her condition. Stan, their lawyer, had said that they should consider countersuing for the cost of the medical care that Elizabeth had needed over the past seventeen years due to the actions of Scott Lewis. Jessa hadn't been sure what to do, and Josh could see that the responsibility for the Collingsworth family weighed heavily on her.

Normally he wouldn't have been as informed about the goings on in the customer's life, but now that Lance and Jessa were back together, Josh heard pretty much everything.

As they finished the walk through, Lance stopped in the large open area that was slowly taking the shape of the kitchen. He stood with his hands on his hips. "You want to talk at all about what happened between you and Cami?"

"Not much to talk about." Josh shrugged. "I just understand some of what she's going through. I offered her that understanding, along with the information that I wasn't married, and suddenly everything changed. She doesn't want anything to do with me now. I would think that would be making everyone around here happy."

Lance cocked his head. "But does that make *you* happy?"

"Well, I wasn't looking to make her uncomfortable. So the fact that she feels like she has to avoid me doesn't make me happy."

"And there's no other reason?" Lance prodded.

"There can *be* no other reason," Josh told him. "While we have a few things in common, the differences are far more significant. And she's leaving as soon as her month is up, so I can't be thinking along any other lines."

"*Can't* be thinking along those lines and *not* thinking along those lines are two different things," Lance said. "I just don't want you to get hurt."

Josh smiled at his cousin. "No worries. That's not going to

happen."

Lance stared at him for a moment and then nodded. "Just concerned, that's all."

"I appreciate that, but don't let it worry you too much."

Lance clapped him on the shoulder. "Now that I'm with Jessa I can't help hoping you find someone, too."

"If it's meant to be, the right person will come along at the right time. I'm not rushing things this time around."

They walked out on to the front porch together. Not really wanting to go hang around all the happy couples, Josh said, "I'm going to take a walk down by the lake. I'll be back in a bit."

Lance nodded. "Don't get lost."

Josh walked around the side of the manor where the skeleton had been found and followed the tree line to the path that led through the trees. As he stepped onto the beach, he walked toward the lake and stood watching the water lap at the sand. The wind had kicked up a bit, so the waves were high. He loved the sound of it, the music and rhythm of the water as it rushed to the shore and then pulled back.

"Are you stalking me?"

Startled, Josh spun around to see Cami on the swing. Her long legs stretched out across the seat as she sat sideways on it. She held a glass in her hand.

"No. I didn't realize you were here." Slowly he approached the swing. "Last I heard, you were headed to town with Lily."

"I was. I needed a few things from the store. She brought me back a bit ago. I bypassed the trailers with all my mothers and headed right down here."

Josh looked from the glass in her hand to the soft-sided cooler sitting next to her. "Decided to skip the bar?"

"Yep. Didn't need the music this time. Just the booze."

She lowered her legs and turned to sit straight on the swing. "Want to sit?"

Even though Josh wasn't sure it was a good idea, he sat down on the far side of the swing. Cami lifted her legs to hook her heels on the edge of the seat. She took a drink from her glass then set it on top of her knees, holding it with one hand and tracing in the condensation with the other.

As he set the swing in gentle motion with his foot, Josh looked away from her and stared out at the lake. They sat in silence for a few minutes.

"No lecture about the drinking?" Cami asked.

Josh glanced over at her. "No. I think you've probably heard them all anyway."

Cami nodded. "And I'm already headed to hell so might as well enjoy the ride."

This time Josh turned more fully toward Cami. "Why would you say that?"

She took another couple of sips of her drink before answering. "Pretty sure I've got a one-way ticket to hell."

"Well, we all do, honestly."

This time she looked at him, her brow furrowed over her baby-blue eyes. "I seriously doubt that."

"You shouldn't. We're all born headed for hell. The Bible says all of us have sinned and fallen short of the glory of God. So if what sends us to hell is sin, then we're all headed there."

Cami gave her head a shake. "You can't tell me that if someone tells a little white lie they're going to go to hell."

"Sin is sin. A few drops of red juice are as noticeable on a white dress as a splash is."

Tilting back her head, Cami drained the last of her drink. Josh watched as she lowered her legs and bent over to reach into the cooler. She pulled out some more ice and then mixed herself another drink. "My dress hasn't been white in a very long time."

"Well, there's a standing offer to switch tracks. To trade in that ticket to hell for one to Heaven."

Cami looked at him. "You're crazy. Do you realize that?"

"What makes me crazy?"

"You're sitting there telling me, without even knowing what I've done, that I could still go to heaven? Pretty sure God's up there wishing you'd shut up. There's no way He wants me in His perfect world."

"Well, I'm pretty sure you're wrong about that. And it doesn't matter if I know what you've done or not. God already knows, and He's the one offering you the opportunity to be forgiven from all your sin. I'm not the one who determines if you go to Heaven or not."

"You'd be the first Christian I've met who thinks that way."

"What do you mean?"

"I've met plenty who tell me I have to quit drinking. I have to quit smoking. Quit dressing like a..." She glanced at him. "Quit singing the songs I sing, in the places I sing them. That God won't let me into heaven if I'm doing all those things."

"You don't have to try to stop all those things before you come to God. If you could make yourself good enough to get into Heaven on your own, God wouldn't have sent His son to die for our sins. It's like trying to get that red stain out of your dress all by yourself. You can't. You need special stain removers. Your sin was already forgiven when Jesus died on the cross. He took care of the stain of sin on your life. You just need to accept that gift and your sins will be forgiven and forgotten."

"Forgotten? By whom? I'm fairly certain *I'll* never forget my sins," Cami said. She continued to sip her drink, and Josh wondered how many she'd had so far. The fact that she was talking so freely made him think she'd likely had a few.

"By God. The Bible tells us that if we confess our sins,

God is faithful and just to forgive us and cleanse us from all unrighteousness. And that He remembers our sin no more. It doesn't say just the small sins, or the socially acceptable sins. No, it's all our sins."

Cami looked out at the lake, drained her glass and made another drink. When she settled back in the swing, feet up on the seat again, she asked, "Even murder?"

Josh tried not to react to the question, but inside his heart had skipped a beat. "Murder? Are you worried that your grandmother didn't go to Heaven because of Scott Lewis?"

Cami shook her head slowly. "No, me. Even if I committed murder?"

"I know I said I didn't need to know your sin, but I can't help but ask...who did you murder?"

Josh stared at her profile and saw her catch her lower lip between her teeth. As she blinked, a tear slid down her cheek. He found it hard to breathe as he waited for her answer. Part of him didn't want to know, didn't want the complication that might come with her confession.

As he watched, Josh saw her take a deep breath even as another tear followed the first. Without looking at him, she said, "My baby. I murdered my baby."

The words were slow to sink in. But then Josh realized what she was saying. "You had an abortion?"

Another slow nod. "I thought it was the right thing at the time." She pressed a hand to her stomach. "But since then...when I see Laurel with Rose. I know it was wrong. Very wrong."

"Do you want to tell me what happened?" Josh still wasn't sure he wanted to hear this, but he had a feeling that she needed to talk about it. And sometimes drunken confessions were the easiest.

She swiped her fingertips across her cheek and took another sip of her drink. "When Laurel got pregnant, Gran sent us both to that special school. The one for troubled girls.

I guess I was getting into enough trouble that Gran saw a chance to get rid of me for a while, too. It was horrible. Laurel knew what was going to happen when she had the baby. We both did. She didn't even get a chance to hold Rose. Or name her. Gran came as soon as she was born and took her back to the manor."

The words came out rushed and disjointed, but Josh thought he got the drift of what she was sharing. Cami stared out toward the lake, but Josh wasn't sure she actually saw it.

"I remember walking into our bedroom at the school to find her weeping. Her milk had come in, and she was in pain but didn't have a baby to nurse. Gran hadn't even cared about that. All she cared about was the family name, and that no one would realize that yet another Collingsworth girl had gotten herself knocked up. I cried with Laurel that day and vowed I would never find myself in that same position."

"But you did?" Josh prompted when Cami fell silent.

She nodded slowly. "I made the mistake of getting involved with the pastor's son. Neither of us could risk buying protection without word getting back to his parents or Gran. So we took a chance. Just once. But it was enough. As soon as I found out I was pregnant, I knew what I had to do. I felt I had no other choice." Cami took a deep shuddering breath. "When we got back from the school, Gran didn't let Laurel anywhere near Rose. She wasn't allowed to hold or feed her. Nothing. Rosie's mother was right there, but Gran made good and sure that Laurel never had a chance to bond with her. I couldn't do that to my baby. I couldn't let her be raised that way."

"Her?" Josh asked.

"I was sure I would have a girl, just like Mama and Laurel. And I was sure that wherever babies went when they weren't born had to be better than the life she'd have with Gran." Cami glanced at him. "Do you think babies who die before they're born go to Heaven?"

Josh felt the air squeeze from his lungs. Unbidden came

the memory of his own child, born without life. Rejected by her mother. He had been the only one to hold the soft body. He had clutched her to his chest and cried to God for strength to endure the loss and to know why. But there had been no answers that night nor in the years that followed. "I certainly hope so."

"I killed my baby. And I could have had her now. Just like Laurel has Rose. But I...didn't know." Cami bent her head as sobs wracked her body.

Josh didn't know what to do, but finally he reached out and took the glass from her. He dumped its contents on the sand and set it down. Then he slid down the swing so he could gather Cami into his arms. Something told him this was the first time she'd let it all out. He had no idea why she'd chosen to reveal it all to him, but he hoped this would be a turning point for her. And he hoped the words of Scripture he'd shared with her still lingered in her mind once the fog of the alcohol had gone. He hadn't realized he had it in him to share those verses, even though they were slightly paraphrased. It had been so long since he'd last thought on them.

Cami kept her face buried in her hands and wept. Josh prayed silently for her and the obvious pain she felt. He hoped God would answer this prayer of his, even though he wasn't sure He was listening to his prayers much anymore. When he had no more words to pray and yet Cami continued to weep, Josh found the lyrics of a hymn come to mind. He and his quartet had sung it many times over the years they were together.

I hear the Savior say, "Thy strength indeed is small;
Child of weakness, watch and pray,
Find in Me thine all in all."

Jesus paid it all,
All to Him I owe;
Sin had left a crimson stain,
He washed it white as snow.

For nothing good have I whereby Thy grace to claim;

I'll wash my garments white in the blood of Calv'ry's Lamb.

And now complete in Him, My robe, His righteousness, Close sheltered 'neath His side, I am divinely blest.

Lord, now indeed I find Thy pow'r, and Thine alone, Can change the leper's spots And melt the heart of stone.

And when before the throne I stand in Him complete, I'll lay my trophies down, All down at Jesus' feet.

The song, as always, wrung emotion from his heart. His own garments had been stained by sin as surely as Cami's had. And though he'd had the right words to say to Cami, he himself had a hard time accepting that God had forgiven him and chose to remember his sin no more.

He wasn't surprised to find that Cami's weeping had abated. Experience had shown him over the years that music could calm emotion as much as it could arouse it. Though she was still in his arms, Josh didn't immediately release her. He wanted her to make the move when she was ready. With her head tucked under his chin, he gazed at the forest, enjoying the sound of the leaves as the wind set them to rustling. Though he understood that this woman was not for him, Josh also knew that he was where he was supposed to be right at that moment.

Chapter Four

CAMI lifted her head, and when his gaze met her shimmering blue eyes, Josh's heart skipped a beat. On so many levels he could relate to this woman, and yet on the most important one, they were oceans apart. Still, when she lifted her hand to touch his cheek, gently stroking, he didn't pull away. And when she moved closer and pressed her lips to his, he closed his eyes.

It had been so long since he'd allowed himself to feel the things Cami stirred within him. He'd done all he could to keep his thoughts and desires on a short leash over the years. They had done too much damage in the past, but now, holding Cami in his arms, Josh felt the flicker of desire. He knew he needed to pull back. Move away. Put distance between himself and Cami. Fight the temptation.

But the emotion of the moment was too strong for feelings long denied. Though she was the aggressor, he didn't resist. Her hands crept behind his neck and held him close as the kiss deepened. Without breaking the kiss, Josh felt her move in his arms, and before he realized her intent, she had moved to sit on his lap, her thighs pressed alongside his.

Alarm bells went off for Josh then and somehow he found the strength to end the intimacy and move her onto the swing beside him. He took several deep breaths, willing the emotions and desires of the past few minutes to calm.

"Guess I'm not good enough for you, huh? Now that you know what I've done." Accusation laced Cami's words.

Josh glanced over and saw her sitting with her arms wrapped across her waist. And there was hurt mingled with anger on her face. He ran a hand through his hair. "No, it's not that. Don't ever think that, Cami. This is about me. I can't do this."

"With me," Cami stated baldly.

"With anyone," Josh told her. "I can't become physically involved with someone I'm not married to."

"So you're a Mr. Goody-Two-Shoes who has never sinned," Cami said with an edge in her tone and her eyes flashing with anger.

"Don't believe that for a minute, Cami," Josh said. "But I have promised God that I would learn from my mistakes."

"And your mistake was having sex when you weren't married?"

"No, my mistake was having sex with someone while I was married to someone else." Josh didn't know why he'd told her, though all she had to do was do a search of his name on the Internet, and she'd dig up all the dirt.

When Cami didn't reply, Josh looked over at her. She was staring at him, eyebrows raised, eyes wide. "You had an affair? I find that hard to believe."

"Believe me. It's true. I lost my career over it."

"Because you had an affair? What kind of job did you have?"

"I was part of a Gospel quartet. Once news of the affair came to light, we were dropped from every radio station that played our music. Any concert dates we had were cancelled.

There was nothing left."

Cami shook her head. "I can't believe it. I mean, I know you can sing. I just heard you. But that you'd lose your career over something like that. Gotta love the Christians."

Josh understood where she was coming from, but he also knew there were always consequences for sin. His had come in the loss of the career he loved. He leaned forward to rest his forearms on his thighs. This change of subject had effectively killed the moment. It was a stark reminder of the damage that had resulted from the last time he'd given his passion free rein.

"I've made mistakes in my past that damaged a lot of people, not just me. I won't be doing that again." Josh turned to face Cami. "You're a beautiful woman. What I feel when I'm with you tempts me, but I can't go down this path again. We have different perspectives on life and faith, and I can't allow myself to get involved with someone who doesn't share my belief in God."

Even as he said the words, Josh cringed inwardly. His belief in God certainly wasn't what it once was, even if he did know all the right words to say.

"So basically you're saying that, because I'm not a Christian, you won't have anything to do with me." It wasn't a question as much as it was a statement.

"I'll always be your friend, Cami."

Cami stood and slipped her feet into the shoes that she'd dropped in the sand in front of the swing. "Well, too bad I'm not in the market for more friends."

Before Josh could respond, Cami walked away. He watched as she moved down the beach and headed north along the shoreline. It didn't take long for her slender figure to disappear behind the trees that ringed the lake.

Josh lowered his head and stared at the sand. He hadn't handled that as well as he could have, but he really didn't know what he could—or should—have said differently. The bottom line was the same. He couldn't get involved with her, knowing she wasn't a Christian, even if he was struggling with his own faith. And it was clear that she didn't hold physical intimacy to the same standard as he did. No matter what his heart was telling him now about Cami, she would be leaving his life soon, and he would have to move on.

Cami hated that her tears were flowing yet again. She brushed at them angrily. Between the emotional upheaval and the alcohol, her head was throbbing. She wanted to go back to the trailer and crawl into bed, but she had needed to get away from Josh. When tears had threatened again, she knew that she couldn't stay there with him. She also didn't want to be seen by any of her sisters while such a mess so going back to the trailer was out of the question until she'd settled down.

She still couldn't believe that she'd told him about her abortion, but there had just been something about him. He seemed so much more caring and concerned than the guys she usually came in contact with. Other guys wanted her body, but when she'd offered herself to the one man she really wouldn't have minded being intimate with, he'd rejected her. Cami pressed a fist to her chest and swallowed hard. She couldn't say she loved Josh, but he had definitely captured a part of her she hadn't been in touch with for a long, long time. In the end, though, it didn't matter.

Cami knew she needed to stick to her plans and move forward. She'd tuck away the memory of this evening with Josh and cherish it. Even though he'd rejected her in the end, she'd always remember the way he'd listened to her without judgment. The memory of being held in his arms so tenderly and hearing him sing would never be far from her thoughts.

Her fingers touched her lips. And the kiss would be a private memory she would share with no one else. Though pain had initially clouded her response to him, ending their embrace, she knew now that he had been telling the truth when he'd said it had been him, not her.

Cami came to a stop where the beach narrowed and turned to face the lake. She'd finally found a man who seemed to care more about what she was like on the inside than the outside, and he was still out of her reach. She hadn't known that men like him existed. She knew the men her sisters had chosen were good ones, but she had never imagined she'd want one like that. But just an hour with Josh had her imagining long walks on the beach, hand-in-hand with him, or standing in his embrace to watch sunsets like the one taking place in front of her right then.

They were just distant dreams. It seemed that all her dreams were destined to be out of her reach. But she wouldn't give up, because that would mean that Gran had won. She would try until her dying day to achieve them. Unfortunately, having Josh wouldn't be part of that, but she wouldn't give up on anything else.

She turned back the way she'd come. Light was slipping from the sky, and she didn't want to get caught out in the dark. As she neared the swing, she could see that it sat empty now. Ignoring the pang of disappointment, Cami picked up the cooler and glass she'd been using. While part of her longed to drink away the memory of the evening, she didn't want to forget all parts of it, so she'd take the bad with the good.

Over the next week, Cami found herself watching for Josh. Knowing that her days with him were numbered, she tried to capture as much as she could to remember when she finally left Collingsworth behind. She'd even managed to take a picture of him on her phone. It would be a reminder to her that good men did exist.

On Friday afternoon, Cami went with her siblings to Stan's law office. They'd fulfilled the conditions of Gran's will and needed to meet with him to finalize things. Cami had booked a flight out of Minneapolis on Monday. Matt and Laurel had agreed to drive her to the Twin Cities, since Laurel had lined up a doctor's appointment for that day as well. Cami wasn't quite as eager to get away as she had once been, but she knew it was time.

"As you've requested, I will make arrangements to have the inheritance money transferred to the accounts you've given me. I would recommend meeting with an accountant to help with the tax issues and to figure out the best way to invest it. There will continue to be income from investments and the properties that the estate still owns." Stan handed them each a small binder. "These have information on all the investments and properties that are still part of the Collingsworth estate. You can sell off anything in the portfolio, but it has to be agreed on by all six of you.

"I've met with the lawyer your grandmother had been dealing with regarding your mother, and she had set up a trust fund already for the care and treatment of Elizabeth. No further money should need to come out of the estate for her care." Stan looked around at each of them. "If you have any questions, please don't hesitate to give me a call. I will continue to work for the Collingsworth estate until such time as you decide otherwise. And if you ever have questions or concerns about my fees, I'm always willing to provide you with a breakdown of them. It has been my honor to be able to work with your grandmother, and I hope you will allow me to continue to work with each of you as well."

"Thanks, Stan," Jessa said. "I think this whole thing has been a lot less stressful than it could have been because of your help. I don't think we have any concerns or plans to replace you. Just be sure to let us know if there are more secrets we should know about, and if there is anything more we need to know regarding the situation with the Lewis family."

"Last I heard from their lawyer was that they were reconsidering the lawsuit, so I think that's a dead issue. For now, at least."

As they left the lawyer's office, Cami breathed a sigh of relief. She'd set up a bank account earlier in the week and would transfer the money to an account in California when she was settled there. Just two more days and then she'd be on her way to a new life. Hopefully one that would offer her more success than the last one had.

Josh joined the family for dinner in town on Sunday night. It was the night before Cami was to leave, so they were all getting together for one last meal. Josh knew he'd been included mainly because of Lance, but he'd attended anyway.

As he watched Cami interact with the others at dinner, he tried to ignore the knot in his stomach. For reasons he wasn't even sure of, he felt a huge sense of concern for Cami. He had an idea of the kind of life she was returning to, and it wouldn't be an easy or safe one. Each night since that time on the beach, Josh had prayed for her. Most of all, he prayed that he had planted seeds that might bear fruit someday. It wasn't always the best idea to have a conversation like that with a person who was intent on getting drunk, but he knew God could still bring to mind what they'd talked about. After all, God had brought all of that to his mind, even though he'd not thought of it for a long time.

He assumed that they'd see each other again at some point. Lance had confided in him that he hoped to propose to Jessa in the next few months. Josh figured that Cami would come home for the wedding, and he would definitely be there, but he had no idea when that might be. And if there had been no change in her spiritually, things would be no different from how they were now.

Back at the manor, Josh went right to the trailer to get ready for bed. Morning would come early, and he tried to get adequate sleep, so that he was always alert on the job. As he pulled his shirt over his head, he heard a knock on the door of the trailer. He knew Lance would get it, so Josh dropped the shirt on the bed.

"Is Josh here?"

His hands froze on his belt buckle at the sound of Cami's voice. He reached for his shirt and quickly slipped it back over his head.

"Yep. Just a second." Lance rapped on the partially-shut sliding door. "You decent?"

"Be right there." Josh slid open the door and met Lance's gaze with raised eyebrows and a shrug. He didn't bother with shoes as he stepped down out of the trailer onto the grass.

Cami stood there, facing away from the trailer. She glanced at him as he moved to her side. "Sorry. I know it's late."

"That's okay. I wasn't in bed yet." Josh shoved his hands into his pockets, waiting to see what Cami would say.

"Can we walk for a few minutes?" she asked, gesturing to the back yard.

The sun had set, so it was fairly dark, but they could probably skirt the perimeter and not run into too many obstacles. "Sure."

Josh fell into step beside her, still curious about what she might have on her mind.

"I'm leaving tomorrow," she said, her voice soft in the night air.

"I know," Josh replied. "Are you looking forward to getting back to New York?"

"I'm not going to New York. I'm going to give LA a shot. New York didn't pan out the way I had hoped. Now with a little more money, I'm hoping I can catch a break on the west coast."

Josh wasn't sure how he felt about the revelation. In the end, she was still going to be part of a lifestyle that could be dangerous. But he understood the desperation to be able to use the one thing she was good at to make money. He had felt that same way, but for him, fame had come quickly. Probably too quickly.

"I hope it works out for you," Josh told her.

"Thanks." They walked in silence for a little while then

she said, "I want to thank you for what you've done for me."

"Done for you?" Josh asked.

"You could have made things much more difficult that night at the bar. Thank you for understanding why I needed to be there. I know you don't agree with the drinking, but I was there more for the music that night. You seemed to understand."

"I didn't realize the passion you have for music until I heard you. Once I understood and realized that you weren't causing any trouble, there was no reason not to let you continue."

"I know it probably wasn't a big deal to you, but it meant a lot to me." She cleared her throat. "And for the night on the beach. I know I'm not the sort of girl a guy like you would go for, but still I appreciate that you didn't take advantage of what I was offering."

Josh stopped walking and laid a hand on her arm. He waited for her to turn toward him. "Listen, the reason I stopped was not because you aren't desirable. You are. And you're also very beautiful. I stopped because it was wrong. With any woman it would have been wrong. And just so you know, you're worth more than that. You realize that, right?"

Cami didn't answer right away. Then she asked, "What do you mean?"

"You deserve more than drunken sex on the beach. You're worth more than that. I know you've got stuff in your past that might make you might think you aren't, but you are."

"How do you know that?" Cami asked. "You don't know everything in my past."

"True. But God does, and He would still say you're worthy of more. I choose to view you as God does, not as how the men in your past have."

"You'd be the first," Cami remarked wryly.

"Well, you need to be the second. Until you accept that you're worth more, people will treat you like you aren't."

"Are you a shrink as well as a renovation guy?" Cami asked with a bit of sarcasm.

"I don't need to be a shrink to help someone who's traveling a path similar to one I've been on."

"You've drunk-propositioned women?"

"No, but I've gone through a very long period of feeling that I didn't deserve anything good in my life. I'd already screwed up a career that was a dream and a marriage that, although struggling, was still a gift. When I threw away what God had given me, I didn't dare to even dream of being worthy of anything else good." Josh swallowed hard, thinking about the nights he'd pleaded for God to just take him from the mess he'd made of everything. God hadn't answered that prayer or many of the others he'd prayed in the last few years. "Believe me, I know what it feels like."

"Sounds like there's more to your story than what you shared on the beach the other night," Cami said.

"There is. I'm actually surprised you remember any of what we talked about."

Cami gave a little laugh. "I'm surprised, too, but it's all very clear in my mind which is unusual for me. I drink to forget, so to have already been drunk and still remember what we talked about is nothing short of a miracle."

Josh was surprised to see this answer to one of his prayers. If she remembered his story, then surely she remembered the verses he'd shared with her as well. "Well, there is more to my story, but I'll save that for another day."

"We don't have another day," Cami said, her voice subdued.

"I think we will," Josh told her. "If Lance and Jessa make it official, we'll practically be family. I doubt we've seen the last of each other."

They had circled the yard and were now passing behind the manor. Just outside the ring of illumination cast by the lights, Cami stopped. Josh turned toward her, wishing he could see her face.

He felt her hands grip his upper arms and then sensed as she leaned close to brush her lips to his cheek. The scent of her perfume teased his senses as did the silky strands of her hair.

"Thank you. What you've done for me, even though I didn't deserve it after how I started out treating you, has been special."

Before she could step back, Josh wrapped his arms around her and pulled her close. He couldn't explain what he felt. He only knew that though she left physically tomorrow, she was going to linger much longer in his heart and mind.

He pressed his cheek to her hair and said, "Take care of yourself. I'll be praying for you."

He ended the hug before it went any further, and Cami didn't attempt any further physical intimacy.

"Thanks. I will," she said and then turned away from him and headed to the trailer.

Josh watched as the light spilled over her when she opened the door. Once she'd climbed the steps, she turned back toward him. Though he wasn't sure she could see him, Josh lifted a hand. She returned the wave before closing the door.

Uncertain how to process what had just gone on, Josh was reluctant to return to the trailer and his cousin's questions. Unfortunately, he couldn't stay outside all night. No doubt Lance would come looking for him if he didn't show up soon.

With one last look at the trailer into which Cami had disappeared, Josh let out a deep breath and headed for what was no doubt going to be at least twenty questions. If not more.

Sure enough, Lance was sitting at the table with his laptop and looked up as he climbed into the trailer.

Chapter Five

HOW'S Cami?" Lance asked.

Mindful of Will's presence in the trailer, Josh didn't want to go into too many details. "She's fine. She just wanted to say goodbye."

Lance raised a brow. "And she couldn't do that tomorrow when she said goodbye to everyone else?"

Resigned to the questioning, Josh slid into the booth across from Lance. "She wanted to thank me for not making a scene when I came to get her at the bar."

"And here I thought she was ticked off at you about that," Lance commented.

"We've had a few conversations since then."

"Are you saying that you're interested in her? Romantically?"

Josh shook his head. "That's not possible. But I did want her to know that just because she may have some things in her past that she's not proud of, it doesn't mean she doesn't deserve better than what she thinks."

"Sharing a lesson learned, huh?" Lance said.

Not exactly learned, Josh wanted to say, but he'd been careful to keep his family from knowing how confused he'd been since Emma's death. "I figured that maybe, more than anyone else here, I understood how she's feeling. I shared some scriptures with her, too." Josh shrugged. "I don't know if it will make any difference, but I felt that I had to at least try. I remember that verse Dad used to always quote about God's word not returning empty. I learned from him the importance of planting seeds when God presents us with the opportunity. Maybe those seeds God gave me to plant in Cami's heart might one day bear fruit. In the meantime, I'll pray for her."

Lance had a thoughtful look on his face. "I apologize."

"For what?"

"For assuming that your interest in her was strictly romantic. It seems that you, out of all of us, saw her troubled soul and tried to make a difference."

"We've all played a role, I think. She's a different person now than when she arrived. That wasn't just my doing."

Lance nodded. "I'll join you in praying for her. I know Jess is worried about her leaving, but she seems very determined."

"She is, but this may be God's plan for her. Though Violet and Laurel have both ended up back in Collingsworth, it doesn't mean that's what He has planned for Cami. We all have our own journeys to make. Some of us have to go through more heartache and troubles before we get to where God wants us. But we will get there. Eventually."

When it appeared that Lance wasn't going to pursue the subject, Josh said goodnight and headed back to what he'd been doing before Cami had shown up.

Cami stared up at the bottom of the bunk above her. It was hard to believe her month was up. She'd survived and was now richer for it. Having made the decision to not return to New York, she was a little more nervous about leaving Collingsworth. She wasn't sure why. At eighteen, she'd left for the Big Apple with only the guarantee of one thousand dollars a month from Gran. It was what she had promised to each of them upon them turning eighteen. That was seven years ago. She was older and wiser. Setting up shop in LA should be much easier with a chunk of change to help make the transition.

She turned on her side, pulling the sheet up under her chin. Closing her eyes, Cami allowed her thoughts to go to her walk with Josh. She'd never met a man quite like him. Even Will, Dean, Matt and Lance were different from Josh. All good Christian men, from what she'd been told and had seen over the past four weeks, and yet Josh seemed more introverted than the other four. She could count on one hand the number of times she'd seen him smile spontaneously. The first time had been upon hearing Will speak a language he understood. It was like he had just been waiting for someone to connect with him.

Cami didn't think Josh knew just how much of a connection she'd felt too. Unfortunately, she had a feeling that it was mostly one-directional. It wasn't hard to see that he viewed her as someone who needed saving. And not necessarily for his own benefit. Though he'd been kind when explaining why he'd rejected her on the beach, Cami didn't doubt that he was on the lookout for a woman much different from her.

And that was fine. She pushed herself up on an elbow and punched her pillow to fluff it then plopped back down. She wasn't looking for a religious man any more than he was looking for a lounge singer with a penchant for drinking. Still, he'd gone from target to...friend. And so far, he'd been a better friend than most she'd had. But now it was time to leave this life behind and move on to the one that waited for her on the west coast. She'd visit again, there was no doubt about that, but this still didn't feel like home to her and likely never would, even without Gran around to frown with disapproval at her.

The next morning, Cami said goodbye to everyone except Josh. He was conspicuously absent when it came time for her to leave with Laurel and Matt. She knew it was ridiculous to feel disappointed, especially since they had already said their goodbyes the night before.

"Be sure and call one of us at least once a week," Violet said as she gave her a tight hug. "You haven't been so good at keeping in contact."

"I'll try harder," Cami told her. "Just seems that sometimes there's nothing to really talk about."

"Just call." Violet stepped back, and Jessa took her place.

"Take care of yourself," Jessa said in her ear. "I do love you, sis. And I'm proud of you."

"For what?" Cami asked as she pulled back to look at Jessa.

"Well, for a lot of things, but one thing in particular is that you quit smoking. I didn't see you smoke at all while you were here."

Cami stared at her for a moment and then laughed. "Oh, that. Well, to be honest, I just smoked during that time I was home for Gran's funeral to jerk your chain."

Jessa lifted an eyebrow. "You don't smoke?"

"Not much, if at all, most of the time. It isn't good for my voice." She tilted her head and gave Jessa a smile. "I'm sorry, but I knew you were expecting the worst of me, so I figured I'd give it to you."

Jessa laughed. "Okay, you got me. Try to keep yourself out of trouble and come home again soon."

Cami nodded. "I'll try."

She hugged Lily, Rose and Will and then climbed into the back seat of Matt's truck while Laurel got in the front. The group stepped back as Matt started up the engine. Just before he pulled away, Cami looked up at the manor and spotted a tall figure standing in an upper window.

Josh.

Like the night before, he lifted a hand, and she responded, pressing her fingertips to the glass. She lowered her hand as Matt drove the truck around the circular driveway and out toward the highway.

Four hours later, Laurel and Matt dropped her off at the airport. She was a few hours early for her flight, but she knew that they had appointments they had to take care of, so she didn't mind. After the final goodbye had been said, Cami breathed a sigh of relief. Hopefully, the next time she saw them all, she'd have finally made some progress with her singing. She was tired of coming home a failure, with nothing to show for all her efforts. Surely her luck would change this time around.

Six months later

"You heading out?"

Cami turned, surprised to see that her neighbor from the apartment next door was up so late. "Just for a few weeks. I have some family stuff going on."

"Well, I hope they feed you good," the older woman commented. "You're nothing but skin and bones anymore."

"I'm sure my sister will be cooking up a storm," Cami told her as she slipped the key into the lock and turned it. "Do you have plans for Christmas?"

"My daughter will be flying in to spend the holiday with me. And no doubt there will be some here who need a place to go. I would have invited you if you were going to be around."

"Ah. Thanks, Grace. And I would have definitely accepted."

"Is your friend going to be here?"

"No. She's gone home to New York." Cami tried not to frown at the reference to Janey. They'd had a big fight a week ago when Janey had suggested they find a new place to live, a more expensive place. Cami had been footing the bill for their current apartment and hadn't been interested in moving since it wasn't a bad place in a fairly decent neighborhood. Though she had never given details of her inheritance, Janey had somehow figured out that she had come into money. In the past couple of months, her friend had been giving subtle hints about them "moving up" in the world.

When Janey had finally come right out and accused her of being selfish and stingy, Cami knew their friendship had reached its conclusion. In a flurry of angry packing, Janey had let Cami know in no uncertain terms what she thought of her. It had been a rough time because Cami had tried to be generous without being frivolous with her money. She'd covered the rent and most expenses, since she felt somewhat obliged after convincing Janey to move to LA with her. But she'd worked in much the same way she had when she'd lived in New York and didn't think it was unreasonable to expect the same of Janey.

The night before, Janey had called to see when she could get her stuff shipped to New York. Cami had told her she wouldn't be able to do anything until January when she came back from Collingsworth, since she was leaving the next day. Janey had been surprisingly conversational, asking about her plans for the trip. And she'd seem fine with waiting for her stuff until January. Cami had been relieved that Janey had calmed down, but she doubted they'd ever be close friends again.

Pushing aside the dour thoughts, Cami reached into the side pocket of her purse and pulled out an envelope. "I was going to leave this in your mailbox, but since you're here, I'll give it to you now. I hope you have a wonderful Christmas with your daughter."

"Why, thank you, darling." Grace took the envelope. "I'm afraid I don't have anything for you, but I'll cook you a good meal when you get back."

Cami smiled. "That's a deal."

The older woman gave her a tight hug. "I'll be praying you have a safe trip and a good time with your family. Don't forget the real reason for the season."

"I won't. Take care of yourself."

The older woman helped Cami take her bags down the stairs to the waiting cab. She waved to Grace and then settled back in the seat as the driver pulled away from the apartment complex.

Cami let out a long breath. She was returning to Collingsworth with mixed feelings. First of all, she wasn't looking forward to leaving the mild winter of California for the harsh one in Minnesota, but more than that, she was once again returning with dreams unfulfilled. She'd worked hard these past six months, but in the end she'd basically ended up no differently than when she'd lived in New York. Mainly a lounge singer, but she could now add wedding and funeral singer to that resume. She'd started the process to record some songs, but hadn't gotten very far, and right now it felt like just one more futile attempt to make her dreams come true.

She stared blindly out the window at the passing lights of the evening traffic. One question had plagued her over the past few weeks. If she gave up on her dream to sing, what else could she do? Sure, she had a high school diploma, but she didn't have credentials to give voice or piano lessons. Was she destined to sing in bars for the rest of her life? To serenade the love of others at weddings? To comfort in song at their funerals? The thought caused a pit to open in her stomach. Music was her passion; she could never give it up. She wasn't trying to get famous for the money. Clearly she had plenty of that now, but just the validation that something she loved so much was something she was really good at, too.

There were plenty of people in LA who were famous for nothing more than being famous. Was it too much to want to be recognized for a talent she was passionate about? She could have gone the route of party girl and maybe hooked up with enough people to get to the "right" person, but she hadn't wanted to achieve her dreams that way. Each time she'd considered it, Josh's words echoed in her mind.

And just so you know, you are worth more than that.

She still wasn't sure he was right, but she hadn't been able to ignore the words even all these months later. Just like she hadn't been able to forget about him either.

Starting that first Friday in LA, he'd sent her a text each week. It would come in around eight o'clock and always said the same thing. *Always remember, you are worth more. Praying for you. Take care of yourself. J*

She hadn't known how to respond to that first text, had even thought it was a one-time thing. Though she'd saved the text, she hadn't replied. But even though she hadn't responded, he'd continued to text every single Friday night as if knowing that weekends were a time when the temptations were the greatest.

She'd kept in contact with her sisters, as well. At least once a week she had called or texted one of them. She'd even had several reasonable conversations with Jessa. Somehow, they were finding their way to a relationship that worked. It made returning to Collingsworth somewhat more tolerable.

When they pulled up at the airport, the cab driver helped her unload her bags, and she went into the terminal to check in. It was going to be a long night. The flight she'd ended up on left just before 11:30 pm and would arrive in Minneapolis at 10:30 the next morning. It wasn't ideal, but it worked with her schedule. She hadn't told anyone she was coming early. When the party she had been booked to sing at that weekend had cancelled, there had been no reason to hang around LA.

Cami was beat by the time her flight landed in

Minneapolis. The flights hadn't been bad, and she'd been able to catch a little sleep, but the almost-four-hour layover in Chicago had been a killer. As she pushed her cart toward the car rental kiosk, she took another sip of the cup of coffee she'd bought as soon as they'd landed. Caffeine was about all that was keeping her going at this point. And she still had a three-hour drive ahead of her.

As she stood waiting for the attendant to look up her reservation, Cami continued to sip her coffee. She let her tired gaze roam over the people milling around the airport. It drifted past a solitary figure, and it took a moment for the recognition to register. When her eyes made the connection with her tired brain, her gaze darted back, adrenalin pounding through her body.

Had it been her imagination? She turned fully around and scanned the faces of the people nearby but couldn't spot him again. It had to be a fluke. There was no possible way he'd know where she was. By not returning to New York and singing under another name in LA, Cami was sure he wouldn't have been able to find her. Periodically she checked her old address, and it was still flooded with emails from him, but there was no indication at all that he had found her.

Blowing out a long breath in order to calm down, Cami turned back around when the attendant spoke to her.

"Here are the keys to your car." He gave her directions for finding it. "If you have any problems, don't hesitate to give us a call."

After signing the papers, Cami gathered up her purse and the keys and pushed the cart with her bags out of the terminal. A blast of cold air helped to clear the sleepiness from her head, and she was glad she'd put on the jacket she'd brought with her. It didn't take long to find the car and make her way out of the airport parking lot.

The warm air from the vents soon began to lull her to sleep, so she found a fast-food restaurant and went through the drive-thru to get a large coffee and something to munch on. She made quick work of that coffee and stopped for one more before she headed north out of the Twin Cities. Though the caffeine definitely helped, it did a number on her bladder, and it wasn't long before she had to pull into a rest area. At this rate, the trip was going to take well over the three hours it usually did.

The rest area was fairly deserted, although another car pulled in as she was hurrying toward the building. The cold air was more than she wanted to deal with right then so was grateful when she entered the building which housed the restrooms. Not wanting to dawdle too much, Cami quickly used the bathroom and washed up.

As she left the women's restroom and headed for the front door, she heard words that filled her with a greater chill than the weather outside.

"I've been looking for you."

Cami spun around just in time to feel his fist clip her temple. She staggered back but managed to stay on her feet as she lifted her head to look into the wild, crazy eyes of Albert Smythe. A gasp escaped her as she pressed a hand to her head. Before she could gather her wits, he was on top of her. Her head slammed against the wall as he pushed her, and the pain that exploded drove all ability to remain upright from her body.

He straddled her hips and began to strike her. The blows rained down on her body. Any spot he could reach as she struggled beneath him. Finally, his hands settled on her throat. Blackness edged in, but Cami fought desperately to maintain consciousness. She was scared that if it pulled her under, she'd never surface again.

When she felt him move and begin to rip at her clothes, she increased her efforts as much as she could. There was no way she'd let him rape her. No way. She just couldn't allow it.

"Hey!" The shout seemed to come from very far away, but it galvanized Albert into action in another direction.

Cami felt his weight lift off her, and suddenly she was blessedly free.

"Are you okay?" The woman's question broke through the haze in her mind.

"I'm fine." She tried to speak the words clearly, but Cami knew her answer was as ludicrous as the woman's question had been. Surely her face bore the evidence of the battering she'd just taken.

"Jeff, where did he go?" Cami heard the woman ask.

"He took off in a red car. I got the license plate. I'm going to call the police."

Cami struggled to her feet.

"You should stay seated," the woman said. "Wait for the ambulance."

Cami shook her head. "No. I'm okay. I just want to get home."

"You're in no condition to drive," the man told her. "You need to wait."

On her feet finally, Cami took several deep breaths, willing away the pain that pulsed through her body. *Home.* All she wanted was the safety of her family and her home. "Could you get me some water?"

The woman went to the vending machine and got her a bottle of water. She opened it and handed it to Cami. As she took a sip, she recognized the metallic taste of blood. Though she understood why the two people wanted her to stay, Cami was still scared that Albert would be back. She wanted to get away before he did.

"Thank you for your help. I need to go." She forced herself to take careful steps to the door, ignoring the protests of the couple as they followed her.

"You need to make a police report. What's your name?"

"You need to press charges."

"I don't want him to know who I am. I don't want him to know where to find my family. I need to go."

She moved as fast as she could toward her rental car and fumbled to get the keys into the ignition. Every part of her body hurt, but she had to get to the safety of the manor. Fear kept the adrenaline high and kept her alert enough to press forward.

Not wanting to draw the attention of law enforcement, Cami drove the speed limit but kept a close watch on any traffic that approached from the rear. She remembered that the man had described the car Albert had left in as red. As she drove, the pain increased and it was getting harder to see, particularly out of her right eye, but she didn't want to pull over. She fumbled through her purse for her Tylenol and took a couple with the water the woman had given her. Hopefully, she could just get to Collingsworth.

Everything would be okay once she got home.

Josh stepped back from the ladder and leaned over to plug in the lights. Jessa had asked him to string a whole bunch lights in the living room and in the chapel they'd built out by the lake. Instead of the gazebo, the building of which had unearthed the skeleton, Jessa and Lance had decided to build a log chapel that could be used year-round for weddings or whatever people might want it for. The first to use it would be Violet and Dean when they were married in just over a week. Then it would be Lance and Jessa's turn. And sometime in the near future he figured there would likely be a child dedication, too.

As he surveyed his handiwork, he heard the muffled hum of a car engine. Frowning, he turned toward the large window facing the driveway. He was pretty sure that no one was due home for a couple more hours. Lily had gone into town with Jessa to meet Violet and Laurel about the wedding. Lance was at the apartment he shared with Josh, working on business stuff.

He pushed aside the filmy curtain that blocked his view of the driveway and spotted a silver car sitting there. The engine continued to run, but no one got out of the vehicle. Curiosity got the better of him as he released the curtain. He grabbed his jacket and shoved his arms into it, zipping up as he reached the front door.

Cold air bit at him as he stepped down the stairs leading to the driveway to where the car was parked. He looked through the front windshield and saw a blond head bent forward.

Cami?

Chapter Six

HEART pounding, Josh reached for the door handle. She didn't move when he opened the door, even with the blast of cold that rushed in.

"Cami? Darlin'?" Josh reached in and touched her chin to turn her toward him. At the sight of her face, his heart stopped and then began pounding again at an alarming rate. "Oh God, please let her be okay."

He quickly reached around her and undid the buckle of the seat belt and turned off the ignition. "Cami? Can you answer me?"

She moaned but said nothing. All he could see of her beautiful face was swollen skin and smeared blood. Anger warred with panic as he lifted her into his arms. He kicked the door of her car shut with one foot and strode across the driveway to where he'd parked his truck earlier. He opened the passenger door and slid her onto the seat and used the remote on his key fob to start the truck.

Trying to keep his thoughts together, Josh ran to lock the door to the manor and, as he headed back to the truck, he pulled his cell phone out and called Jessa.

He climbed behind the wheel as it started to ring and began to back out, phone pressed to his ear.

"Are you finished lighting up our world, Josh?" Jessa said when she answered, humor in her voice.

"Jessa, it's Cami. I'm taking her to the hospital in town."

There was dead silence for what seemed like forever then Jessa said, "What? Cami's there? What's wrong?"

"I don't know for sure. She just pulled up a few minutes ago but didn't get out of her car. When I went to check on her—" Josh paused as his voice cracked. He swallowed hard. "Someone's beaten her up. Bad."

Josh could hear Violet and Laurel asking her what was wrong.

"We'll meet you at the hospital," Jessa said. "I'll have Violet call Dean. See you in a few minutes."

Josh hung up the phone and glanced over to where Cami slumped against the seat. What on earth had happened to her? He'd prayed for her safety each night. Why hadn't God answered his prayer? Having her show up like this was gut-wrenching. All he cared about now was getting her to someone who could take care of her and make sure that she would be okay.

He pulled up in front of the emergency department and sprinted around the truck to lift Cami out. The glass doors slid open as he walked toward them. There were a few people in the room, but a nurse spotted him right away and headed toward him.

"She's been beaten," Josh told her. "She's a Collingsworth."

The nurse's eyes widened, and she gave a quick nod. "Let's get her onto a bed." She motioned for Josh to follow her and led the way to a curtained-off area. "I'll need some more information."

"I don't know any of her medical information, but her sisters should be here soon. They can help you with that."

The nurse was joined by another one and almost immediately a man in a white coat stepped into the area around the bed. They were talking and using terms Josh didn't understand, but he couldn't leave her. As the nurse pulled her shirt open to reveal her torso, Josh felt no stir of desire, only waves and waves of anger at the huge area on her ribs that was already darkening to a bruise. And his hands clenched to fists when he saw more bruising around her neck. Who had battered her so badly?

"Josh?"

He turned from the sight of Cami sprawled unconscious on the bed and moved past the curtains to where her sisters stood.

"What's going on?" Violet asked. "Is she there?"

Josh nodded. "I have no idea what's happened. I heard a car pull up and looked to see who it was, but when no one got out, I went to investigate and found her."

"You said she's been beaten?"

"That's the only explanation I can think of. The car's in perfect shape, so I doubt it's from a car accident. And it looks recent. Like, I mean, within hours."

Jessa walked past him and into the curtained area. He wanted to follow her but instead allowed the other three sisters that privilege.

"I'm Jessa Collingsworth. She's my sister. Is she going to be okay?"

Josh was sure that had they been anyone but Collingsworths, they'd probably have been politely asked to leave.

"We're still checking her over," a male voice said. "She appears to have sustained a beating."

Josh felt movement beside him and saw Laurel come out, one hand over her mouth, another tight on her swollen stomach. He quickly put an arm around her shoulders and guided her to a chair in the waiting room. "Are you okay?"

Laurel took several deep breaths. "She looks...horrible."

Josh nodded. "I'd like to get my hands on whoever did this to her."

She looked up at him, her eyes so much like Cami's now filled with tears. "Did she say anything to you?"

"No. She was unconscious when I found her."

"Josh!" Looking up, he saw Dean headed in their direction.

Josh stood as the man reached them. He was dressed in his sheriff's uniform and looked all business. "What's going on? Violet called and said something about Cami being assaulted? I didn't even know she was here."

"No one did. She just showed up at the manor." Josh repeated his story to Dean, who made notes on a small pad.

"So she was driving? Was it a rental?"

Josh shrugged. "I'm sorry, man. As soon as I saw her face, I didn't look at anything else."

"And the beating looked recent?"

"I'm not able to tell for sure, but I'd guess it was within the past two or three hours."

"So possibly she was attacked on her way here," Dean said, reaching for his phone as it rang. He turned away from where Josh stood.

Josh glanced back at Laurel. She sat with her head bent, both hands on her stomach. He really hoped that this didn't send her into labor. Though he knew Matt was on a job site in a neighboring town, Josh didn't hesitate to pull out his phone and call him.

"Let me talk to Laurel," Matt said when Josh had explained what was going on.

Josh held out the phone. "It's Matt."

A relieved look crossed her face as she took it.

"Well, that answers a few questions," Dean said as he slid his phone into its holder on his belt. "The office got a call asking about Cami. Apparently a couple found her in a rest area building getting beaten up by some guy. They tried to stop him, but he took off. The man managed to get his license number and called police. Unfortunately, Cami was determined to leave as well, and by the time the cops arrived, she was already gone. Smart bystander managed to get her license plate, too. They traced it back to the rental agency and got the information on who had rented it. They've also picked up the guy who was beating her and are holding him, pending more information."

"How long ago did this all happen?" Josh asked.

"Sounds like it was about three hours ago."

"The cops worked fast. Didn't they try to catch Cami on the highway?"

"I guess they didn't realize she'd turned off on the road coming here. It was the rest area right before the two highways diverge." Dean glanced toward the doors leading to the triage area. "We'll need to talk to Cami."

Josh shrugged. "You're not going to get much out of her at the moment. She was out cold when I found her and hasn't woken up yet."

"I'm going to go see what's happening," Dean said.

As he walked away, Laurel handed Josh back his phone. "Matt wants to talk to you."

Josh took the phone and pressed it to his ear. "Hey, Matt. You want to come be with Laurel?"

"I'd like to, but I hate to ask you to leave there," Matt said.

"It's no problem. Laurel's place is with her sister, and she needs you here. I'll head out now, so go ahead and leave. I think they can survive without supervision for half an hour."

"Thanks, bud. I owe you one."

Josh ended the call and turned back to Laurel. "Matt's on

his way."

"Thank you, Josh."

"You're welcome. Please send me updates as you get them. I'll be praying."

Fighting disappointment and worry, Josh left the ER and went out to his truck. He set up his hands-free so he could call Lance and update him on what was going on with Matt and the job site.

"So you're headed there now?" Lance asked.

"Yep. I told Matt to go ahead and leave. There would only be about half an hour without one of us at the site. Laurel needed him."

"Of course, that's fine," Lance reassured him. "I just wish you didn't have to go. I know you'd rather be with Cami. I'm on my way to the hospital now."

"She needs her family. I'm not family," Josh said as much to remind himself as Lance.

The silence from Lance's end of the call told Josh that his cousin wasn't fooled. "I'll give you a call the minute we find anything out. Okay?"

"Thanks. Laurel said she'd keep me updated as well."

After the call was over, Josh put on some Gospel music and had a talk with God about Cami. How he wished it was a two-way conversation.

The blanket was wrapped around her so tightly that it hurt. And it was a hurt she couldn't escape, no matter what she did. The blackness that had swamped her earlier began to recede, and slowly the realization came to Cami that the blanket that was hurting her so badly was her own skin. Everywhere hurt. The back of her head. Her wrists. Her neck. And her ribs. With every breath she took, those hurt the most. Suddenly she wished for the blackness to return. At least then she'd been free from the pain that wracked her body.

"Cami? Are you awake?"

"Vi?" She barely recognized her own voice and winced from the pain in her throat.

"Open your eyes, sweetie," Violet encouraged her.

Her eyes? They hurt so badly. "I can't."

"Okay. Can you tell us what happened?"

The rest area. *Albert.* Pain. *Escape.* "No."

"Cami, it's Dean. We've got some information on your attack. Does the name Albert Smythe mean anything to you?"

No. How could they know about him? If they had found her, he could find her again, too. She tried to shake her head, but pain shot from her neck to the top of her head.

"Jess, can I talk to you outside?" Dean asked.

Cami didn't know if they left the room, but soon felt a gentle touch on her arm. "It's okay, sweetie. You're safe now."

"Hospital?"

"Yes," Violet said, "you're in the hospital."

"How?" The last thing she remembered was pulling up in front of the manor and hearing someone talk to her.

Cami? Darlin'?

"Josh was at the manor when you arrived," Violet told her. "He found you in your car and brought you to the hospital."

So she hadn't imagined his voice through the haze of pain. "Go home?"

"When can you go home?" Violet asked.

"Yes."

"Not for a little while, sweetie. They want to do some xrays to make sure nothing is broken."

"Don't leave me." Cami forced the sentence passed her swollen lips. "Please."

She felt a fluttering touch on her cheek. "You will never be alone. One of us will always be with you."

"I'm sorry to interrupt, Miss Collingsworth, but we need to take your sister for some scans now."

"Can I come with her?" Violet asked.

"Yes, but you'll have to wait when we take her in."

"Thank you."

Cami tried to see what was happening around her, but her eyes were so swollen that she could barely open them a slit. She stifled a moan as the bed was set in motion. The next half hour passed in a blur of pain as she was scanned to check for broken bones and internal bleeding.

She tried to think of other things to keep her mind off the pain, but, unfortunately, the thoughts that came were just as painful. Albert had been waiting for her. She was sure of it. There was no way it was just bad luck that he happened to have been in the Minneapolis airport when he lived in New York. And there had been only one other person who had known of her travel plans. She hadn't given Janey the flight number but had commented about taking the red eye. It wouldn't have taken long for someone like Albert to figure out which flight she was on.

Janey must have been angrier with her than she had thought. No doubt Albert had paid her something for the information. The pain of the betrayal hurt almost more than the bruises that now covered her body.

"Your sister is very fortunate." The words drew Cami back from her painful thoughts. She didn't feel very fortunate right then. "The scans show no internal bleeding, but she does have a couple of bruised ribs on her right side. The damage to her face is all on the surface. None of the bones were broken. The swelling will take a little while to go down, so she'll likely need to take painkillers for a bit."

"So we can take her home?" Cami realized that Jessa must have returned when she heard her ask the question.

"Not right away. I'd like to keep her until we can get her pain under control. We'll be moving her to a private room and giving her something for the pain. I'd also like to get some fluid in her to make sure she doesn't get dehydrated."

Cami wanted to leave the hospital, but she also wanted to be free of the pain. So, if that meant she had to hang out here a bit longer, she would do it. And she had no doubt that as soon as she was clearly coherent, Dean would have more questions for her. It sucked that her sister had to be engaged to the sheriff. She might have gotten away with lying to someone else, but there was just no way she could pull that off with Dean. Soon the whole family would know about her stalker...even Josh.

~

It was just past six when Josh left the job site and headed for Collingsworth and the apartment he shared with Lance. Once he'd gotten back together with Jessa, Lance had had no interest in returning to Fargo and neither had Josh. Thankfully, they had found enough work in towns around Collingsworth to make it worthwhile. Lance had agreed to let Dave and his family continue to stay in the house in Fargo since he wasn't going to be moving back there. After the wedding, Lance would take up residence in the manor with Jessa.

The next few weeks promised to be super busy with two weddings, a birth, and Christmas. His parents and siblings would be arriving for Christmas and Lance's wedding. This whole situation with Cami certainly added a new twist to things. Last he'd heard, she was supposed to have arrived the next week. Why she was there early would probably be just one of the questions asked of her over the next few days.

He had been glad to hear that she wasn't seriously injured, though she sure *looked* messed up. There had been little to show of the beautiful young woman who had left Collingsworth six months ago. He hated that she had endured such an assault, but from what Laurel had told him when she'd called, Cami wasn't exactly forthcoming with details for Dean to help them charge the guy who had done it.

The shorter days meant that, even though it was just after six, it was already dark as he drove the winding highway back to Collingsworth. Thankfully, tomorrow was Saturday, so he wouldn't have to return to the job site if Matt felt he should stay with Laurel. Josh wasn't sure of her exact due date, but he knew it fell sometime in the next week. It had been planned that he would be at Matt's site next week anyway. Lance had work for Matt closer to Collingsworth in case Laurel went into labor during the day. Thankfully, this job was just about complete, and then all jobs would be done until the new year.

As he neared Collingsworth, Josh was undecided about where to go. Last he'd heard, they'd released Cami to go home to the manor. He really wanted to see her again, to see her responsive, since the last look he'd had of her had been when she'd been sprawled unconscious on a hospital bed.

Using his hands-free, he called Lance for an update.

"Why don't you just come to the manor?" Lance said after Josh gave him the final update for the day on the project. "We're all here, and there's food."

"Okay. Will be there shortly."

The driveway of the manor was full of vehicles when he pulled in. Josh parked behind Lance's truck and then crossed to the front entrance of the house, his booted feet crunching on the snow. The temperature had dropped with the setting of the sun, and it promised to be another brisk night. It was unseasonably cold for this time of year, and even after living through several winters, Josh still couldn't get used to or appreciate the cold.

Jessa had long ago given him permission to just walk in,

but for some reason, he felt uncomfortable doing it now. He couldn't pinpoint why. He'd been welcomed and treated like family for the past six months, but somehow Cami's arrival shifted his perspective of the group gathered here.

Still, he opened the front door and let himself in. After taking off his boots, he walked down the hallway to the kitchen where the family was gathered. The smell of food caused his stomach to rumble, reminding him that he hadn't really eaten anything of substance since breakfast that morning.

"Hey, Josh," Lance said when he spotted him. "Come grab some food."

Josh nodded and made his way to the counter. His gaze swept the room, and he noticed that Cami and Violet were missing. He took the plate Jessa held out to him.

"She's upstairs in her room with Violet," she said even though he didn't ask the question.

"How's she doing?" Josh asked as he dished up some food.

Jessa shrugged. "Hard to say. The meds seem to be keeping the pain under control, but she's still not saying much about what happened. Dean has most of the information on the actual attack and the guy who did it to her, but she's not saying if she knows him or why he would attack her. Dean's pretty sure it wasn't random because of some information they've given him."

"But physically she's okay? I mean, no broken bones or signs of...rape?" Josh felt his throat tighten as he said the word. She'd been through so much already in her life. Rape would have been too much.

Jessa shook her head. "Scans revealed no broken bones or internal bleeding. And she insisted there had been no sexual assault, though she wouldn't let them examine her."

Though that didn't surprise Josh, it did worry him. It was possible that she was hiding it just like she had with other things in her life.

"Fortunately, the witnesses' stories seem to back her up. They said that though her clothing was ripped, they didn't think the guy had raped her. But they told the cops they were pretty sure he intended to because his belt was undone when they happened upon them."

The knot in Josh's gut loosened a bit at that information. "God's timing in protecting her from further injury."

Jessa nodded, but her eyes filled with tears. She blinked rapidly and wiped away a couple that slid down her cheeks. "I try not to think about how close we came to losing her. I just want her to come home. Not just to visit, but to stay. It's not safe out there for her."

"I agree. I've prayed for her each day since she left," Josh said. He'd never revealed that to anyone, but he wanted Jessa to know that she wasn't the only one who was worried. "But I don't know if this will be enough to convince her of that."

"I'll be praying it is." Jessa motioned to his plate. "You go ahead and eat. I'm going to go see how she's doing."

"Um, if she's up to it, I'd like to talk to her," Josh said, "if she agrees."

Jessa stared at him for a moment and then nodded. "I'll ask her."

Josh joined Lance, Dean, Matt, and Laurel at the table. They had already finished eating, so he bowed his head to say a silent prayer for his food.

"I guess Jessa caught you up on how Cami's doing," Laurel said as he began to eat.

Josh nodded and then glanced at Dean. "What do they know about the guy who attacked her?"

"Not too much," Dean said. "He's from New York, but he's not saying anything, and neither is Cami."

"You think he knew her from when she lived there? Is it

possible he's one of the reasons she left New York for LA?" Josh asked between bites.

"It is possible. One thing the officers did mention was that he didn't seem to recognize her name when they asked him why he'd beaten her. So either he really doesn't know her, and it was a random attack, or he knows her by a different name."

"A stage name?" Josh asked. "It's possible that she didn't use her real name when performing."

Dean nodded. "I was wondering about that. Unfortunately, she's not being any more forthcoming with details than he is."

"I want to thank you, Josh," Laurel said quietly. "If you hadn't reacted so quickly, she might have been much worse off sitting out there in the cold."

Josh turned his gaze to Laurel. "I'm just glad I was here. Did anyone know she was coming home early?"

Laurel shook her head. "I didn't know anything. Last I heard, she was supposed to arrive next Friday."

"Hey, babe," Dean said, his gaze going to the entrance of the kitchen.

Chapter Seven

JOSH looked over to see Violet walk into the kitchen. She met his gaze and gave a slight shake of her head. It wasn't unexpected, but he still felt the sting of disappointment. He tilted his head to let her know he understood and then returned to his supper.

"Did she say anything more to you?" Dean asked.

"Not really. She did say that she decided to come home early when her gig for the weekend cancelled, but other than that, she's not talking about the attack at all."

"Do you think she remembers it?" Laurel asked. "Could that be why she can't talk about it?"

Violet shrugged. "She could just say she doesn't remember, but she's not. I think she remembers but for some reason doesn't want to discuss it."

Josh finished his meal as they continued to talk. He took his plate to the sink and rinsed it off before putting it in the dishwasher. He'd been around the manor so much during the past six months that it was basically a second home now. It was good of them all to include him in anything they had going on.

He was surprised to see Jessa walk into the kitchen a short time later.

"Is she all right on her own?" Violet asked.

Jessa nodded. "She said she was okay. I think she needed a little space. She has her phone within reach if she needs us."

At the mention of Cami's phone, Josh glanced at the clock on the wall above the fridge and saw that it was almost eight o'clock. Though it was usually ten o'clock when he sent the message, it was eight o'clock when she received it on the west coast. Rather than wait until ten to send it, Josh pulled out his phone

As conversation continued around him, he debated the message to send. The same one he usually did, or one that was more pertinent to the situation? He sat for a minute then slowly tapped out a message for her.

Always remember, you are worth more. Praying you are able to sleep tonight. Take care of yourself. J

She didn't reply. But then, she never did.

A short time later, Josh pushed away from the counter where he stood. "I think I'm going to head for home. I'll come back tomorrow to finish the lights in the chapel, since I didn't get those today."

"Thanks again, Josh, for taking care of Cami so quickly," Jessa said.

Josh nodded as he pulled his jacket on. "See you guys tomorrow."

Though he wished he had the right to stay and care for Cami, he knew it was not his place and most likely never would be.

Cami stared at the message on the display of her phone.

She should have said yes. When Jessa had asked if he could come up and see her, she should have said yes. But her pride had kept her from letting him see her so battered. Not that he hadn't already seen her that way, but she'd been unconscious, so she hadn't known what was going on.

She lifted a hand to her face, wincing as her fingertips brushed across swollen flesh. At least she could open her eyes enough to see a little bit. Chewing still hurt so she'd had to be content with sucking some protein drinks through a straw. Hopefully, by tomorrow she'd be feeling better.

But tonight, before the swelling went down, there was something she had to do. Lifting the phone in front of her, Cami fixed it so she could see herself on the screen and then took a picture. The position hurt her ribs, but thankfully the first attempt worked. It took a couple of minutes, but soon she had sent the picture attached to a message.

Was it worth it?

Once it was sent, Cami settled back against the pillows and closed her eyes. Jessa had helped her go to the bathroom and had given her more meds before she left, so she hoped that she'd be able to sleep for a little bit. And at some point she was going to have to figure out what to tell everyone...particularly Dean, who was not likely to give up without some answers. But that could wait for tomorrow.

Cami slowly maneuvered herself into a sitting position, gritting her teeth against the pain in her side.

"Just take it slow, sweetie," Violet said.

"If I take it any slower, we'll have another problem on our hands," Cami commented. Though the swelling was still present, she was at least able to talk a bit better. The hoarseness of the night before had also lessened, though she could still feel the bruises on her neck.

Violet helped her to stand and then walk the few steps to the bathroom. The room spun a bit at first but soon she gained her equilibrium. Thankfully, walking itself didn't hurt since her legs had escaped injury. He'd focused his attack on her torso and head. It was just the pain and dizziness in her head that knocked her off balance.

"I would like to take a shower," Cami told Violet after she finished using the bathroom. "I feel...yucky."

"Do you think you can manage on your own?"

"Yes. Maybe stay within shouting distance just in case."

Violet got her shower products from her bag and helped her get the water temperature right. It took much longer than usual, but Cami felt decidedly more human when she finally climbed out. The pain she'd had to endure had been worth it to wash away the blood and dirt that had remained on her skin and in her hair.

She let Violet help her get dressed and then blow dry her hair. Before leaving the bathroom, Cami looked in the mirror.

"A real horror show," she commented to Violet, who stood waiting in the doorway.

"Well, I just tell myself it could have been so much worse."

Cami nodded slowly. She couldn't imagine what might have happened if that couple hadn't arrived when they had. Everything she'd learned about self-defense had gone completely out of her mind with the surprise of the attack, but she hoped that she would have been able to fight back at some point.

After slipping into a pair of loose sweats and a baggy sweatshirt that Laurel had picked up for her, Violet helped her put on a pair of thick socks. It wasn't her usual attire by a long shot, but it was comfortable, and that counted for a lot right then.

Cami was sitting at the table eating small spoonfuls of yogurt when she heard the front door open. She heard male voices, and her stomach clenched. Her first instinct was to go hide. For some reason, it was important to her that Josh not see her all messed up. Realistically, it was already too late.

She braced herself for Josh's arrival, but when Lance walked into the kitchen, he was alone.

"Where's Josh?" Jessa asked.

"He's taking the lights around to the chapel. I'm going to go help him, but just wanted to check in with you ladies first." Lance snagged Jessa around the waist and pulled her close for a kiss. Without releasing her, he looked in Cami's direction. "How are you doing, Cami?"

"I've been better," she managed to say without too much pain.

Lance nodded. "I can imagine. Hopefully, they've given you some good stuff to help with the pain."

"I think she could make some money off what they've given her," Violet said with a grin.

"Luckily, I need the meds more than the money," Cami replied but didn't attempt a smile. Even with strong pain meds, talking still hurt a bit. She couldn't imagine what smiling would be like.

"Well, I'm going to go help Josh. Why don't you come out in about an hour to check it out?"

"I can't wait to see it," Jessa said. "I think it's going to be beautiful."

After Lance had left, Cami asked, "Chapel?"

Jessa sat down at the table with her. "Yes, after they found the body while digging for the gazebo, we decided not to build it. But since we'd decided to go ahead and convert this into a bed and breakfast, we thought it might be nice to offer wedding services as well. That's when we came up with the idea of a small chapel. It's back along the tree line by the lake. It seats about sixty people. I think you'll like it."

"You're both getting married there?" Cami asked.

"Yep. Violet and Dean will be the first ones, though."

"And I can't wait," Violet said, her eyes sparkling.

"You really want me up there like this?" Cami gestured to her face. "I look hideous."

"We have a week," Violet reminded her. "And I'm still hoping you can sing."

Cami hadn't allowed herself to think about that. Her voice sounded a bit closer to normal, but she hadn't tried to sing. "We'll see. No promises at this point."

Violet nodded. "I know. But just so you know, it doesn't matter to me what you look like the day of the wedding. I'm just so glad you're going to be here."

Conversation moved onto the wedding plans as Cami finished her breakfast, and a short time later the front door opened again. This time it was Matt and Laurel with Rose.

Cami was a little concerned about how the young girl would react to her appearance and didn't know what her parents might have told her about the attack.

Rose approached her, brow furrowed. "Hi, Cami. Mama said you'd been hurt. Are you okay?"

Cami reached out and touched the girl's cheek. "I'm sore, but I'm going to be just fine."

"I'm glad to see you up," Laurel said as she slipped an arm around Cami's shoulders and gave her a quick hug. "Did you sleep well?"

"Better than I would have without the painkillers."

Laurel lowered herself onto a chair, her hand resting on her swollen abdomen. "I could use some of those. This baby is killing my pelvis."

"Any day now?" Cami asked. As she watched her sister, she wondered how it felt to have a child growing within her body. She had never gotten that far, and probably never would. If children came from God, Cami couldn't imagine that He would ever entrust her with something so precious again. He'd given her that gift once, and she'd killed it. There was no getting around that. And she was pretty sure, no matter what Josh said, that God couldn't forgive something like that.

"I would love it to be today," Laurel said with a sigh. "We're ready to meet this little one, aren't we?" She glanced over at Matt and smiled.

Matt leaned over to run his hand over Laurel's belly. "Very ready."

"Did you find out what it is?" Cami asked.

"Nope," Matt said. "We decided to be surprised."

"It will probably be a girl," Cami said. "Boys are a rarity in this family."

"I want a sister," Rose said. "I thought I had five sisters, but now I have none."

Cami realized that must have been quite an adjustment for the young girl. "A sister would be nice. And then the next one can be a brother for you."

"Next one?" Laurel arched a brow. "At this point, I can't even contemplate another one."

Jessa's phone chirped and after checking the display, she said, "Do you guys want to go see the chapel? Lance says they're done with the lights."

Violet immediately got to her feet. "I can loan you a jacket, Cami. That thing you brought isn't up to this cold."

Cami wasn't sure about going, but she did want to see the chapel. And, surprisingly, Josh. She couldn't hide from him forever, so she might as well see him sooner rather than later. "Okay. I'm interested in seeing this place."

As everyone got bundled up to brave the cold, Cami took another pill to keep the pain at bay as it began to edge back in. She knew it would be easy to get addicted to them, so she was trying to only use them when necessary. She'd been cautioned at the hospital to not let the pain get too bad because then she'd be playing catch-up and taking even more than she should.

A pathway had been shoveled from the back porch to a log building tucked against the trees. Cami fell in love with it as she walked along the path. It was a much better idea than the gazebo had been. And she had no doubt it would become a popular place for weddings.

Matt opened the door and held it while the ladies stepped inside. The scent of burning wood greeted them as she followed Violet into the foyer of the chapel.

"Smells like they've got a fire going," Jessa said.

Violet gestured to the door to their left. "There is a room over there for the bridal party, so they can wait without being seen."

"Is that my beautiful girl I hear?" Lance asked as he came through a set of double doors.

"Yep. And Jessa's here too," Violet quipped with a smile.

As she listened to the banter between her sisters, Cami knew that nothing like this would ever have been possible if Gran had still been alive. How sad was it that it had taken her death to finally bring peace and happiness to her granddaughters? Though Cami couldn't claim the level of peace and happiness that her sisters had, she was in a much better place in her relationship with them than she'd ever been before.

For a while there, she'd wondered if Jessa planned to step into Gran's shoes. That would not have boded well for the relationship between them, but it seemed that Jessa had seen the error of their grandmother's ways and had determined not to repeat the mistakes the older woman had made.

"Come see the sanctuary," Violet said, tucking her arm carefully through Cami's. "You're going to love it. Since I can't get married outdoors, this is the next best thing."

When Cami stepped through the double doors, she found herself in a room that, although not small, still managed to be cozy. There were six dark pews on either side of a wide aisle. They weren't as long as the ones in a church, but they looked like they could seat six or seven people each. It wasn't a place for a super fancy or large wedding, but for the couple looking for an intimate, less formal ceremony, it would be perfect. She could see why Violet was so enamored with it.

The warm smell of pine came from the large stone fireplace at the front of the church, and as Cami looked up, she could see the result of Lance and Josh's work. Small white lights hung suspended from the ceiling above the pews and the stage at the front. With the daylight spilling in through the windows lining the walls, their effect wasn't immediately apparent, but Cami had no doubt that in the evening, their twinkling would add to the atmosphere.

Finally, her gaze landed on the man she'd been trying to tell herself didn't mean anything to her. She'd purposely tried to look everywhere but at him when she'd walked in. But finally, there was no denying her hunger for a glimpse of Josh.

Cami? Darlin'? Even now his voice with its Southern edge echoed in her mind.

He stood, hands on his hips, watching her. When his blue gaze met hers, she saw the corners of his mouth edge up slightly. As if of their own accord, her steps took her to where he waited. Though she knew she looked horrible, Cami figured it didn't matter. Josh didn't care what she looked like. She was well aware that whatever he felt toward her, it had nothing to do with loving her.

"Thank you," she said as she came to a stop in front of him.

He stared at her for a long moment before he said, "You're welcome. Although you did scare about ten years off my life."

"I'm sorry."

I can't believe you made it to the manor like that."

"I don't even remember driving the last bit," Cami told

him. Except for *Cami? Darlin'?*

"How are you feeling?" His gaze roamed her face and neck though it was covered by a scarf. "You had some pretty fierce-looking bruises on your ribs and neck."

Cami's eyes widened. "My ribs?"

Josh must have realized what he said because his brows drew together. "Uh, yeah. Sorry. I was still with you in the room when they began to examine you. They just opened your shirt, nothing more, while I was still there."

Cami struggled to understand why she cared that he had seen her in her bra. In truth, she'd worn skimpier swimsuits and more revealing outfits over the years. But for some reason, she was embarrassed to think that Josh had seen that much of her. When she'd first met him, she'd attempted to get his attention through provocative clothes and actions, but in the past six months, Cami had taken to heart what he told her each and every week. *You are worth more.* She'd tried to be a better person, to be worthy of the faith he had in the person he thought she was.

He reached out and touched her jacket-covered arm. "I'm sorry. I didn't realize what they were going to do, but I also didn't want to leave you alone. As soon as your sisters arrived, I left."

"It's fine," Cami assured him. "Just surprised me. That's all."

Josh tilted his head. "Are you sure you're okay? That was quite a beating you endured."

Cami realized that Josh was the first one, aside from Dean, who had broached the subject directly. "I'm in some pain, but I'll be fine."

"Remember what I've told you? You're worth more, right?"

"Yes, I remember."

"Well, you're worth having the person who did this to you brought to justice," Josh said, his voice low, but Cami could hear the determination in it. "You need to talk with Dean and tell him what happened."

If it had been anyone but Josh, she would have just brushed it aside, but for some reason she found it hard to resist his request. "I just want to forget about it."

Josh shook his head. "You can't do that. He'll just come back again or even attack another woman. Why don't you want him brought to justice? What are you scared of?"

Cami could hear the murmur of voices from the other side of the room, but no one approached them. No one gave her an out from having to answer his questions. She shoved her hands into the pockets of Violet's jacket and stared past Josh to the snowy scene through the window behind him. "I didn't want him to know who I was. If I tried to get a restraining order or press charges against him, he'd know my name."

"What do you mean? You know him?"

What was it about this man that made her want to spill all her secrets? She didn't even have the excuse of alcohol this time, although maybe the pain meds were dulling her senses in the same way. "Yes. I met him at a lounge that I sang at in New York. He was a regular, so we started talking off and on, but then he started following me to my other gigs. He asked me out, and I said yes, but there was just something...off about him, so after those first couple of dates, I turned him down any time he asked. He didn't like that."

"So he's been stalking you?"

Cami nodded. "That's one of the reasons I moved to LA instead of going back to New York."

"What did you mean when you said you didn't want him to know who you were?"

"I never used my real name for my work. I didn't want to be known as a Collingsworth anymore. I figured if I filed for a restraining order, he'd find out my real name. I couldn't let that happen."

"Do you know how he found you this time if he didn't

know your real name?"

Cami nodded and explained what had happened with Janey. "I thought I saw him at the airport in Minneapolis while I was picking up my rental car, but I really didn't think it was possible. Then when he found me at the rest area..." Cami drew her arms in tight against her sides, wincing as they pressed against bruised ribs.

The fear that had overcome her with his first blow to her face flooded back. She bent her head and swallowed hard. Each breath she took became more difficult, and suddenly Cami felt like she was drowning in an ocean of fear.

She felt Josh grasp her arms. "Hey. Breathe. Take a deep breath in and let it out. You're safe."

Cami tried to focus on his words as he continued to urge her to breathe in and out. Her breaths came in jagged pants as she tried to control the fear that engulfed her. She pulled her hands from her pockets and grasped Josh's forearms, hanging on for all she was worth.

"You're safe, darlin'. Breathe."

Her legs momentarily gave way, but her grip on Josh's strong and steady arms allowed her to regain her balance.

"Here. Sit down." Josh guided her to one of the front pews and allowed her to sink down onto the padded surface.

Cami bent her head and covered her face with her hands as she took in deep, ragged breaths that bordered on sobs. Now that she'd lost control, she didn't know how to pull herself back together.

She felt an arm settle around her shoulders. "You're safe, sweetie," Violet murmured. "We're not going to let anyone hurt you again."

Though she missed Josh's presence, she was grateful for the support Violet offered.

Conversation swirled around her, but Cami wasn't able to focus on it. She was trying so hard to deal with the fear, to not allow it to pull her back down again. When Violet moved, another person took her place.

"You're going to be okay, Cam. Just hang in there." Jessa, this time. She ran her hand up and down Cami's back. "It's going to be okay."

She continued to take deep breaths and gradually the shuddering sobs subsided, and the drowning feeling eased. More movement, but this time she recognized Josh from the scent of his cologne as he sat back down next to her.

"Can you look at me?"

Chapter Eight

CAMI lowered her hands and stared into Josh's deeply concerned blue gaze. Her eyes hurt from the tears, and she blinked a couple of times to try to clear her vision.

"Listen. Dean's here. Can you tell him what happened?"

Dean. At once, Cami felt a mixture of panic and relief. Slowly she nodded. "I guess so."

"We'll be right here with you. Just tell him what you told me." Josh's gaze went past her, and he nodded.

Cami slowly turned and saw that Dean was now sitting on her other side. Violet, Laurel and Jessa were seated in the pew behind her, and Laurel reached out to rub her arm in encouragement. Matt stood a couple of feet away, his arms crossed, and a fierce look on his face.

"I'm going to record this, Cami. Okay?"

Cami nodded that she understood.

"So Josh tells me that you know the man who attacked you," Dean prompted.

Haltingly at first, Cami told Dean what she'd revealed to

Josh earlier. "I changed my stage name again in LA, so I thought I was safe. I didn't get any emails on my new account, and there were no phone calls to my new cell number. I didn't think Janey would do something like this."

"I'm sorry you've had to go through this, Cami," Dean said when she fell silent. "We *will* make sure this guy pays for what he's done."

Cami stared down at her hands where they lay fisted in her lap. There was relief now at having shared her story.

Dean laid his hand over hers, waiting until she looked up. His brown eyes showed the same concern as Josh's. "You're going to need to answer some questions from the law enforcement officials who picked him up. I'll arrange for them to come here, though, so you don't have to leave Collingsworth. You've done the right thing."

"I just...just didn't want to involve you guys. It was my problem."

"Your problem is our problem," Matt said, speaking for the first time. "We're all family now. You don't have to deal with things like this by yourself."

Cami took a deep breath and let it out. "Thank you."

As she sat there, Cami realized that at that moment, her path had diverged from the one her mother had ended up on. Though there were many similarities in their lives, by revealing what had happened to her, Cami had taken a step toward being free from the man who had terrorized her. It was something Elizabeth Collingsworth had never done. Cami didn't doubt for a minute that the beating Scott Lewis had inflicted on her mother at Collingsworth had been just one in a long line of abuses.

"Why don't we pray about this?" Lance suggested.

Cami bent her head, but kept her eyes open as the man who was soon to be her brother-in-law prayed for her healing, for wisdom for those involved in the investigation, and for her safety through all of it. As she listened to his words, Cami was grateful that someone was there to put into words what she couldn't. Maybe God would listen to Lance.

When Lance ended his prayer, the others there echoed his "amen." This spiritual bond they all shared was something Cami would never be a part of, but there was a longing in her heart to feel the confidence and trust in God that was apparent in Lance's prayer. She just kept messing up. Even when she tried to do the right thing, it turned out wrong.

"We should head back to the house," Jessa said. "I think Cami could probably use a little rest."

Cami wanted to argue with her, but after the emotional upheaval, her body was rapidly unwinding. Josh got to his feet and then offered his hand to help her stand. He released it as soon as she was up. Cami longed for his continued strength and support as she made her way down the aisle, with Violet beside her. The walk back to the house was made in silence, and Violet didn't say anything until she was back upstairs in her room, tucked into the bed she'd left a few hours earlier.

Violet brushed her fingers across Cami's forehead. "You think you can sleep?"

Cami nodded. "I'm exhausted."

"I can imagine. Sleep as long as you need to. Just text me when you're awake. Okay?"

"I will," Cami said, her eyelids already drooping. And before Violet had even left her side, the oblivion of sleep pulled her under.

❧

Josh stood with his hip braced against the counter and took another sip of the coffee Jessa had offered him when they'd returned to the manor. He was only half-listening to the conversation. His gaze was on the entrance to the kitchen as he wondered if perhaps it would have been wise to get out of Dodge before Violet showed up. The look she'd shot him after everything had gone down at the chapel had been anything but happy.

When she finally appeared, she marched right over to him and planted her hands on her hips. Her brown eyes flashed with emotion, and her brows were drawn together as she regarded him.

"I'm trying to decide if I should hug or slug you," she said.

Before Josh could say anything, Dean approached them and slipped an arm around Violet's shoulders. "Definitely hug, babe."

Violet looked up at her fiancé. "He made her cry."

"She needed to cry. She needed to get it all out," Dean told her. "Yes, it was difficult to watch, but I'm pretty sure it was the best thing for her."

Violet crossed her arms, and the frown remained firmly in place. "And I suppose you're happy that you got what you needed from her."

Dean turned her toward him, his hands grasping her upper arms. "No, I'm not happy she had to relive what she went through. And really, I didn't need her to give me details about the attack. The witnesses plus the evidence that was on the guy along with the pictures of Cami in the ER would be enough to charge the guy. Their background interaction was helpful and supports what we've found out about this guy since he was picked up." Dean ran his hands up and down her arms. "C'mon, babe. You know I would never want to hurt Cami or any other member of the family. What I did today was more for her than the case. She needs to feel in control, and talking about it will help her move past what happened."

Josh watched as Violet leaned her head against Dean's chest. The lawman wrapped his arms around her and pulled her close. No one said anything, and when Violet moved out of Dean's embrace to face him again, Josh held his breath.

"I guess I owe you a hug," Violet said.

Josh set his cup down on the counter, and Violet wrapped

her arms around him in a quick hug. When she stepped back, Josh said, “I didn’t mean to make her cry.”

“I know.” Violet tilted her head. “What exactly is it between you and her? None of the rest of us could get her to talk.”

Josh picked up his cup and took another sip of coffee. “When she was here before, we kind of had a moment.”

“A moment?” Jessa asked from where she sat at the table. “What kind of moment?”

Josh wondered how much to share. He didn’t want them to read anything into what had gone on between them, but saying nothing might lead to the same result. “I went for a walk one evening and ran into her down by the lake. She was a little...drunk. And drunk people like to talk sometimes. She shared some things. I shared some things. Let’s just say we managed to clear the air. We became...friends.”

He glanced at Lance, since of all of them, he knew the most about what had gone on that night. Obviously, his cousin hadn’t shared any of it with Jessa.

“So you’re not...involved?” Laurel asked.

Josh shook his head. “It’s not that type of relationship. She needed someone to talk to, and I happened to be there. We have some things in common, which helped.” He cleared his throat. “To be honest, I’m more concerned about the state of her heart spiritually than romantically.”

Jessa nodded. “I am, too. She had the same exposure to church and the Bible we all did, but she had absolutely no interest in any of it. I’m not sure she’s even a Christian.”

“She doesn’t think she is,” Josh said. “So I’ve been praying for her and just waiting for any opportunity to help her if she has questions .”

“Well, do you think that if you get the chance, that you could encourage her to come home for good?” Violet asked.

Josh paused and then shook his head. “To be honest, I’m not sure Collingsworth is the best place for her. She is very gifted musically. I think it would be wasted here. And if she can't use that gift, I think she would slowly lose the essence that makes her who she is."

"That's not exactly what I wanted to hear," Violet informed him. "Back to wanting to slug you. Just so you know."

"I understand," Josh told her, because he really did. There was a part of him that wanted Cami to come back to Collingsworth. That part of him that he tried to ignore and push aside, since he knew it couldn't lead anywhere. "What I will do—what we should all do—is try to lead her back to God and then trust Him to guide her to the place where He wants her. Maybe it is Collingsworth. God does work in mysterious ways sometimes."

"Thank you for caring for her, even though she started out trying to make your life miserable," Jessa said.

Josh smiled at the memory. "Yes, she certainly did that." He drained the last of his coffee and set the cup back on the counter. "And on that note, if you don't have anything else around here for me to do, I'm going to head back to the apartment."

"I think we're good for now. Thanks for your help with the chapel," Jessa said. "Will you be back later?"

Josh shook his head. "I have practice at church."

"Okay, but we still expect you for dinner after church tomorrow as usual."

"I'll be here," Josh said.

As he made his way to the hallway, Lance said, "Wait up."

Josh waited for Lance to join him and then walked to the front door.

"Listen, I hope you're okay with their questions about you and Cami."

"It's fine. I understand their concern."

Lance tilted his head. "Actually, I'm not sure you do."

Josh frowned. "What do you mean? I thought I made it clear how things were between me and Cami."

"I'm pretty sure that all they see right now is that you were able to get Cami to open up in a way none of them have been able to. That says that she trusts you."

"Yes, I understand that, and I think she does."

"You might not be feeling romantically inclined toward her, but that doesn't mean she might not feel the same way toward you. I think they're worried she'll get hurt."

"I don't want to hurt her," Josh told him.

"Sometimes that's not something you can really prevent. You can't control how she feels about you. But the more you're around her, playing the understanding friend, the more likely it is that she'll feel something for you."

"So you're suggesting I back away?" Josh shook his head. "I can't do that, man. I'll do my best not to unintentionally lead her on, but I'm not going to push her away if she needs to talk."

"Just keep it in mind. That's all I'm saying."

"I will," Josh assured him. "See you later."

Lance's words kept going around in his mind as he drove back to the apartment. Over the months since that night down at the lake, the idea of a relationship with Cami had come to mind more times than it should have. He would be an idiot if he denied that there were things about her that he found very attractive. Yes, she was a beautiful woman, but it was the other things they shared that usually drew his thoughts in her direction. The wounds they both carried from past mistakes. The love of music that was more than just a passing fancy. But he knew there could be nothing more serious between them if her heart wasn't set on the same things his was, spiritually.

Since he'd taken off his ring and opened himself up to the possibility of moving forward, Josh had thought he'd find at least one woman who piqued his interest. But in the time since removing that symbol of his previous marriage, not one woman had snagged his interest the way Cami had. He had gone out once with a woman from the church in Collingsworth, thinking maybe it was just because he hadn't gotten to know anyone well enough, but there had been nothing there for him.

And there was no denying the absolute panic and fear that had engulfed him at finding Cami the way he had the day before. Somehow he needed to keep his eyes fixed on God in this whole situation. He was well aware that what he wanted and what God had in mind for him could be two completely different things, which was why he was having a hard time putting his complete trust in God's plan for his life.

Cami woke with a groan the next morning. The pain in her ribs took her breath away as she rolled over and pushed herself to a sitting position. They'd told her it might get worse before it got better, and clearly they'd known what they were talking about. Unfortunately.

The sight that greeted her in the mirror was a mix of good and bad. She braced her hands on the counter and leaned toward her reflection. The swelling looked like it had gone down more than she had thought it would. The puffiness was barely obscuring her vision, but the discoloration around her eyes was something to behold. She touched the bruising under her right eye. The stinging that resulted reinforced what she already knew. There was no way she could apply the makeup necessary to cover the bruising. Plus, the redness of the broken blood vessels in her one eye was just disturbing.

With a sigh, she brushed her hair into some semblance of order and then turned away from the mirror. No going out in public just yet. Moving slowly, she pulled on a pair of leggings and another loose sweatshirt that Violet had loaned her. Cami was grateful for the thickness of the sweatshirt as a bra was still beyond her, and she didn't want it obvious that she wasn't wearing one. She would have laughed at herself had it not hurt so badly. There was a time when she went without a bra just so she would get attention.

All these changes she'd made and still the results were the same. Still no man who was interested in her for anything other than the physical. Still no record deal. Still singing in bars and lounges. What was she supposed to do now?

The silence of the manor greeted Cami as she left her room. It had been pretty obvious the night before that she wouldn't be going anywhere the next day, but Violet had stopped in earlier before leaving for church to make sure she was okay on her own. She'd assured her that she was and had managed to fall back to sleep again. But it wouldn't be long until church was out and the family returned to the manor.

She moved carefully down the stairs, appreciating the smell of dinner that lingered in the air. Jessa had apparently put something in the oven before she'd left. She made herself a cup of coffee, and then, uncertain of what else to do, she took a slow tour of the downstairs of the manor. It hadn't even been close to finished when she'd left six months ago, so it was nice to finally see the finished product.

As Cami stood in the living room, she realized that, while the layout was basically still the same, the changes to the décor and furniture were significant enough that it didn't even feel like the same place in which she'd grown up. And if she were totally honest, the place felt like home to her for the first time...ever. Gran's overbearing presence had been removed from the manor with the completion of the renovations. Cami doubted that that was what Gran had intended when setting it all up, but, in her opinion, it had been the result.

She wondered at the lack of Christmas decorations as she surveyed the room. There were small white lights hung around the window similar to the ones in the chapel, but other than that, the room was devoid of any holiday décor. She couldn't imagine that there would be no decorating for the holidays, which meant they were probably going to do it within the next few days. It would be the first time she'd been home for Christmas since before she'd graduated from high school. Surprisingly, it felt right.

She settled down on the couch in front of the window, coffee in hand, and watched for the first of the family to return home from church.

~

Josh was the last to arrive for dinner. He'd swung back by the apartment to pick up his heavier jacket after hearing that they would be going to cut down the Christmas tree for the manor later.

Voices and the heavenly aroma of roast beef welcomed him when he walked through the front door. He found the family gathered in the kitchen, but knew they'd be eating in the more formal dinner room. There were too many of them to have a sit-down meal at the breakfast nook.

"Hey, Josh," Matt said when he walked in. "Good job with the worship team this morning."

"Thanks. It's a joy to be back doing what I love," Josh told him. All of them gathered there now basically knew his story and understood why being part of the worship team was such a big thing for him.

"Here you go," Jessa said as she shoved a basket of rolls into his hands. "Take this to the dining room, please."

"Sure thing." Before heading there, Josh glanced around the kitchen. Cami was nowhere to be seen, and he wondered if she was still resting. He found her in the dining room, slowly walking to each place setting, laying a napkin down. "Hey."

She looked up and gave him a small smile. "Hi."

Josh leaned forward to place the basket of rolls in the center of the table. "How are you feeling today?"

"Still pretty sore." She touched her cheek. "But at least some of the swelling is starting to go down. Here's hoping I can cover what's left by the wedding on Saturday. I hate the thought of being in Vi's wedding pictures looking like this."

Josh shoved his hands into his pockets. It was the safer thing to do since right then he wanted to reach out and pull her close for a hug. "I think she'll just be happy to have you in her pictures, period. Are you coming to cut down the tree later?"

"Are you doing that today?"

Josh nodded. "Jessa has it all planned for this afternoon. I think it's being decorated tonight."

"I might get in on the decorating, but still don't think I'm in any shape to be chopping down trees."

Before Josh could respond, Matt and Lance entered the room, carrying more food. Within a few minutes, the rest of the family and food made it to the table. As they settled into chairs around the large table, Josh found himself across from Cami. After Jessa said grace for the food, conversation flowed as they ate.

Josh watched Cami, noticing that she didn't engage in any of the conversations. She picked at her food and seemed such a shell of her former self. While he'd prayed for changes in her life, he hadn't wanted her to lose the spark and wit that had made her unique and special. He hoped it was just a temporary thing brought about by the attack, but part of him worried it was more. It almost seemed like the life had gone out of her. His heart clenched at the thought.

"You're not hungry, Cami?" Jessa asked her. When she didn't reply, Jessa said, "Cami?"

Cami glanced to where her sister sat to her left. "Huh? Sorry. What?"

"You're not eating very much. You not hungry?"

Cami touched her cheek. "Still kind of hurts to chew."

"I'm sorry. I didn't think about that when I made a roast. Fill up on potatoes and gravy at least. That should be easier."

Cami nodded, but Josh noticed she didn't add anything

more to her plate. He knew it was unrealistic to expect her to be her normal perky self so soon after such a trauma, but it concerned him nonetheless. Maybe forcing her to face it and talk about it hadn't been the right thing. Josh found his own appetite slipping away at the thought that he might have caused more harm when he'd only meant to help her.

❧

"Do you want to come with us?" Violet asked. "You wouldn't have to do anything. You might have to walk a little bit, but we won't make you swing the ax."

Cami didn't really feel like going, but she could feel herself slipping into...something. A dark place she didn't want to be. Maybe an outing like this would help keep her from sliding further down. Being left alone with her thoughts was probably the last thing she needed right then. "I'd come, but I doubt I have adequate stuff to wear."

Violet smiled at her. "That is not a problem. Come with me." As they headed for the stairs, she called back over her shoulder. "Don't leave without us. Cami's coming, too."

Within five minutes they were back downstairs, and Cami was dressed to survive the cold afternoon. She'd taken another dose of her pain medication, so hopefully she'd be able to enjoy the outing.

"Why don't you ride with us?" Jessa suggested.

"We're going to ride with Laurel and Matt in their new van," Violet said. "Rose and Addy can hang out together."

"I'm going with Nick," Lily said. "You could ride with us."

"Thanks, hun, but I'm sure you'd rather not have me tagging along with the two of you. I'll inflict my presence on Jessa and Lance."

Lily smiled and then took Nick's outstretched hand. They went down the stairs to the old car that Nick drove and were the first to leave. Jessa opened the back door of the cab of Lance's truck. Cami managed to get up onto the seat without too much pain and then waited as Jessa closed the door and climbed in the front. A blast of cold entered the cab when both doors on the driver's side opened. Cami watched in surprise—though she knew she shouldn't have been—when Josh swung up onto the seat next to her.

He gave her a wide grin. "Missing the balmy temperatures of California yet?"

Cami nodded. "Winter was definitely something I never missed about Minnesota."

"I hear ya. I moved here in the summer and didn't know what I was getting into. Growing up in Kenya, we never had a white Christmas."

"Do you have siblings?" Cami asked.

"Yep, though not as many as you do." Josh pulled out his wallet and opened it. "I have two sisters and one brother. All younger."

Cami took his wallet when he held it out and stared at the picture in the plastic pocket. Along with the three young people, the photo included a middle-aged couple. All of them were smiling, and she could see where Josh got his looks from. "They look very…happy."

"Yes, they do. And they are." He took the wallet back when she held it out to him. "You'll get to meet them."

"I will?"

"Yes. They're all coming for Christmas and Lance's wedding."

Well, if she'd had any thoughts of getting involved with Josh, they were gone now. His family would no doubt take one look at her and strongly advise Josh against getting anywhere near her. "Where do they live?"

"My mom and dad live in Texas now. They work at their mission headquarters there. My one sister is a nurse in Dallas and is married with no kids yet. My brother is going to college, and my youngest sister is still in high school."

"And they're all coming for Christmas?" Cami asked.

"Yep. Jessa was gracious enough to offer rooms at the manor for them."

Cami glanced at her older sister, who nodded as she looked toward the back seat. "We'll have a full house for Christmas this year. I'm excited about it."

While Cami could understand why Jessa was excited, she wasn't feeling that way herself. She knew it was all because of the way she looked right now. She was a performer. She could have performed her way through any situation. With her makeup and outfit in place, she could play whatever role she wanted to. Her singing had allowed her to adapt to that. Sometimes her songs were sweet and innocent. Other times they were sultry and seductive. Sometimes fun, sometimes sad. She dressed accordingly and played it up with her body language. But now, with a battered face and body, no matter what role she chose, the one that screamed out the loudest was victim.

"What do you usually do for Christmas, Cami?" Josh asked.

Cami thought back over the past few years. "I usually spend Christmas Eve with friends. A couple of years I had a gig. It was generally pretty low-key. New Year's Eve was the big celebration."

"Well, I hope you're ready to celebrate Christmas this year," Josh said with a smile. "I've already warned Jessa that my family loves to celebrate—and I mean *celebrate*—Christmas."

She just hoped they'd be too caught up in their celebrations to notice her. She also hoped that by then the worst of the damage to her face might have faded. After seeing herself in the mirror that morning, Cami was surprised that any of her family could stand to look at her face to face without wincing.

Chapter Nine

"So, who has the final say on the tree today?" Cami asked.

"That would be me," Jessa said without hesitation. "Of course, I welcome input."

Lance laughed. "Sure you do,"

"Are you calling me controlling?" Jessa asked.

"Only in the most loving and affectionate way," he told her.

Cami saw the smitten look on his face as he glanced toward Jessa. Though she hadn't always liked Jessa, now that Gran wasn't there to dictate how she should be treated, her older sister seemed to have mellowed toward her. She was happy that Jessa had been able to take on the role of head of the family without turning into their grandmother. Cami was sure she hadn't been the only one to wonder if that was possible. No doubt, part of the change was due to Lance and the love they shared.

"Here we go," Lance said as he turned off the highway into the parking lot of the Christmas tree farm.

Once the vehicle stopped, Lance and Josh opened their doors and climbed out.

Before opening her door, Jessa turned toward Cami. "If you need a break at any time, just let me know. You can come back and wait here."

"I think I'll be fine. I'm feeling okay at the moment."

Her door and Jessa's opened at the same time. Josh stood there. "Need a hand?"

She slid her gloved hand into the one he held out and slid from the seat to the snowy ground. It was definitely easier getting out of the truck than into it. The rest of their group gathered around and then moved toward the entrance to the farm. There were lots of other cars in the parking area, but it wasn't crowded as they walked up and down paths looking for the perfect tree.

Cami crossed her arms in an effort to keep warm as she followed Jessa and Lance. Josh stayed fairly close to her although he didn't stick right beside her.

"Are you doing okay?" Cami asked Laurel as they stopped to look at one large tree.

Laurel smiled. "I'm great. I figured some walking might get this kid moving."

As they continued to walk, it slowly dawned on Cami what Josh was doing. Whether walking or stopping to view a tree, Josh was positioning himself to shield her from the wind that had kicked up. The thoughtfulness of his actions gripped her. While she'd dated some real jerks, she'd also had a couple of relationships with men who hadn't been that bad. But none of them would have done for her what Josh was doing. Here was this man who didn't claim to love her or even want her, and yet through his actions he showed the kind of man he was. Cami couldn't imagine how he would treat the woman he did choose to love.

And a large part of her hoped she wasn't around to see it. Could she stand to see him choose another woman to love when each time she saw him, she lost a little more of her heart to him? She knew it wasn't his intention to have her fall in love with him. How could it be when he'd made it clear that there could be nothing between them? And yet still, as she watched Matt care for her pregnant sister, and Dean tease Violet while Lance catered to Jessa's demands for the perfect tree, Cami found herself longing—for the first time ever—for that type of relationship for herself.

It surprised Cami to admit that. She hadn't been one to ever think of settling down with just one man. Without having had a good example of what a loving relationship could really be, marriage had never been on her to-do list. But seeing her sisters find love was making her reconsider her stance. She knew, however, that it would take a very special man to know everything about her and still love her. So far, she hadn't been the best judge of character when it came to men. And that continued with Josh. While he was a fine man, he obviously wasn't for her.

"Okay. Let's take a vote on this one," Jessa said as she pointed to a large pine tree. "I think it would work perfectly in the living room."

The vote didn't take long. If Jessa liked it, that was pretty much good enough for everyone. Cami stood with Laurel and watched as the others each took a whack at the tree. Even Rose and Addy got in on the action. Lance finished it off and then he and the other guys had the pleasure of carrying it back to his truck.

Josh shrugged out of his jacket and hung it in the foyer closet before rejoining the family in the living room. The tree had been wrangled from the truck into the house and was now set up and awaiting decorations.

"We've got new lights," Jessa said as she pointed to a few bags sitting near the tree. "Who volunteers to string them onto the tree?"

Josh glanced around, noticing almost immediately that Cami was missing. His concern kicked into overdrive, but there was nothing he could do about it. He was pretty sure that at least one of her sisters was aware of her absence and the reason for it. Before he could wonder further, a box of lights was shoved into his hands. Apparently, volunteering and conscription meant the same thing in Jessa's book. Not that he minded. He was grateful that the family included him in their gatherings, even though, at most, he would be cousin-in-law when Jessa and Lance married in a few weeks' time.

"I'm going to get something for us to drink. You have two options. Hot chocolate or coffee." Jessa took a count and then left with Rose and Violet to get the drinks. Laurel had settled herself in one of the easy chairs and didn't look to be moving any time soon.

After Laurel freed the lights from their boxes, the guys made quick work of stringing them. By the time Jessa and the others were back with the drinks and some cookies, the small white lights were twinkling on the tree. But Cami was still absent. He'd been surprised on the way back from the Christmas tree farm that she'd chosen to ride with Lily and her boyfriend. They'd gotten back to the manor first and by the time everyone else had arrived, Cami had disappeared. It was hard not to take it personally, but Josh also knew he had no right to take anything Cami did that way.

"She said she was just going to lie down for a little while."

Josh turned to see Violet standing at his elbow. He thought about pretending ignorance, but knew Violet wouldn't buy it for a second. "Okay. I hope the outing wasn't too much for her."

Violet's brows drew together. "I don't think it was that. I think she still struggles with being around all of us, not really knowing where her place is."

"Yes, I'm sure there's some adjustment since your

relationships with each other were dictated very much by your grandmother."

"That's for sure. I'm just glad that Jessa and Cami seem to have gotten to a place where they can co-exist without too much friction. I must say that I wondered if that day would ever come." Violet glanced up at him. "Did you hear about Jessa's latest purchase?"

"I don't think so." Though honestly, Jessa had been buying quite a few things the last few months, so it was possible he had and just didn't realize it.

Violet smiled. "A baby grand piano."

"Really? For Cami?" Josh could only imagine what Cami's reaction would be to that.

"Not for her, necessarily, but because of her. Jessa never realized until you told us that night about how much Cami really loved her music. I think we all figured it was a bit of a phase. Even though our mom, from what we have heard over the years, was also musically gifted. I'm guessing Jessa is hoping to show Cami that we support her in this."

"When is it coming?" Josh asked.

"Sometime this week, I think. Maybe it will help pull Cami out of whatever she's sinking into." Violet paused and then said, "And on that note, I think I'm going to go check on her."

"I'm sure she'll appreciate that."

"Not too sure about that," Violet said. "But it will put my mind—and yours—at ease, I think."

Josh watched her walk away and hoped she returned with Cami in tow. He thought the fun of decorating would help buoy her spirits.

Violet was gone about ten minutes, and when she returned, she wasn't alone. With her blonde hair pulled back in a ponytail, Cami looked more like a teenager than a young woman in her twenties. She had the sleeves of her sweatshirt pulled down past the end of her fingers, and when she sat down on the couch next to Laurel, she tucked her hands under her thighs.

Josh noticed that she kept her gaze on the activity around the Christmas tree. Not once did she look in his direction. A battle kicked to life within him then. He remembered the words Lance had said about Cami getting hurt by him, even if it was unintentional. It wasn't doing him any good to be focused on her like he was, either.

He knew there could be nothing between them until she understood and accepted God's love for her and what that meant for her spiritually. Allowing his emotions and feelings to get so caught up in her was futile unless he was prepared to wait indefinitely. Part of him was more than willing to do that, but Josh had to wonder about his ulterior motive for wanting her to give her heart to God. He needed to be able to say that he wanted that for her, regardless of what it meant for them. At that moment, he wasn't sure he could say that and truly mean it.

Cami didn't come anywhere near him for the remainder of the evening and disappeared without saying goodbye. That was a pretty clear indication to Josh that she was putting distance between them, so he would respect that and try to give her the space she needed.

Though her sisters were careful to make sure she got her rest, Cami found herself tiring easily. Monday she was at the sheriff's station to make her formal report. And on Tuesday she went along for the final fitting for their bridesmaid dresses and tried to ignore the looks of curiosity on the faces of the salespeople at the bridal salon. Violet insisted that she still wanted her to be part of the wedding party, regardless of the state of her face. She also wanted Cami to sing, but Cami wasn't sure yet if she was feeling up to that.

Thursday afternoon, Cami was upstairs in her room working her way through a couple of possible song choices for Violet when Jessa popped her head in.

"Hey. Can you come downstairs for a minute?"

Cami nodded as she slipped the ear buds out. "What's up?"

"I just want you to try something out for me."

Jessa wouldn't volunteer any more information, and when they got to the bottom of the stairs, she told Cami to cover her eyes. Cami gave her an exasperated look, but decided for her sister's sake to play along.

With her sister's hands on her shoulder to guide her, Cami kept her eyes covered. She guessed they were in the living room when they finally came to a stop.

"Okay," Jessa said, an edge of excitement to her voice. "You can open your eyes."

Cami slowly lowered her hands and opened her eyes. In spite of the pain, her jaw dropped when she saw the shiny black piano in front of her. She reached out and ran her fingers along the edge of it. "Wow. Just...wow."

"C'mon. Sit down and play for us," Violet urged.

Cami glanced around and saw that all of her sisters were gathered there. Nerves fluttered in her stomach. She had never performed for family before. Clenching and unclenching her hands, she slid onto the padded bench and then adjusted its position. Figuring it would be appropriate, she chose to play one of the Christmas songs she'd been rehearsing for the gig that had gotten cancelled.

Because she'd memorized the songs she'd planned to perform, she was able to play without music. She began tentatively, getting used to the feel of the keys, but after she'd played the song through once, Cami began to sing.

Silent night, holy night!

All is calm, all is bright.

'Round yon Virgin, Mother and Child.

Holy infant so tender and mild,

Sleep in heavenly peace,

Sleep in heavenly peace.

Cami felt movement on the bench beside her and looked over to see Lily seated there. Her younger sister gave her a smile, and as Cami began the second verse, Lily joined in with her. Singing brought some pain to her face, but she pushed on and soon, from behind her, she heard the others join in. As she finished the song, she moved into another familiar carol. She didn't know how long they sat there, but she went through five of the more familiar Christmas carols before lifting her fingers from the keys.

She sat for a moment, and then turned on the piano bench, her gaze searching for Jessa. Cami was surprised to see her sister sitting on the couch, tears streaming down her face. Jessa got up and came to where she sat and knelt beside her.

"I'm sorry. So, so sorry." Jessa grasped Cami's hands in hers. "I didn't know."

Cami stared down at her sister. "What do you mean?"

"Josh tried to explain to us what music meant to you, but until this I didn't understand what he meant."

"Josh?" She'd been trying to avoid thinking of him, so to have his name pop up like this brought with it a flutter in her stomach.

"After he brought you home from the bar that night, he said it took so long because he stayed to let you finish your set. I didn't understand why he would do that, even though he said that you needed the music." Jessa swiped at the wetness on her cheeks. "It wasn't until now that I understood what he meant. I'm so sorry none of us realized what music has meant to you. I realize now just how much Gran hurt you by trying to keep music from you. It's who you are."

Cami felt as if a band on her heart popped open at her sister's words. Even though they had accepted her talent, which was evident by them asking her to sing at their weddings, she had never expected that they would ever get what music was to her. She knew that what drew her to Josh was that he understood that part of her like no one else ever had. But today it seemed that Jessa—the one sister she'd conflicted with the most—finally grasped what made her who she was.

Mindful of her sore ribs, Cami hugged Jessa. "Thank you."

When the hug ended, Jessa pulled back, her eyes still wet. "I know that you probably won't ever call the manor home, but just know that this will always be waiting for you when you do come back."

"It's beautiful." Cami ran her fingers over the ivory of the keys. "So much nicer than the electronic piano I have in my apartment. I love it."

"And I don't know about Jessa," Violet said as she joined them at the piano, "but you're definitely singing at my wedding."

"I have a feeling you're going to be the true star," Jessa said with a grin.

Cami shook her head. "No, you will both shine like you should on your wedding days."

"I just hope I can make it to both of them," Laurel piped up from her spot on the couch.

As the conversation moved into the area of babies and weddings, Cami didn't feel she had much to offer, but she was content to just be there with her sisters, talking. It was the way it should have been since they were younger, but Gran had made sure that never happened. Thankfully, it wasn't too late.

Cami woke early Friday morning, glad to feel a little more like her old self. Unfortunately, a sneeze reminded her just how far her ribs were from being totally healed. They were her greatest concern when it came to singing at Violet's wedding. She'd been practicing slow deep breaths to try to get used to the feeling.

Standing in front of the mirror, she carefully pulled off her top to view the damage. The bruises around her neck, which had been the least serious, had faded the most, but her rib area was a nice map of purple and yellow. Thankfully, the dress Violet had chosen covered more than it revealed, and makeup would take care of the rest. The swelling around her eyes was way down, but there was still discoloration around them and on her jaw that she'd need to cover up.

Cami hated that Albert had been able to do this to her. She should have been able to defend herself better. But she'd let her guard down and was paying the price now. He was just lucky she hadn't been ready for him. He'd be having a few physical problems himself had she been prepared.

After she finished checking her bruised body, Cami got in the shower and managed to wash her hair, though it was a slow and painful process. She was determined to do it on her own, but it still winded her enough that she had to sit down on the bed for a few minutes after she was all dressed in order to catch her breath.

There was a lot of activity in the manor, as preparations were underway for the rehearsal dinner and then the wedding the following day. Will and his family were due to arrive at some point, though they would be staying with Sylvia through Jessa and Lance's wedding.

Concerned about her music for Violet's wedding, Cami slipped out of the manor and headed for the small chapel. Jessa had mentioned that a piano had been delivered there as well, so Cami wanted to try it out before the rehearsal that night. She still hadn't decided on what song to sing, but hopefully spending some time there might help her make up her mind.

The chapel was empty, but still had a cozy feel to it as she walked down the aisle to where the piano sat. It wasn't as grand as the one in the manor, but it suited the size of the chapel. She hoped she'd be able to practice some before people came to decorate.

ঌ৵

"Anything I can do?" Josh asked as he stood in the doorway of the kitchen.

Laurel was seated on a stool at the counter, cutting vegetables. He wondered how much longer it would be before she went into labor. She looked like she couldn't get much bigger without popping. It was no wonder Matt wanted to stick close to home.

"Can you take that to the chapel?" Jessa asked, pointing to a box sitting on the table. "It's candles and wreaths for the window sills. I'll send Cami out to help set them up once she comes downstairs."

At the mention of Cami, Josh's heart skipped a beat. He'd steered clear of the manor all week to give her the space that she seemed to want. And if he was honest, it was space he needed as well. She was stirring too many things to life within him, and none of them were appropriate given their situation.

"Okay. I'll take this out and be back if you have more to go," Josh said as he lifted the box and headed for the back door.

It was a perfect winter morning...if there was such a thing. It had snowed lightly the night before so everything was pristine white, and there was no wind which kept the cold from biting through to his bones. Someone had already used the snow blower to clear a path from the porch of the house to the steps of the chapel. The snow still on the ground crunched beneath his boots as he walked.

As soon as he opened the door to the foyer, Josh realized that Cami wasn't upstairs at the manor like Jessa had thought. The sound of the piano and her voice drifted out to him as he stood there. Moving slowly, he entered the sanctuary and set the box down on one of the pews. The way the piano was positioned, he could see her profile as she played. Apparently she was too caught up in her music to realize that she was no longer alone.

He debated leaving but just couldn't. Just like it had that night at the bar, Josh found himself mesmerized by the sound of her voice. He really couldn't understand how she hadn't managed to get herself discovered with her talent. She had a voice quality that rivaled some of the talent out there and even exceeded some, in his opinion. And given that music had been his business not that long ago, he figured he was a fair judge of talent.

She stopped in mid-song, and Josh wondered if she was aware of his presence, but she didn't turn his way. She straightened her back and appeared to be taking several deep breaths. The image of her bruised ribs flashed in his mind, and he realized that she had to sing with that pain.

After about a minute, she began playing again and almost immediately Josh recognized the song. He had sung it himself at weddings back when he'd still been singing publically. Though it was an old song, he knew it would be perfect for either Violet or Jessa's wedding. He was somewhat surprised, given its spiritual content, that she knew it, but if she was performing at weddings, no doubt it had been requested a time or two.

Lance had asked him to sing at his and Jessa's wedding and listening to Cami now, Josh wondered if he could convince her to do a duet. As he stood there listening to her, his phone suddenly sounded a text message alert.

Cami immediately quit playing and turned toward him. "It's usually good manners to turn off your phone when you're attending a performance."

"Well, to be honest, I didn't know you were giving one," Josh said as he walked down the aisle after a quick glance at his phone. "As far as anyone knows, you are upstairs in your room at the manor. Jessa just texted me to ask if you were here." He quickly responded then slid the phone into the pocket of his jacket.

Cami swung sideways on the bench and slid her hands under her thighs as he approached. "I wasn't trying to avoid anyone, but needed to get some practice in. That wouldn't happen at the manor."

Josh nodded as he sat down on the front pew, a few feet from the piano. He was relieved to see that the bruises were fading on her face. Aside from the discoloration, she was looking much more like the woman he remembered. "Have you decided what you're going to sing?"

She shrugged. "I figure I should sing something with a spiritual tone to it since this is for the ceremony, but there are a couple of other songs I like as well."

Josh leaned one arm along the back of the pew. "Are you singing at Jessa's wedding, too?"

"Yep. And I'm assuming that most of the same people will be at both, so I need to do something different."

"Interested in a duet?" Josh asked.

Cami's eyes widened. "With you?"

Josh nodded. "Lance asked me to sing at their wedding, too."

"I'm not really one to sing with others."

"Let's give it a whirl," Josh suggested, though a voice in his head was screaming that this was a very bad idea. "I can harmonize if you sing the melody."

After giving Josh a long look, Cami swung back around to face the keys. "What song?"

"How about that one you were playing by Shania Twain?"

Cami hesitated. "Do you mean 'From This Moment'?"

"Yes. Just let me find the lyrics. It's been awhile since I've sung it." It didn't take long to find what he was looking for on his phone, but as he looked up, Cami didn't appear to want to play it. Her hands were clasped in her lap.

Cami glanced sideways at him. "I'd kind of decided not to

do that one."

"Why's that? It's a very beautiful love song." Josh leaned forward. "I think it would be great for Jessa and Lance. Maybe we could even sing it as she walks down the aisle if she wants."

He saw her take a deep breath and place her hands on the keys. "Okay. We can give it a whirl."

~ Chapter Ten ~

As she started the song, Josh immediately sensed a change in how she was singing it now with him from how she'd sung it before she'd been aware of his presence. Though he'd initially been thinking about making the duet something special for Jessa and Lance, as the song progressed and their voices blended in a way he hadn't imagined, he quickly began to understand Cami's reluctance. He touched Cami's shoulder lightly, and she lifted her hands from the keys without looking at him.

"Yeah, I think maybe you're right. It would be best if we just did our own thing." Josh cleared his throat. "I'll leave you to your practicing. I'm sure anything you choose will be beautiful."

Without waiting for her to respond, Josh spun on his heel and walked toward the back of the sanctuary, berating himself with every step. He didn't know where his mind was. It had been great to see her again, and that should have served as a warning right there. But his common sense had clearly taken a hike when he'd walked into the chapel and realized she was there singing. It was hard to have such a powerful thing in common with her, and yet have an even more powerful thing standing between them.

"God, help me!" Josh said the words aloud as he walked back to the manor. "Give me strength to not think of her in any way but friend. I know it can't be anything else. Help me let her go, even as I pray for her to find You."

He didn't want to go back into the manor, but he'd promised his help, so he had no choice. It was going to be even more difficult to give her space as time progressed. Work was basically on hold until the new year. The last job had wrapped up the day before, and with his family arriving soon and staying at the manor, he'd be over even more. If God was testing him, it was a doozy. And while he'd given into temptation in the past, Josh wouldn't allow that to happen again. He liked to think he was a stronger, if not wiser, man than he had been all those years ago.

It would have been easier if the attraction to Cami was just physical. And while that was part of it, ever since that night at the bar and then the one at the beach, it had become so much more. Too much more. She occupied far more of his thoughts than she should.

"Everything okay?"

Josh looked up to find Lance standing in the doorway of the manor. He took the steps to the porch in one bound. "Yep. Box delivered as Jessa requested. I'm assuming there's still more."

"Jessa said that Cami's at the chapel," Lance said, stepping back so that Josh could enter the manor.

"Yes. She's practicing for the wedding." Without waiting for Lance to continue the conversation, Josh waded into the wedding preparation chaos in the kitchen.

Cami stared at the piano keys. Her emotions were a tangled mess after the encounter with Josh. She wished she played classical music, because right then she wanted to be able to vent all the emotions in a resounding symphony of sound. Anger slowly burned away the other emotions. Anger at herself. At Josh. At God.

At first she hadn't believed that Josh was suggesting they sing a romantic song as a duet. Then she realized that he really was just focused on doing a special song for Lance and Jessa. Of course, it had eventually dawned on him. Or at least she assumed that's why he'd backed away from the duet. Was he really that clueless, or did he just not feel the same pull toward her that she felt toward him?

All of it just made her feel frustrated and angry. She knew that there could be nothing between them. He'd made that pretty clear. But that didn't stop her wayward heart from hoping. She knew if she did what he'd told her to do that day at the lake—give her heart to God—it would be one less obstacle, but then, what if she did it and he *still* didn't want her. It was easier to tell herself that it was because of his faith. But deep down, she was pretty sure that neither God nor Josh was interested in her since they both know her deepest, darkest secret. The one thing she could never undo.

Pushing aside her dour thoughts, Cami once again rested her fingertips on the keys of the piano. The one song she kept coming back to for Violet and Dean wasn't a new one, but the classic had spiritual undertones with parts of it taken from the Bible. She hoped that they would appreciate it. And between now and Jessa's wedding, she'd try to find another appropriate song. Because even if she had wanted to sing the Shania Twain song, it wasn't going to happen after singing that little bit with Josh.

She ran through the song a couple of times before deciding it was good enough to perform that night at the rehearsal. Hopefully Violet and Dean would approve, because she really did want them to be happy with it.

Cami stood, sucking in a breath as her ribs protested the change of position. The pain pill she'd taken earlier was beginning to wear off. She waited for a minute, hand braced on the piano, and took a couple of slow, deep breaths. Just as she began to walk toward the back of the chapel, the doors opened, and several people walked in.

"Hey, Cami," Violet said, her face beaming. "How are you doing?"

"Probably not as good as you," Cami replied with a smile. "Did you think this day would ever come?"

"It's taken its sweet time, that's for sure," Violet agreed.

Behind Violet came their other sisters. The men came last, each carrying boxes which they set on the floor in the foyer.

"Hey, while we're decorating, can you sing for us?" Violet asked. "Just the song you've chosen for the wedding. And maybe Josh can get the microphone set up properly for you."

Cami nodded. "If you'd prefer a different song, just let me know."

"I'll get a mic," Josh said and disappeared into a small room just off the foyer.

"What about microphones for you guys?" Cami asked.

"They designed this place to have the microphone for the bride and groom suspended from the ceiling," Violet said, pointing to a long cord that hung down. "That way, they don't have to fuss with a microphone during the ceremony."

Josh came back out of the room with several things in his hands. He moved to the front of the chapel without looking Cami's way and began to set up. Cami didn't really want to go back to the piano until he was done, but as the others began to empty boxes of the things Violet had chosen for her decorations, she knew she couldn't avoid it.

"Have a seat," Josh said as she approached. "Let me make sure it's at the correct height."

She settled back down on the bench she'd so recently vacated and tried to ignore his closeness as he worked with the stand to get it right.

"Is there a mic for the piano as well?" she asked.

"Yes, so while you're singing I'll see what I can do to set the blend and balance correctly. Don't want it to overpower your voice." He pointed to a small area at the back of the sanctuary that had a half wall around it. "I'm going to be there in the sound booth. Start to sing and let me see what I can do."

Cami nodded and watched as he made his way around the people decorating to reach the booth. He sat down and bent his head. She waited until he straightened and gave her a thumbs-up. Suddenly nervous, she played a longer intro than usual, then leaned a little closer to the mic and began to sing. Not wanting to be distracted by the others in the sanctuary, she closed her eyes.

The familiarity of the words and music helped wash away her nerves, and her voice gained strength as she started the second verse. When she got to the end, she let the note linger before lifting her foot from the pedal. She took a deep breath and opened her eyes.

Seeing Violet and Dean standing by the piano, watching her, took Cami by surprise. "Um, is that okay?"

Dean smiled. "Perfect. I think I'd like to have you sing that during the lighting of the unity candle." He glanced at Violet. "What do you think?"

Violet slipped her arm around his waist, resting her head against his shoulder. "I think that would be a perfect place for it." She gave Cami a soft smile. "Thank you for doing this for us."

"It's my pleasure." She glanced toward where Josh sat. "Were you able to do what you needed, Josh?"

"I think so, but run through it one more time just to make sure."

Cami nodded and began the song again, this time keeping her eyes open. Violet and Dean moved away to help with the decorations, and when she finished it, Josh called out that it was fine. She left the piano then and was going to help, but Violet told her to go back to the manor.

"We've got it all under control here," she said. "I know you're still in pain, so just rest up."

With the pain in her ribs becoming more than just a nuisance, Cami knew it was better to do as Violet said. Besides, putting some distance between herself and Josh would be a good thing.

"So much better than poufy dresses in vibrant colors," Jessa commented as she smoothed her hands down the chocolate-brown satin of the dresses Violet had chosen.

Though brown wasn't Cami's favorite color, she had to admit it suited each of them. The gowns had an empire waist that worked well with Laurel's burgeoning stomach. Though the long dresses were strapless, each of them wore a small bolero-style jacket with sleeves that reached their elbows. Violet's best friend from Seattle had flown in, and they'd all been in agreement that she should be her matron of honor. Addy and Rose were the flower girls.

Cami had been surprised to find out that Lance, Josh, Matt, and Will were Dean's groomsmen. He had chosen Matt to be his best man, and she wondered how Laurel felt about not being paired with her husband for the event. Thankfully, Josh was paired with Laurel and Cami would be with Will. The last thing she had needed was to be paired with the man she was trying to avoid. Apparently, Violet felt the same way.

The wedding progressed smoothly, which wasn't a big surprise since the rehearsal had also gone off without a hitch. The only difference was that the pastor gave his full message to Violet and Dean. As she listened, Cami found her interest piqued by his words. He spoke of the importance of having God as a part of their relationship, which was something she hadn't heard about in the weddings she'd attended either as guest or performer.

"Think of your relationship like a triangle. God is the top, and each of you represents one of the lower points. As you grow closer to God individually and as a couple, you'll grow closer together. He is the strong foundation on which you need to build your marriage and family."

The concept was foreign to Cami, but she supposed it made sense to someone who believed in God in that way. Not just as an entity out there beyond the clouds watching them scurry about, but a God who they believed was actively involved in their lives.

If she'd put her faith in God, would He have protected her at that rest stop? Would He have made sure that Albert wouldn't have been able to find her, let alone assault her?

Cami pushed aside her thoughts when it was time for her to sing, while Dean and Violet lit their unity candle. And then there was plenty of whooping and hollering when the pastor pronounced them husband and wife and told them they could kiss. She couldn't help but smile when Dean cupped her sister's face and sealed their union with a gentle kiss. Then he took her into his arms and dipped her for another, slightly more passionate, one.

The reception was scheduled for two hours later at a hall in Collingsworth, so they had time to take pictures. Though it was chilly, Violet had arranged for a few outdoor shots. They all had wraps that they put on before leaving the chapel. Knowing it would mean less time in the cold if no one fooled around, they followed the instructions of the photographer to get the group shots out of the way. Cami was relieved to step into the warmth of the manor while Violet, Dean, and Addy stayed outside for a few more shots.

Whether it was just the excitement of the day or just time, Cami woke to the news the next morning that Laurel was at the hospital in Collingsworth. The news brought mixed feelings as she vividly remembered the last time Laurel had gone into labor. She hadn't wanted Cami to tell anyone. She hadn't wanted to deliver because, as long as the baby was within her, no one could take it away. Cami had stayed with her throughout the whole long labor, crying with her as she moved into the final stages and then delivering a squalling, red-faced little girl. That brief glimpse had been all either of them had had of the baby until they got back to Collingsworth.

"Okay, God, if you're out there, be with Laurel as she goes through this and please keep her from remembering what happened before." Cami leaned on the bathroom vanity and stared at herself in the mirror. The outward bruises were fading well, but she was finding that the inner wounds she bore were getting worse. She didn't know if it was seeing her sister get married or being around Josh, but there was a constant ache in her heart. An ache edged with hopelessness.

Cami took a deep breath and let it out. She had always thought of herself as fairly upbeat and determined, but lately it seemed that she kept finding herself thinking that there was no hope for her dreams. No music. No love. No family. Was that her destiny?

"Cami?" Her name was accompanied by a knock.

Turning, Cami saw Jessa coming toward her open bathroom door.

"What's up?"

"Matt just called. Laurel is asking for you."

"Me?"

"Yes. He said that she's asked several times for you to be with her." Jessa gave her a quizzical look. "Did you talk about being with her during the delivery?"

Cami shook her head. "I think it might have something to do with Rose's birth."

Comprehension dawned on Jessa's face. "You were with her."

Slowly Cami nodded. "Yes."

"Can you go to her now?"

"If I can get a ride. I just need to get changed."

"That's not a problem. We'll drop you off on our way to church. I don't think Laurel needs all of us hanging around there right now."

After Jessa left, Cami quickly changed into a pair of jeans and a long-sleeved t-shirt and then applied enough makeup to cover the bruises. She wasn't completely sure she wanted to be with Laurel, but if her sister needed her there, then that was where she'd be.

Once at the hospital, the nurses directed her to Laurel's room. It was surprisingly calm and quiet when she walked in. The lights were turned low, and music played softly. Cami glanced around and spotted Laurel lying on a bed facing the window. Matt sat next to her in a chair, his head tilted back and eyes closed.

A nurse stood at a high table making notes on a chart. She smiled and said, "Are you Cami?"

At the nurse's words, Laurel stirred as Matt stood.

"Cami?"

She rounded the end of the bed and went to where Matt stood holding Laurel's hand. Cami leaned forward and rested her hand on Laurel's face briefly. "I hear you were asking for me."

"Here," Matt said, motioning for her to change places with him. "I'll let you guys talk. I'm going to walk for a few minutes."

Cami took Matt's place, grasping Laurel's hand in hers. She sank down on the chair, so that she was at eye-level with her sister. Softly she said, "I didn't think you'd want me here. Won't it bring back bad memories?"

Laurel shook her head. "You got me through that labor and delivery. I want you here for this one, too. I think we both need to go through this together."

"Matt is okay with that?"

"He understands."

"How are you doing?"

"Better now that they gave me an epidural. I said I didn't want one, but I forgot how much it hurts."

"Are you dilating?"

Laurel nodded. "Last time they checked me I was at six."

Cami remembered well everything she'd learned about childbirth ten years earlier. She'd studied what she could, once she'd realized that she would be with Laurel during the delivery. She had never dreamed that there would come a day when she'd once again be supporting Laurel through this process. Thankfully, this time her sister would get to keep the baby.

"What can I do for you?"

Over the next few hours, Cami and Matt took turns caring for Laurel and when she was finally given the okay to push, they each took up position on either side of her. Cami tried to ignore the sick feeling in her stomach as the painful process brought back a flood of memories. She had to remind herself over and over again that this time Laurel got to keep the baby.

"It's a boy!"

The words were accompanied by a hearty cry. Cami stared at the baby as they laid him on Laurel's chest. Matt bent close to give his wife a kiss and to meet his new son.

Feeling overwhelmed with every kind of emotion, Cami took a step back and then another before turning to flee the room. She found a bathroom and took refuge in a locked stall and wept silently. Though Laurel had likely thought going through the birth would be a healing process for Cami, she didn't know what had happened two years after Rose's birth. The secret Cami had told no one but Josh.

What had she done? Seeing that newborn baby placed on Laurel's chest, it was the only thing going through her mind.

What have I done?

"It's a boy!" Jessa exclaimed as she disconnected the call.

Josh smiled. They had all been so sure it would be another girl, since Will had been the only anomaly in the family history of giving birth to girls.

"A boy?" Rose shrieked. "I have a brother?"

"That you do, sweetheart." Jessa gave her a hug.

"What's his name? Can we go see him?"

"I don't know his name. Matt said they'd tell us when we got there. So yes, we can go see him."

Rose's excitement bubbled over as she urged them to get ready to go. They'd finished their lunch a few minutes earlier, so they just donned jackets and boots and left. Josh hadn't been sure about going since technically he wasn't family, but Jessa said he was welcome. And being friends with Matt now, Josh was anxious to congratulate him on the birth of his son.

Once at the hospital, they were all allowed to go into Laurel's room. Josh didn't know if that was common practice or if it had to do with who the patient was, but he figured it wasn't going to be too crowded since Violet and Dean weren't there. They had left the previous evening for their honeymoon. He was pretty sure they were headed somewhere on a plane, so they wouldn't be able to meet the new baby until they returned at the end of the week.

"Oh, he's beautiful," Jessa said as she and Rose bent over the baby in Laurel's arms. "Okay. What's his name?"

Laurel and Matt glanced at each other and then Laurel said, "Benjamin Matthew Davis."

"I like that name, Mama," Rose said, her face beaming.

Josh knew that Cami had been at the hospital, so he glanced around the room in search of her. She was nowhere to be seen. Concern that he'd been pushing aside now came to the forefront. Knowing what he did about her past, he wondered how she was handling this.

When the door slowly opened a few minutes later, he glanced over in time to see Cami walk into the room. Their eyes met for a second, and the emotion there hit him like a punch in the gut. He knew she was just barely holding it together, had maybe even had to pull herself back together in order to come into the room.

"Cami! Where did you go?" Laurel asked as she waved her sister close.

"I just wanted to give you guys some time together with your son."

"Well, come meet your nephew, Benjamin Matthew."

Josh saw the slowness in her steps as she moved to stand beside Rose.

"I want you to hold him, Cam," Laurel said.

Josh held his breath as Cami allowed Laurel to place the baby into her arms. From his position behind Matt on the other side of the bed, he had a clear view of her face. She lowered her cheek to press it against Benjamin's, but when she lifted her head, the shattered look on her face took his breath away.

Chapter Eleven

SHE quickly returned the baby to Laurel and spun from the bed to once again leave the room.

"What's wrong?" Jessa asked.

"I thought it might help her get over the trauma of the last time," Laurel said, "but maybe I was wrong."

Josh was sure it had less to do with that than the decision she'd made a few years later.

"I'll go check on her." He didn't know if it was the smartest move, but of everyone there, he was the only one who knew her secret and why she was reacting the way she was.

He didn't spot Cami in the hallway, so he asked a woman at the nursing station if she'd seen her.

"She went to the restroom near the waiting room," the nurse said and pointed down the hallway.

Josh thanked her and walked toward the closed door. He wasn't sure what to do when he got there. No way would he go in there after her, but he wanted her to know she wasn't alone. Josh settled into one of the chairs in the waiting room that gave him a view of the restroom door.

As he sat there watching, Josh prayed for God to help Cami. He truly did want to show her God's love and how He could make a difference in her life. Unfortunately, their emotions and attraction seemed to keep getting tangled up in their every interaction.

Even now, Josh wondered how he should approach her. He wanted to hold her and give her a shoulder to cry on it if that was what she needed, but no doubt that would just complicate things further. There seemed to be no right way for him to deal with her. But now he didn't know what to do. He'd told Jessa and Laurel he'd check on her. He couldn't very well go back without being able to tell them that she was okay.

He let out a long sigh. Sometimes his best intentions got him into the worst situations.

He'd just about decided to give up when the door to the bathroom opened, and she stepped out. Josh quickly stood and walked in her direction.

"Cami," he called out.

She stopped walking and swung around to face him. He could see the strain of emotion on her face. "Are you okay?"

Her eyes narrowed briefly as she crossed her arms. "I'll be fine."

"I'm sure this has been difficult for you," Josh said as he shoved his hands into his pockets. It didn't appear that a hug was wanted or needed.

"It's had its ups and downs. I didn't know that Laurel wanted me to be with her for the delivery. It was a bit of a shock." She glanced down the hall in the direction of Laurel's room. "I'd better get back before they get too worried."

Josh nodded and stood, legs braced apart, hands on hips, watching as she walked away. He decided not to return to the room since he'd already seen little Benjamin, and it was time for their family to be together. And he wasn't family.

With a sigh, he turned and headed for the elevator that would take him to the lobby floor and the exit of the hospital. What was it about him and wounded women? It had been the same with Emma. They'd started dating in high school and even then it was apparent she had some emotional issues, but neither he nor her parents had realized how bad they were. They had all been guilty of thinking they could just love her out of the depression she kept sinking into.

First they'd dismissed it as teenage moodiness, then hormonal issues. She'd gotten better for a short time after their marriage, and Josh had thought the worst was behind them. Little had he known. She'd wanted to get pregnant right away, but it hadn't happened like that which had started another downward spiral. Then his group had started up, and they'd begun to travel. He'd asked her to come on the road with them, but she'd refused.

He had breathed a sigh of relief when she'd finally gotten pregnant, only to have the bottom drop out of their world when their daughter was stillborn. Emma had sunk to a scary low. And Josh had done the unthinkable. The affair was already over by the time the news broke. But two days after his lapse in judgment was made public, Emma committed suicide. The media had had a heyday with that, saying that Josh's affair had caused her to take her own life. Josh knew in his heart that that had not been the case. At that point, Emma had had no access to any type of media, and her parents would never have told her, knowing what that would do to her. But it was so much more sensational to spin it the other way.

And now here he was again drawn to a woman with troubles of her own. Though he doubted she had the emotional problems Emma had, she was still dealing with a lot. He did see strength in her that Emma had never had, so maybe it was unfair to compare them. All he knew was that, unless things changed considerably with Cami, there was no happy ending for him there.

Cami pushed open the door of the room, hoping they wouldn't ask too many questions. She planned to just brush off her emotional response as a reaction to what had happened with Laurel at Rose's birth. As she stepped into the room, she glanced back over her shoulder, expecting to see Josh behind her, but instead she saw him standing at the bank of elevators, hands shoved into his pockets, head down.

She paused for a second, wondering if her response to his concern for her had sent him away. She hadn't meant to be brusque with him, but if she'd let even a little emotion show, the dam would have broken. Again. As it was, she was hanging on by a thread. Determined to get through this without breaking down again, Cami pulled her gaze from him and walked into the room.

Calling on every bit of strength she still had, she walked to Laurel's bed again. She pasted a smile on her face for the sake of her sisters. "Sorry about that. It's all just a little emotional for me."

Jessa slipped an arm around her shoulders and gave her a quick hug. "It's okay. I think we're all a little emotional today. I'm upset because I have to take back all the adorable pink things I'd bought for the baby."

Matt chuckled. "I did warn you that there was a fifty-fifty chance it would be a boy."

"Well, given Collingsworth history, I was pretty sure that Laurel's eggs would flat out reject a Y chromosome." She reached out and stroked a finger down Benjamin's cheek.

Lance's phone made a sound, and Cami looked over in time to see him glance at the screen and then up at her. He looked back down and tapped out a message before returning the phone to the holder on his belt. Cami guessed that it was a message from Josh explaining why he hadn't returned to the room with her. If only he'd sent her a message, too, so she knew if it was something she'd done.

They didn't stay too long, since Laurel still hadn't slept since giving birth. They took Rose with them when they left, after assuring her that she could come back to visit Laurel later that evening. Cami stared out the window of Lance's truck as he drove them back to the manor. Already she had decided that she needed a break. Cami was sure people would say she was just running away, but right then she was thinking more along the lines of self-preservation. Hopefully, no one would give her grief over her plan, but it didn't matter. She was going to do what she needed to in order to keep from totally falling apart.

Josh looked up from his computer when Lance walked into their apartment. He'd just finished reading an email from his mom, detailing the itinerary for their trip to Collingsworth for Christmas and Lance's wedding.

"What's up?" he asked as he clicked to reply to the email.

Lance grabbed a soda from the fridge and sat down on a chair across from him. "Cami's gone."

Josh jerked his head up. "What?"

"She told Jessa she had some things she needed to take care of in California."

"Is she coming back?"

"Apparently she said she'd be back before Christmas."

"Is Jessa upset?"

Lance shrugged. "I don't know. She didn't seem to be, but I know she's been trying to just accept Cami without getting upset by what she does."

"One of these days, the girl's gonna have to stop running," Josh said as he bent over his laptop.

"Maybe. There's never a guarantee that someone will get their life on track. Jessa and I pray for her each day, but in the end, Cami's a grown woman and is responsible for her own decisions."

Josh sighed and sat back in his chair. "Yes. You're right. I just wish I could figure out what I'm feeling for her and somehow get over it."

"I had kind of hoped you'd find a nice, uncomplicated woman at church to date."

"You and me both." Josh crossed his arms across his chest. "I don't know why I feel so concerned. I don't understand why I feel this attraction to her. I just don't get it. It's really a temptation I don't need right now."

"I didn't realize you felt that strongly about her," Lance said. "I mean, I knew there was something there. I just didn't know what exactly."

"Well, that makes two of us. She seems to want nothing to do with me, so, in a way, that makes it a bit easier, but honestly I feel like God is testing me. Maybe this is His way of seeing if I'll fail in this area of my life twice." Josh sighed. "Maybe if I pass this test, He'll send me a woman who loves me and who I can love."

"Perhaps. Clearly you're not going to be able to move on as long as Cami is around. Although, you didn't exactly move on when she wasn't around either."

Josh tossed Lance a frustrated look. "Don't you think I'm aware of that? I just don't understand it. I know we have some things in common. Well, one major thing with our love of music. But the most important thing is something she's not interested in. Why can't my heart understand that that's the only thing that matters and move on?"

"Sorry, I have no answers for you, bud. All I can say is to keep praying about it. God may have a plan that none of us sees right now."

Josh blew out a long breath. "Well, it would be nice if He clued me in."

Lance laughed. "I'm sure you're not the only one who has ever felt that way. But I guess that's where trust and faith come in, right?"

"You'd think I would have learned that already," Josh said

with disgust. “Either I’m stupid or I’m a slow learner.”

“You’re neither. You’re human. You’re not supposed to lean on your own understanding. We all have our own struggles on what we trust God with and those things we keep trying to take care of ourselves. This situation with Cami is particularly complex, so I would just suggest that you continue to pray and take it a step at a time.”

“I know you were worried about Cami getting hurt, but I’m starting to feel like I may be the one in danger of that.”

“Well, don’t let fear of being hurt stop you from following God’s will. Whatever that might be.”

“I guess it’s kind of out of my hands for the next little while anyway.”

Lance leaned forward and set his can of soda on the table. “I’ve found a couple of places that we might be able to flip in the new year. Interested in taking a look?”

Josh nodded. “Definitely. Anything to take my mind off all this.”

Cami lifted her suitcase and carried it up the stairs to her second-floor apartment. She slipped her key into the lock and opened the door. It was so nice to be away from the bone-chilling cold of Minnesota. Hoping to air the place out a bit, Cami opened some of the windows. Before unpacking, Cami went back downstairs to get her mail.

She decided to check on Grace before returning to her apartment. She knocked on her neighbor’s door and as she waited she flipped through her mail. When she didn’t answer, Cami knocked again. “Grace?”

While it wasn’t unusual for the woman to go out sometimes, something just felt off to Cami. She went to the window beside the door and, using her hand to shield her eyes, she tried to peer into the apartment. A shadowy figure on the floor made her heart jump into her throat. She moved back to the door and tried the handle, surprised—and grateful—when it opened.

"Grace!" Cami rushed to the woman's side and sank to her knees. "What's wrong?"

"You're my...miracle...baby girl," the woman said in a weak voice. "I prayed...for help. Here...you...are."

"Hang on. I'm going to call for an ambulance." Cami found the woman's phone and dialed 911. "Please help. My neighbor has collapsed. We need help."

Grace gripped her hand. "Call my...pastor. Please."

"Where is his number?" Cami asked. "What's his name?"

"My Bible." Grace lifted a shaky hand to point to a table beside her recliner. "Please call...him."

"I will, sweetie. Just relax."

"Sing...for me."

Knowing Grace liked hymns, Cami settled on the only one she knew by heart.

Stroking the woman's wiry gray hair, Cami leaned close and began to sing.

Amazing Grace. How sweet the sound.

That saved a wretch like me.

I once was lost but now am found,

Was blind, but now I see.

For the first time, she really thought about the words as she sang them. She only knew the first verse, so she sang that one over and over, praying as she did that help wouldn't be too late.

It seemed an eternity before the ambulance showed up. They asked for information on Grace, but beyond her name, Cami couldn't give many details. And she had no idea about her medical information. When Grace took a turn for the worse, they moved quickly to get her to the ambulance.

Cami asked them which hospital they were taking her to as they wheeled her away. Remembering her promise to Grace, she found her Bible and flipped through it. The only thing that had phone numbers on it looked like a program from a church. It listed a pastor's name, so Cami decided to take a chance that he was the person Grace wanted her to call.

She took the paper back to her apartment where she got her phone and dialed the number. It rang twice before it was answered.

"May I please speak to Pastor David Miller?"

"Speaking. How can I help you?"

"My name is Cami Collingsworth. I'm calling on Grace Olson's behalf. Do you know her?"

"Grace? Yes, I know her very well." The man paused. "Is something wrong?"

"Yes. I just got home and found her collapsed in her apartment. She asked me to call you. I'm her neighbor." Cami gave him the information about the hospital where they'd taken her. "I'm going to be going there right away myself."

"I know she'd appreciate you being there. I will also be there as soon as I can."

After she hung up, Cami returned to Grace's apartment and found her purse. After a brief pause, she also picked the Bible up and slipped it into the handbag. She tried not to think how long Grace had been laying there. Or what might have happened to the woman had she not come home when she did.

You're my...miracle...baby girl. Cami didn't recall anyone ever calling her a miracle before. She was just grateful that she had come when she had in order to help Grace.

At the hospital, Cami approached the front desk to see about getting some news on Grace's condition. "A friend of mine was just brought in by ambulance. Can you tell me how

I would find her?"

"We don't give out information to non-family members," the woman said brusquely.

Cami lifted the purse she held. "I have her bag here which probably has all her medical information. I assumed that it would be needed."

"The ambulance staff should have gotten that from her."

"I'm pretty sure Grace was in no condition to tell them anything, and I didn't know where her purse was when they came to get her. All I could do was give them her name."

The woman held out her hand for the purse, but Cami said, "I'm not sure I should give it to a non-family member."

The woman shot her an unpleasant look.

"Listen, you won't even tell me she's here. I'm not handing over her purse without some kind of confirmation." Cami opened the bag and pulled out Grace's wallet. "I'll give you her medical card and you can photocopy it if you need to, but I won't let go of this until I can make sure Grace is actually here."

With a scowl, the woman behind the desk grabbed the card from Cami's hand. She sat at the computer punching keys for several minutes. Cami stood to the side when someone else approached the desk.

"I'm wondering if you could direct me to where Grace Olson is," a man asked.

Cami touched his arm. "Are you Pastor Miller?"

The man turned to her and smiled. "Yep. Are you Cami?"

"Yes." She held out her hand. "It's a pleasure to meet you, though I wish it were under better circumstances."

"I agree. Has there been any word on her yet?"

Cami shook her head. "They won't tell me anything because I'm not family."

The man smiled and turned back to the woman. "Could

you please let them know that if Grace asks for us, Pastor Miller and Cami are waiting here? We would be very grateful."

Cami saw the woman immediately respond to the pastor's graciousness and felt a pang of remorse for her own petty replies. The woman nodded and typed some more information into the computer before handing the card back to Cami.

"Why don't we have a seat over here?" Pastor Miller suggested as he pointed to a row of seats in a waiting area.

Cami led the way and sat down on one of the padded chairs. "Thank you for coming."

Pastor Miller smiled. "I would come in a heartbeat for Grace. She's a very, very special person to my family and to our church."

"She's special to me, too," Cami said. "I'm just glad that I came home unexpectedly. I wasn't scheduled to be home again before Christmas. It seemed like she had already been laying there for a while."

"I last spoke to her Saturday afternoon. She said she wasn't feeling well and would likely not be at church on Sunday. Later on that day, my wife called her but got her answering machine. That isn't unusual, so she left a message. We were actually just talking about how we should stop by to check on her when you called. She has had some health issues in the past, but nothing like this."

"She spoke to me a bit when I first found her, but I didn't ask how long she'd been there. By the time the ambulance arrived, she'd lost consciousness." Cami stared down at her hands. "I hope she's going to be okay."

"Me, too. We'll certainly be praying for her to get better quickly." The pastor fell silent then said, "Grace spoke a lot about you."

Cami glanced at him. "Really?"

"Yes. She cares a great deal for you. Recently she'd asked

us to pray for an opportunity to share her testimony with you."

"Her testimony? She never spoke about her past."

Pastor Miller nodded. "It's a painful part of her life, but for some reason she felt it was important to share it with you."

"I hope she'll be able to tell me about it soon."

"Actually, she asked me to share it if something should ever happen to her and I had the chance. It seems that right now, she's unable to, but I have the opportunity. Would you like to hear it?"

Cami nodded suddenly curious about the past of the elderly woman who had befriended her six months ago.

"Grace was raised in a Christian home but struggled through her teen years. By the time she was eighteen, she'd already had one baby and by nineteen, there was another. At twenty-one, she found herself pregnant again, but this time she married the father of her baby...which turned out to be twins. So she found herself at twenty-two, the mother of four children under four. She shared how overwhelmed she felt trying to deal with them all. How inadequate she felt. With her husband working to support them, and too proud to ask her own family for help, Grace turned to alcohol to help her get through the day.

"The problem escalated, though no one knew how much she was really drinking at home until the day she decided to take her kids to the store to pick up some milk and bread. Her husband was sleeping, so she took the keys and their car. Unfortunately, in her inebriated state, she didn't properly buckle them into the car, so when she ran a red light and hit another vehicle broadside, two of the children were thrown from their seats and died instantly."

Cami felt her stomach churn at the revelation. She had such a hard time reconciling a woman who would do that with the Grace she knew.

Chapter Twelve

GRACE was charged with various offenses. Drunk driving. Manslaughter. I'm not sure about all of them, but she didn't even try to defend herself. She pled guilty and was sentenced to ten years. Her husband divorced her and took their surviving children to his family in Florida. Once in the prison, Grace tried to commit suicide, but she was found before any serious injury occurred. It was as she was recovering from that attempt that she met a Christian woman who visited the prison. That woman was my sister, which is why we care so much for Grace. It took a while, but eventually she told my sister her story and why she knew that God would never forgive her. After all, she'd failed to properly care for the children He'd blessed her with."

The words pierced Cami's heart. How well she understood that sentiment. "Things must have changed for her though. I know she's all about God now, and her daughter was supposed to come visit her for Christmas."

The pastor nodded. "Grace said it wasn't an instantaneous thing, her belief in God or the relationship with her daughter. What Grace came to realize—and what is true for all of us—is that God offers forgiveness for all our sin. He doesn't pick and choose which sins He'll forgive of us if we are truly repentant. Grace said that the verse that made a difference for her was the one that says, *for all have sinned and come short of the glory of God*. She told me it was when she accepted that it wasn't just that one act that made her a sinner but that, in fact, without God, she was a sinner, period. Whether it was a lie or whether it was something like she had done, as long as she didn't accept God's forgiveness for her sin, she was a sinner."

"You really think God views the sin of a lie and the sin of murder as the same?"

"Each sin is like a red blot on a garment of white. If you were wearing a white dress and got a drop of something on it, would the stain not be as noticeable as if it were a splash? Big or small, it is still stained and no longer pure white. Our sins, big and small, are like red stains on garments of white. In fact, there is a verse in the Bible that says, '*Though your sins are like scarlet, they shall be as white as snow; Though they are red like crimson, they shall be as wool.*'"

Cami remembered Josh saying something similar, but part of her had wondered if he was just saying that to get her to become a Christian so that whatever was between them would be "right." But here was a man who had no vested interest in the state of her soul, with nothing to be gained, saying the same thing as Josh. Could she really find forgiveness for the decision she'd made so many years ago that still ate away at her soul?

"You need to understand, though, that God wants you to repent of all your sin, not just the one you think is the worst."

"All my sins?"

"Any blot on your garment is what He wants to wash away, but you need to present it all to Him and repent."

Cami thought back over her life and knew there was much more than just the abortion that she needed forgiveness for. "There is so much. I know I've done a lot of things that weren't right, but I figured since I was already damned to hell by my actions in high school that anything else I did wouldn't make much difference."

"Well, you are quite right that our sinful actions put us on a path for hell, but God in His infinite mercy gave us a way to be cleansed of all our sin and to experience everlasting life with Him in Heaven. When He sent His son Jesus to die on the cross, He died for all our sins. The Jews had been sacrificing a lamb as a way to gain forgiveness, but when Jesus came, He became the sacrificial lamb for all our sins. All we have to do is confess our sins and accept the gift that is offered to us because of Jesus' death and resurrection."

All? It seemed like a lot to have to bring up her sins and confess them. There were so many. Though she hadn't paid much attention to what went on in church, Cami still knew the general rules. The Ten Commandments and things like not having sex before marriage. But when you had no hope, the rules didn't seem to matter. She was pretty sure that whatever garment she wore was not white with a few small blotches of red. It was solid red. And what was so special about her that God would care if she confessed her sins or not? Did He really want someone who chose to kill their own child in His heaven?

"Pastor Miller?"

Cami looked toward the woman who said the pastor's name. He stood and identified himself to the nurse.

"Grace is awake and asking for you. And also for someone named Cami?"

At the sound of her name, Cami also stood and moved to Pastor Miller's side. "That's me."

"You can both go see her for a few minutes. She is still not completely stable but was most insistent that she see you both." The nurse motioned with her hand. "Please follow me."

Cami pressed a hand to her stomach as she followed the nurse and Pastor Miller. She really didn't like hospitals, and it felt like she'd spent too much time in them lately, even if it was for a good reason like Laurel's baby.

On one hand, the sight of Grace alert was reassuring, and yet she still didn't look anywhere near her normal self. The pallor of the woman's skin concerned Cami. She was no doctor or nurse, but Cami was fairly certain that the older woman's appearance wasn't normal.

When Grace lifted her hand barely an inch off the mattress, Cami moved to her side and took it in hers.

"Thank you, Cami." Her words were weak but still clear. "God sent you at just the right time."

Cami ran her fingers over the delicate skin of Grace's hand. "I'm just glad I decided to come back to LA unexpectedly."

Grace smiled, but it was missing its normal vibrancy. "God knew I needed you." Her gaze moved to Pastor Miller. "Will you pray for me?"

The man took Grace's other hand in both of his. Cami listened as he asked God to comfort Grace and keep her from pain and that He would heal her body and renew her strength. It wasn't a long prayer, but Cami could see the peace on Grace's face when her pastor ended the prayer.

"Can you call my daughter?" Grace asked him.

"I will do that for you. I still have her information."

Grace's eyes closed, but then she struggled to open them again and looked straight at Cami. "What happened to you?"

Cami lifted her free hand to touch her face, aware that although the bruises had faded, they weren't completely gone, and makeup didn't completely cover the damage yet. "I had a run-in with a not so nice man. But I'm fine. They caught the guy."

Concern was evident on Grace's pale face. "You need to take care of yourself."

"I will. Everything's fine now." Even as she said the words to reassure Grace, Cami struggled to feel the confidence of them. She really wasn't feeling that anything in her life was fine, but all she could do was press forward and hope that somehow she'd figure out how to get to that point.

"You're going to need to leave now." Cami glanced up to see a nurse standing at the foot of Grace's bed. "We still need to do more tests, and she needs to rest."

Cami wanted to ask what they thought was wrong with her, but was pretty sure they weren't going to tell her anything since she wasn't family. Instead, she bent and pressed a kiss to Grace's cheek and gently squeezed her hand. "See you later."

As she followed the pastor from the room, Cami hoped that she would. Grace seemed so much more fragile than when she'd left not that long ago. To her knowledge, the older woman hadn't had any health problems since she'd moved in next door to her.

Pastor Miller stopped at the nurses' station. "I'm going to be calling Grace's daughter to let her know what's happened, but she lives out of town. In the meantime, could you please make sure to call me if she takes a turn for the worse? I'm her pastor, and I don't want her to be alone."

The nurse took down his information and assured him she'd call if anything came up. Back in the waiting room, he turned to her. "I need to leave for a while, but I'll be back this evening. Are you going to stay here? If not, I can give you a call if they contact me."

Cami didn't have anything to do at the apartment, but she also didn't want to hang around the hospital. She still hadn't fully regained her strength after the attack, so exhaustion was pulling at her. "I think I'll be heading home, so I'd appreciate that."

As he nodded, Pastor Williams reached into his pocket and pulled out a card. He held it out to her. "Here is my information. If you have any questions about what we talked about, feel free to give me a call."

Cami gave him her cell number as well. "Thank you."

As she walked out into the bright, warm sunshine, Cami marveled at the circumstances of the past twenty-four hours. Had God really had a hand in getting her back to California? She'd felt like she was running away from Collingsworth, but maybe God had been drawing her to Grace's side. The thought amazed her if that was the case. Would God really use someone like her to be there for Grace? Why not just another neighbor in the apartment block? But as the story Pastor Miller had shared came to mind, Cami realized that perhaps God guided her back here not just for Grace's sake but for her own as well.

A rush of heat greeted Cami as she opened the door to her car. She slid behind the wheel and started it up so the A/C could begin to cool the interior. As she drove home, she couldn't seem to block out the words that she'd heard now twice. First from Josh and then from Pastor Miller. Still, she had a hard time believing God could forgive her for that fateful decision made so many years ago.

On the way back to her apartment, she stopped and picked up some food since she knew the fridge was empty. After making herself a sandwich, she sat down and stared at the suitcase that still stood by the door. She couldn't stay here long. She'd promised to be back for Christmas.

Cami let out a long breath. She couldn't believe she'd just up and left Collingsworth. She wasn't one to run from difficult stuff. Usually she just toughed it out, but for some reason Laurel's baby had pushed her to a place she hadn't been to before. Now she didn't know what to do. Given some distance, she wanted to be back with her family, but now Grace needed her. There was no way she could leave her until she knew the older woman was going to be okay.

Without taking her suitcase from where she'd left it by the door, Cami made her way to her room and sank down on the bed, wincing at the pain in her ribs. Now that she wasn't focused on anything else, the pulsing pain drew her attention. She found her pain pills and took one before lying down. Her lack of sleep the night before began to rear its ugly head and pull her toward slumber. Before she completely drifted off, she placed her phone on the bed next to her in case Pastor Miller called with an update.

Cami woke to find herself reaching for the empty side of her bed. A sick feeling flooded her stomach as she realized she was alone. The dream that had captured her so deeply was gone. There was no Josh holding her close. There was no baby cradled in her arms. No feeling of love and peace surrounding her.

Cami squeezed her eyes shut, desperate to slip back into the dream world that had felt so right. So perfect. When sleep didn't return, she rolled onto her back and stared up at the ceiling. *Josh.* The man was everything she'd never known she wanted in a man, but could she ever be the woman he deserved? And how did she separate the longing for Josh from the growing desire to know God? She knew it was the one thing that stood between her and Josh, but it couldn't be the reason she gave her life to God.

She thought about calling the pastor to ask him more about it, but then realized she had access to some answers herself. Though she didn't have a Bible on hand, she did have her laptop and she was pretty sure she could find one online.

Swinging her legs over the side of the bed, she pushed to her feet and went to get her laptop bag. She settled down in her favorite chair and booted it up. As she waited for it to load, Cami thought back over the conversations she'd had with both the pastor and Josh. With the search site up on her screen, her fingers hesitated over the keyboard. Finally, she slowly typed out *forgiveness for abortion*.

She realized that she didn't doubt that God existed or that He had sent His son to die for the sins of mankind. But what she couldn't grasp was that He would forgive the sin she had committed. As she watched the search results load, Cami soon realized she wasn't the first person to have wondered that. Reading through blog posts written by women who had made the same decision she had, Cami felt tears drip down her cheeks. She'd felt so alone in what she was feeling, never wanting to acknowledge what she'd done that fateful day. But here, women shared their pain and heartache. The guilt they carried for years. But then they also shared the freedom they'd found from that guilt.

I lived for years with the secret pain of my abortion. I could never seem to free myself from the guilt that plagued me because I knew what I'd done was wrong. That guilt was my cross to bear for what I'd done. Or at least that was what I thought. It didn't seem right that I be forgiven for choosing death for my child instead of life. But like a wound that never heals and eventually gets infected, the emotions I'd buried deep for so long could no longer be hidden.

It had been my hope that telling even just one person about what I'd done would alleviate some of the guilt I carried. I just couldn't keep it to myself anymore. But then the person I told wasn't willing to just keep my secret without challenging me to seek forgiveness from God. It took quite a while, but finally I came to understand that God doesn't look at our sin, He looks at our hearts. He doesn't care what the sin is. He wants to forgive all of our sins—big and small. But He wants our hearts to be repentant, not seeking forgiveness so we can sin again, but so that we can be washed white as snow. When I came to Him, I brought my sorrowful, broken, guilt-ridden, repentant heart and asked Him to forgive me and heal my heart. And He did!

Does it mean that I never feel guilt over what happened? Or that I don't think about it anymore? No, not at all. My guilt over what I did will always be my weakness, and Satan uses it to torment me at times. But he can't keep me down because now I take that guilt to God and ask Him to help me deal with it.

Cami brushed the tears from her cheeks and allowed the little flicker of hope in her heart to finally burst into a full flame.

She didn't know exactly what to say, but hoped with everything in her that God truly looked at the heart and could see hers. “Please, God, forgive me for what I did to the baby You gave to me. I made so many wrong decisions back then, but that was the worst. I am so sorry.” She paused, remembering the pastor’s words about not just asking forgiveness for the “big” sin, but for them all. As she sat there, the clarity with which things came to mind was surprising. One by one, she confessed them to God and asked His forgiveness.

As she spoke each one, it felt like a string snapped, and the sin was released. It was like nothing Cami had ever experienced before. She knew then that it wasn’t about religion or about some distant deity. This was about having a personal relationship with God. About trusting Him with her heart and her life in a way she’d never trusted anyone before. It was so freeing and exhilarating.

Eager to share with someone, Cami picked up her phone and found the card Pastor Miller had given her and called him.

“Pastor Miller? This is Cami,” she said when he answered.

“Cami! I’m glad you called. I have some good news.”

“So do I,” Cami told him.

There was a pause before he said, “Well, you go first.”

“I asked God to forgive my sins the way you said I should.” The words tumbled out so fast Cami wasn’t sure he’d understand.

But it was clear he did when he said, “That is absolutely terrific news! Thank you, God! How are you feeling?”

“Free. For the first time in as long as I can remember, I don’t feel held down by the weight of the guilt I was carrying for everything I’d done. Does it last?”

Pastor Miller didn’t laugh at her question. “It can last, but God never promised us a life without trials even after we put our trust in Him. What you have to remember is that now, instead of facing those trials on your own, you have God with you. These trials we face are often meant to teach us things and to grow our faith. Don't believe that little voice that may try to tell you that God has deserted you during those tough times. He hasn't. He is always with you and will never forsake you. Trust in that. Believe that."

"Thank you. For everything. I came here with a lot of questions and confusion, and I'll be leaving with a peace I never imagined possible. Thank you."

"I am just grateful that God could use whatever words I said to help you get to this point. And I know Grace will be thrilled. She's carried such a burden for you. There was never a week that went by that she didn't request prayer for your salvation at our weekly prayer meeting."

"How is Grace doing?" Cami asked. "Is that some of the good news you have?"

"Yes, it is. I stopped by again a little earlier, and she was much improved. They said she has stabilized and seems to be doing much better. When I talked with her, I could see that she was stronger than when we'd spoken with her this morning."

Relief flooded Cami. "I'm so glad to hear that. She had me pretty worried."

"Us, as well. The other good news is that I was able to get hold of her daughter, and she's flying in tonight to be with her mom."

"I'm sure Grace was happy to hear that." And so was Cami, because it meant she could leave for home with the knowledge that her friend was out of the woods and had a loved one caring for her.

After making arrangements to go to the hospital the next morning to meet Grace's daughter, Cami sat back in her chair and took in a long breath and let it out. She felt like she'd been on a roller coaster but could finally catch her breath.

As she sat there, she looked around at the apartment she'd lived in for the past six months and knew that it wasn't home to her. LA was no longer where she should be. Though she still wasn't sure that Collingsworth was where she'd put down roots, for now it was a home that was more appealing than the one on the West Coast.

She was eager to get back to the manor and her family, but Cami decided to take the time to tie things up in LA. Getting up from her chair, she went in search of a pen and some paper to make a list of everything she needed to do. She had to get it done quickly because she had to be back in Collingsworth by the end of the week.

After visiting Grace the next morning and meeting her daughter, Cami returned to the apartment prepared to pack up what she wanted to have shipped to Collingsworth, and to call for a pick-up of the items she would donate. Grace had been sad to hear the news that she was leaving LA, but she'd expressed her delight at the news of Cami's salvation and had said she could let Cami go with peace in her heart because of it.

As Cami walked through the apartment, she realized there really wasn't much that she needed to ship to Collingsworth. She was standing in the kitchen looking through the cupboards when she heard the door of the apartment open. Brow furrowed, she walked out of the kitchen, concerned that someone might be trying to break in. Surprise shot through her when she recognized the figure standing in the doorway.

"Janey! What are you doing here?"

Her former roommate paused, a myriad of emotions crossing her face. "I, uh, came to get my stuff. I didn't think you'd be here."

"I didn't plan to be originally, but I'm here for a couple of days to pack up my things."

Janey frowned. "You're leaving LA too?"

Cami nodded. "There's nothing here for me."

"Where are you going to go? Back to New York?"

"No. I'm done with the scene there, too. I'm going home to Collingsworth."

"I thought you hated it there," Janey said, crossing her arms.

"I did, but a lot has changed in the past couple of weeks. It's where I want to be now."

Janey arched a perfectly-plucked eyebrow. "It must have really changed for you to want to be there."

"It's where my family is, and they have been there for me since the attack in a way that my friends weren't." Cami realized it was probably not right of her to make her point in that way and opened her mouth to apologize, but Janey spoke first.

"Uh, about that," Janey began, her gaze lowering. "I had no idea what he was going to do. I would never have told him where you were if I'd known."

Cami wasn't sure she believed her, but quickly realized that it didn't really matter. Whatever anger she'd held toward her friend had dissipated over the past couple of days. "Why did you tell him in the first place? You know I was trying to stay away from him."

Janey looked up, her expression chagrined. "I needed the money. He offered me five thousand dollars to tell him where you were. I couldn't pass it up. And...I was still mad at you."

"I never meant to hurt you, Janey, but our paths were moving in different directions. I just couldn't continue on the way you wanted."

"I understand that now." Janey shifted from one foot to the other. "I'm just here to get a few things and then I'm gone."

"Listen," Cami began, suddenly eager to not leave things on a bad note with her friend. "I'm planning to donate most of the furniture and stuff I bought that's too bulky to ship back to Collingsworth. If you want any of it, let me know and you can have it."

Janey glanced around the room before her gaze met Cami's. "Thanks, but I think all I want to take is the stuff that's mine."

Cami nodded and watched as she walked to her bedroom and disappeared inside. As she stood there, she realized that this was another part of her life that she had needed to resolve. Things still weren't great between her and Janey, but at least what had happened was out in the open now. She wondered about sharing with Janey the spiritual journey she'd experienced the past couple of days. The closed bedroom door made her think that Janey wasn't interested in any sort of conversation. But even if she couldn't share her story, she could at least pray for her friend to also find the peace she now had.

When she finally settled into her seat on the airplane on Friday morning, Cami breathed a sigh of relief. It had been a frantic few days, but she'd managed to get everything done that she'd wanted. Pastor Miller had been a great help in finding a place that could make use of the furniture she wanted to donate. He'd also gratefully accepted the donation of her car to the church. She left it up to him what to do with it. He hadn't known her financial situation, so had protested at first, but she'd assured him she could afford to give it away.

She'd paid the airlines for extra bags for the clothes and other personal items she had decided to keep. In the end, there had been no need to ship anything. Janey had packed her stuff up within a day and had left barely twenty-four hours after showing up at the apartment. It had been a tense good-bye, but at least in her heart Cami knew she no longer harbored any ill-will toward her friend.

As the plane took off, Cami stared out the window to the sprawling city that she'd come to with such high hopes, but there had been no more success there than there had been in New York. She had begun to pray over the past couple of days for God to give her some clear direction on what to do. Not just about her music, but about Josh, too.

His face filled her thoughts. His beautiful blue eyes. His rare smile that caused butterflies to flutter in her stomach. The care with which he'd dealt with her after that night in the bar. And though she knew it wasn't something she should focus on, Cami couldn't help but think about the feel of his strong arms around her. For the short time that he'd held her, she had felt safe. But was any of that love? If she was honest with herself, she didn't know what real love was between a man and woman. And would it make any difference to him that she was now a Christian?

Cami pressed a hand to her stomach at the thought that, in the end, it might make no difference at all on Josh's part. Maybe his care and concern had come from a place of Christian love and nothing more. Would this be one of those trials that Pastor Miller had mentioned? Having her heart broken wasn't something she'd ever imagined having happen. She'd been very careful to never let her emotions get involved in any relationship, but somehow Josh had gotten past all the guards she'd had in place. And she knew how he'd done it, too. Their shared love of music. She'd never had anyone understand how important it was to her. Connecting that way had breached her walls and let him in.

At one time, Cami would have just asked him point blank if he was interested in something with her. But she knew it wasn't just a casual fling on her part. It would be something more. Something permanent. Where that might have once scared her, she found it appealing now. But did Josh?

Chapter Thirteen

JOSH frowned as he looked at the arrivals board. An unexpected storm around Dallas had delayed the departure of his family's flight. And he hadn't bothered to check before leaving Collingsworth, which had been really dumb. At least it appeared that the delay was only thirty minutes. He could handle that.

Looking around, he spotted a place to sit so he settled down and took a drink of the coffee he'd picked up on his way in. Another flight arrived, and passengers began to cluster around the baggage claim carousels. He let his gaze wander over them as he continued to sip his coffee.

When he spotted a woman with blonde curls, he lowered his cup and leaned forward. Surely his eyes were playing tricks on him. Of all the flights arriving, was it possible Cami had come home on one of them? Josh kept his gaze locked on the woman who stood with her back to him as he got to his feet, dumped his nearly-empty cup into the trash and wove his way through the crowd. Just as he reached her, she moved away to grab a large bag from the carousel. He stood there waiting for her to turn around.

His heart slammed in his chest when she did. Her attention was on her bag, but he could clearly see that it was indeed the woman he'd been thinking about far too much lately.

"Let me help you with that," he said and reached to take the suitcase from her.

She looked up, her eyes widening as their gazes met. "Josh?"

"In the flesh." Josh gave her a smile as he took the bag from her now lax grip and lifted it easily onto her cart.

"Why are you here? I didn't tell anyone I was arriving."

Josh had to focus on her words because all he wanted to do was drink in the sight of her. "Uh...my family was supposed to arrive twenty minutes ago. Their flight is delayed."

"Oh." She gave him a small smile. "I should have realized that. I knew they were coming for Christmas."

Before he could stop himself, Josh said, "But if I'd known when you were arriving, I would have been here to meet you, too."

She stared at him without saying anything for a long moment before turning back to the carousel. "I still have a few bags coming."

"Wow," Josh said as he stood next to her. "You travelling with everything you own?"

"Pretty much."

Josh looked down at her. "Really?"

Cami met his gaze briefly before looking back at the bags circling on the conveyor belt. "Yes. I got rid of all my furniture and stuff in LA. I just have my clothes and things I couldn't part with."

"Wait a second." Josh laid a hand on her arm. When she looked at him, he said, "Are you moving back to Collingsworth?"

"For now. I don't think it's a permanent move, but I need a little time to make some decisions."

Josh could hardly believe what he was hearing. After the way she'd left earlier in the week, he'd figured that she'd come back just in time for Christmas and Jessa's wedding before leaving again. He wondered what had happened to change things. The last he'd heard, she had no intention of ever returning to Collingsworth except for the odd visit. And yet here she was waiting for all her worldly goods to arrive on the conveyor belt.

"Do you need a ride back to the manor?" Josh asked.

"I planned to rent a car," Cami replied as she stepped toward the carousel and reached out to grasp the handle of another bag. She hefted it from the belt and set it on the floor.

"How about you just point out your bags so I can get them off that thing?" Josh once again moved the bag to her cart. "No need for you to strain yourself. I imagine you're still in some pain."

"It's getting better every day," Cami told him then pointed to another bag. "That one's mine."

Josh easily lifted the bulky bag and set it with the others. "You don't need to rent a car, you know. My folks had already planned to rent one, so we have plenty of room."

He saw her brows draw together and knew she was most likely trying to decide if she wanted to ride for three hours with his family. "None of them bite. Honest. They're actually a lot of fun to be around."

Cami glanced at him. "I'm sure they are. I guess it would be kind of a waste to rent a car when you have room for me."

"Then it's settled." Josh knew he shouldn't be so pleased that she'd agreed to ride with him, but he was. "How many more bags?"

"Just two."

After the last of her bags had shown up, Josh pushed her

cart to the nearest board displaying flight arrivals. "Looks like they should arrive in about ten minutes. Hope you don't mind waiting."

Cami shook her head. "No, it's not a problem. But do you mind watching my bags while I go to the restroom?"

"Not at all. I'll just be over there," Josh said, motioning to where he'd been sitting earlier.

As he sat down, he pulled his phone from his pocket. He glanced in the direction Cami had gone then tapped out a quick text to Lance.

Found Cami at the airport. Will be bringing her home with my family.

It didn't take long for an alert to sound a response. *Really? That's terrific! Jessa will be so relieved. I will let her know. One more for dinner!*

Josh smiled. He had to admit that he, too, was relieved that Cami was back home safely. A day hadn't passed over the past six months when he hadn't wondered about her and prayed for her safety.

Cami stared at her reflection in the mirror. She was surprised that she couldn't actually see her chest moving with each beat of her pounding heart. It had started the moment she'd looked up to find Josh standing in front of her and was just now beginning to slow.

"Nice sense of humor you have there," she said under her breath. Where she would once automatically have assumed that things like this were a coincidence, after this past week, Cami no longer did.

She'd told Grace that it was such a good coincidence that she'd come home when she did. Grace had quickly corrected her to say that it wasn't a coincidence; it had been God's direction. While Cami understood the obvious benefit of having her return to California to help Grace, she couldn't see the importance in running into Josh at the airport.

Maybe it really was nothing more than coincidence. That's what she would keep telling herself. Adding significance to it would just be setting herself up for disappointment.

After drying her hands, Cami took several deep breaths to get her elevated heart rate back down to where it should be. Not that it was likely to stay there once she saw him again, but she really didn't want him to see how his presence affected her.

The crowd of people had increased while she'd been in the restroom, and it took her a few minutes to return to the spot where she'd left Josh. A quick look revealed that he wasn't there. Glancing around, she spotted him at the bottom of an escalator surrounded by people she assumed were his family. Not wanting to intrude, she backed up against a nearby wall so she wasn't in the way of the people milling around her. Even from this distance she could see that it was an enthusiastic reunion for Josh and his family. He stood with an arm around an older woman who she assumed was his mother. She tried to recall what he'd said about his family. He hadn't ever told her their names, but she was pretty sure he had two sisters and a brother, and one of the sisters was married.

She didn't want to intrude on their reunion and was wishing she had access to her cart so that she could go rent a car like she'd originally planned. But her cart was still with Josh, so there was no way to make her escape. As the group turned toward one of the baggage carousels, Josh looked around, and their gazes met. She felt her heart skip a beat at the smile on his face. Though she knew it was because of his family, she could only wonder what it would be like to be the one to bring such a joyous expression to his face.

He turned back to say something to an older man who Cami assumed was his father then headed in her direction.

"I take it your family arrived," Cami said when he approached her.

"Yep, and earlier than the display said. Want to come meet them?" he asked.

"I think I'll wait until they've got their luggage. It's a bit of a madhouse over there right now."

Josh nodded. "That's true."

"Listen, I was thinking maybe I'll just go ahead and rent a car. I'm sure you'd like to spend this time with your family."

Josh frowned and put his hands on his hips. "It's not a problem. My dad was already going to rent a car so it's not a space issue."

"I know. It's just...I don't want to intrude." She looked past him to where his family was and discovered that the female members of the group were watching them. "Or give them the wrong idea."

"The wrong idea?" Josh asked.

"They're already watching us and no doubt wondering who I am."

"They already know who you are," Josh told her. "They know all about your family. Mom, especially, is curious about the family Lance is marrying into."

Cami wondered how much he'd told them about her. The drunken, unsuccessful sister of the bride. Not that it should matter, but it did. She'd spent years not caring what people thought of her. Suddenly she was caring too much. It wasn't a change she liked. Trying to mold herself into what others thought she should be made her weak. "Well, if that's the case then, there's no chance of them getting the wrong idea about us. I'll take you up on the ride."

Josh stared at her for a moment, his expression dark. "Not certain I want to understand your reasoning, but I'm glad you've agreed to the ride. I'm not sure your sisters would talk to me again if I let you make that drive on your own when there's room in my truck."

Cami nodded. She'd tried not to think about the drive north and having to pass the rest area where the attack had happened. When she'd traveled to the airport on Monday, it had been dark, and she'd been on the other side of the highway, so hadn't been able to see it clearly.

"Don't move," Josh told her. "I'm just going to help them with the bags, and we'll be right back."

As Josh made his way back to his family, Cami opened the zipper on one of her bags and found the heavier coat she'd packed there earlier. She laid it across the handle of the cart and found the boots she'd packed in another bag. Might as well prepare for the cold while she waited. She sat down on the bench and slid off the flats she'd worn on the flight. With a little tugging, she got the knee-high boots on and zipped them up. The boots weren't the height of fashion, but they were practical and would hopefully keep her from ending up in a snow bank. She'd forgotten to bring them when she'd come home the last time. This time she was a little more prepared.

She stood and shrugged out of her light jacket and put it and her flats into the open bag. After she zipped it closed, Cami looked up to see Josh approaching with his family. As they neared, Cami saw that, regardless of what Josh had said earlier, their faces showed their curiosity.

Josh smiled as he reached her. "Cami, I'd like you to meet my parents, Doug and Michelle. Mom and Dad, this is Cami. She's one of Jessa's sisters."

Cami held out her hand to shake their hands. "It's nice to meet you."

"You, as well," Michelle said with a warm smile. She was a plump woman just a little shorter than Cami. Her blue eyes, very much like her son's, were friendly and curious. "What a good thing that our flights arrived close together so Josh could pick us all up."

"Actually, he didn't know I was arriving," Cami said. "I was quite surprised to find him here when I got off the plane."

"As was I," Josh added.

"You didn't tell him you were coming?" Cami turned to

the man at Josh's side and knew she was seeing what Josh would look like in another twenty or thirty years. Like his wife, his smile was warm, and his grey eyes twinkled.

"I actually didn't tell anyone. I kind of have a habit of coming and going without much warning."

"I'm sure your family is glad to see you whenever you do show up," Doug said.

"That's something you'd have to ask them," Cami replied with a smile. "Let's just say I've been more welcome sometimes than others. My fault, not theirs."

Cami saw the curiosity grow on the faces of Josh's parents, but before either of them could say anything more, Josh introduced her to his siblings.

He gestured to a young woman who looked remarkably like Michelle with a little less of the plumpness. "This is Bethany and her husband, Steve. And this is my brother, Colin." The young man looked a lot like his dad and Josh. The genes in this family pool were strong. "And this young lady is my sister, Amy."

"Amelia," the girl corrected. "Call me Amelia." Unlike her sister, it appeared she took after her father in height and build.

Cami greeted each of them in turn. "It's so nice you could come for Christmas and Lance's wedding."

Once the introductions were done, Josh said, "Let's go get the car and then we can head for home."

Home. For the first time, it really did feel like she was heading home. As Cami reached for her coat, Josh took it from her and helped lift it up her arms onto her shoulders. Though it didn't hurt as much doing it that way, Cami was sure it fueled any assumptions his family might have about them. Seeming not to care, Josh took charge of her cart and led the group in the direction of the rental counter. It didn't take long for Doug to get the keys to the car he'd reserved.

"I'm going to go with Dad to get the car, and then we'll

come back around to pick you guys up with the luggage," Josh said as he pulled his gloves from the pocket of his jacket. "Better put your warm stuff on. It's cold out there."

Since they had come from mild temperatures as well, the Moyers also dug out jackets from their bags, and by the time Josh returned about ten minutes later, everyone was ready to face the winter.

"Let's get this show on the road," he said as he once again pushed Cami's cart. Colin, Steve and Amy took charge of the rest of them, and they moved from the warmth of the terminal to the frigid cold of Minnesota.

Josh's dad stood at the side of his rental car and opened the front door as they approached. "'Chelle, come get in out of the cold."

Without argument, Josh's mom slid into the front seat and let Doug close the door for her.

At his truck, Josh opened the door as well. "Why don't you get in the front, Cami? Amy, you get in the back. Slide across so there's room for Colin."

Cami started to argue but decided it would just draw more attention to them than she wanted. Grateful for the warmth of the air flowing from the vents, she turned to see Amy slide across to the seat behind Josh's. It didn't take too long for the luggage to be transferred to the back of the truck, and soon they were headed home with Josh leading the way.

"So, Cami, do you have a boyfriend?" Amy asked from the back seat.

Though not surprised by the girl's curiosity, Cami was a little surprised at the directness. The only thing that might have been a little more direct would have been if she'd asked if she and Josh were an item. She turned in her seat so she could see the girl and said, "No. Not at the moment."

"So you're single and ready to mingle?"

Cami laughed. "Well, single, yes, but no, not ready to mingle."

The girl's brow furrowed. "You're not looking for a boyfriend?"

Cami smiled at the incredulity in the girl's tone. She remembered being her age and thinking that not having a boyfriend was the end of the world. "Nope. I'm quite content being single for the moment."

She saw Amy shoot a look toward the back of her brother's head. When the young girl looked back at Cami, she said, "Josh said you live in California. I'd like to visit there some day."

"It is very beautiful out there," Cami told her. "But I'm in the process of moving."

"Where to? I can't imagine anyone leaving California."

"When I moved there, I couldn't imagine leaving either, but things change. Life throws things at you that can force you to reconsider decisions you've made."

There was a beat of silence before Amy said, "What happened to your face?"

"Amelia!" Josh admonished from the front seat.

"You need to dial down the questions, sis," Colin said, speaking for the first time.

"I was just wondering. She could tell me it's none of my business if she wants."

Cami met Josh's glance and lifted an eyebrow. "I'm fine answering, but if you'd rather she not know the details, I'm okay with that, too."

She saw his jaw clench as he turned his gaze back to the road but then he gave a single nod. Cami looked back over the seat to where Amy sat, arms crossed. "I was attacked almost two weeks ago. My face got pretty bruised from it."

Amy leaned forward, her hands going to the edge of her seat. "Did they catch the guy?"

Cami nodded. "He's in jail right now. I knew him, so it didn't take them long to catch him."

Amy's eyes widened. "You *knew* him?"

"He was an ex-boyfriend-turned-stalker," Cami told her. "I clearly wasn't a very good judge of character."

"Wow. Is he the reason you're not looking for a boyfriend right now?"

Cami heard Josh let out a long sigh and wanted to laugh. She wasn't offended at all by Amy's questions, but clearly Josh was getting a little exasperated. "Well, at the moment, yes, it's one of the reasons. But I have others."

Before she could ask anything else Colin said, "Josh, I think we need to stop and trade Amy for Steve. Pretty sure he won't ask so many questions."

"Oh, shut up," Amy said. "You're just as curious. I know you are. After all, she's right up your alley. Pretty, blonde and all legs. That's what you like, right?"

Colin groaned. "Oh, good grief, Amy!"

Cami turned back around to look out the passenger window so they couldn't see the grin on her face.

"What? Mom's always said if I had questions to just ask. So I'm asking."

"I'm pretty sure this is not what she had in mind, and you know it," Colin informed her.

"Hey, Cami's almost family, so I just want to know about her. Isn't it good to know about people who are going to be a part of your life?"

"Stop it, Amy," Colin said firmly. "Don't pull this innocent act on me. I know what you're up to. Pretty sure you wouldn't be like this if Mom or Dad were in here with us."

"I'm not up to anything," Amy protested. "I'm just curious."

Colin muttered something, but Cami didn't catch what it was.

"Fine. I won't ask any more boyfriend questions."

"How about no more questions, period," Josh suggested.

"It's a long drive. What else are we going to do if we don't talk?"

"You could sleep," Colin suggested. "I'm down with that."

Cami could only imagine the look that got him. She had to admit, she liked the spunk Amy had and didn't mind her questions at all.

"Or *you* could sleep," Amy shot back. "I'm down with *that*."

Cami pressed a hand to her mouth to stifle her laugh. Somehow this was not how she'd pictured Josh's family, but so far it was delightfully refreshing to know that his family had their squabbles as well.

When neither of the guys responded to her, Amy said, "What did you do in California?"

Cami turned from the window, her gaze briefly meeting Josh's when he glanced her way. She gave him a wide smile as if to say *I told you this wasn't a good idea*. Even though she didn't mind, clearly it was making him uncomfortable.

"I'm a singer."

"Really?" The girl's brows drew together. "I don't think I've heard your name before."

"I never made it big," Cami said. "But that's what I was doing out in LA."

"So if you weren't famous, where did you sing?"

"I started out singing in lounges and bars, but I also sang at weddings and other special events. I had one Christmas party I sang at early in December."

"Do you like it?"

"Singing in general? Or where I sang?"

"Um, both."

"I didn't always enjoy singing in the bars. It depended on

the place. Some were better than others. I enjoy singing at weddings, and the Christmas party was fun to do. I love singing in general. Music is my life."

"Josh sings. Did you know that?"

"Yes, actually, I did."

"Have you heard him sing?"

Cami thought back to the night on the beach when he'd held her and sang that soul-soothing song. "Yes, I have. He has a beautiful voice. Do you sing, too?"

Amy paused for a second as if off-balance by the question coming in her direction for a change. "Yep, we all do. Josh is just a *tiny* bit more talented than the rest of us." She held up her fingers to show a small gap between her thumb and index finger.

"Why don't you sing something?" Cami asked. She figured maybe that would curb the questions for Josh and Colin's sake.

"Okay. Let me think."

"Why don't you make it something Christmassy?" Josh suggested.

"Well, this would be rather appropriate," Amy said and started singing 'Winter Wonderland'.

Cami listened to her for the first verse, realizing that the girl had more than just a little talent. As she started the second verse, Cami couldn't help but sing along. Before long, Colin and Josh had both joined in as well. After that song, Amy launched into 'Joy to the World'.

They were so caught up in singing song after song that the rest area where she'd been attacked was upon them before she realized it. It was there, but instead of looking, Cami turned away from the window and continued to sing. And then they were past it. Her heart lightened just a little at having gotten beyond that hurdle.

Cami was surprised when Josh reached over and gave her

hand a quick squeeze. She met his gaze with a small smile and a nod. She hadn't realized he knew exactly where the attack had happened, since there were a couple of rest areas along the route to Collingsworth. But it was clear that he did know the significance of the one they'd just passed.

~ Chapter Fourteen ~

THOUGH she was sure Amy hadn't missed the exchange between her and Josh, Cami didn't glance back at the girl, just continued to sing the latest Christmas song she'd chosen. By the time they arrived at the manor, whatever aggravation the guys might have felt toward their sister seemed to have faded. And as Cami slid from the truck, she knew that even though she'd felt bad leaving Grace, this was where she was supposed to be. Grace had urged her to go, and it was only because the older woman had improved so much with her daughter there that Cami had felt peace at leaving.

The front door of the manor opened, and Jessa and Lance came out onto the porch. Cami climbed the stairs to reach her sister, and for the first time with Jessa, she initiated the hug.

"Welcome home, sis," Jessa said as they embraced.

Cami stepped back from Jessa as Lance moved down the stairs toward his family. Jessa followed him, while Cami turned to find that Lily had come out as well. She hugged her younger sister. "How are you doing?"

"I'm fine. How about you?" Lily asked.

"I'm better. Glad to be home."

"Really? It seemed like you couldn't wait to leave earlier this week," Lily said.

"True, but things have changed a bit," Cami told her. "I'll tell you about it sometime."

Before they could say anything further, people began to get the bags from the back of Josh's truck. Cami walked down to pick up one of her bags, but Josh stopped her.

"I'll take care of them. I don't think you should be lugging these bags around yet."

"Well, who do you think did it this morning?" Cami asked with a smile. "I survived that."

"You don't need to do it now. I can take care of it for you."

Cami tried to hold on to her heart, but she was losing it to this man. One little piece at a time. It scared her more than anything else ever had. She'd been so careful to never give someone the power to hurt her. Albert had hurt her body, but already the bruises were fading and the fear wasn't as strong as it had been immediately following the attack. However, Josh was slowly gaining the power to hurt her so much more. And she wasn't sure he even knew it.

Trying to keep her emotions from showing, Cami climbed back up the porch steps and entered the manor. There was a lot of commotion for the next little while as people were shown to their rooms and bags were sorted out.

"Why so many bags, Cam?"

Cami turned from the bag she'd set on her bed to see Jessa standing in the doorway. "I decided my time in LA had come to an end. But don't worry, I won't park myself on your doorstep too long. I'm thinking I'll see if I can find a short-term lease apartment in Collingsworth until I figure out what I'm going to do."

Jessa stepped further into the room, a frown on her face.

"You will do nothing of the sort. The manor is as much your home as it is mine."

"You and Lance will be newlyweds. I don't want to be in the way."

Jessa laughed. "Don't worry about Lance and me. We will have our suite for any privacy we need. I'm just surprised you decided to leave LA."

"It was time. I don't think I'll be settling here permanently, but I just need some time to refocus and figure out where...God wants me to be."

Jessa's eyes widened. "Where God wants you to be? Since when has that been important to you?"

"Since about two days ago."

"Really?" The excitement in Jessa's voice was clear. "I never imagined... You can't know how happy this makes me." Jessa crossed the room and pulled Cami into her arms. "I know we don't have the time to talk now, but I need to hear all about it."

"I have a lot to tell you," Cami told her. "But it can wait."

"Jessa, babe?" Lance came into the room. "Is everything all right?"

Cami saw a wide smile spread across her sister's face as she turned toward Lance. "Everything is perfect."

"Well, I'm glad to hear that." His gaze went from Jessa to Cami and then back again. "What exactly is everything?"

Jessa turned to Cami. "Can I tell him?"

Cami nodded.

"Cami became a Christian!"

Surprise crossed Lance's face. "That's terrific news!" He moved to give Cami a hug. "We have been so worried about you. No more running off now?"

"Not for a while," Cami assured him with a smile. "I'm actually moving back to Collingsworth for a little bit."

"Wow. The good news just keeps coming," Lance said, his dimples out in full force with his grin.

"Well, I, for one, am very glad you're back because I could use some help with dinner. Everyone is going to be here," Jessa said, a frown worrying her features.

"Everyone? Are Violet and Dean back?"

Jessa nodded. "Yes, they got back today as well. So we've got dinner for seventeen underway."

"Just tell me what to do," Cami said. "I'm here to help."

Cami decided not to do any unpacking right then and headed downstairs with her sister.

"You're going to stay with Lance and me," Josh told Colin. "Hope that's okay."

"That's more than okay," Colin said with a grin. "I love women, but there's just a bit too much estrogen here."

Lance laughed. "Well, a few of us are doing our best to even it out. Three down, two to go."

"Why don't I drive you over to the apartment so you can drop off your stuff and then we'll come back?" Josh said. "Give you a bit of a break."

Colin agreed, so the two of them headed back out into the cold. His family had actually been to Collingsworth in the past, though it had been many years. They'd come to spend time with Lance's family when they'd been home on furlough from Kenya. But that had only been once every four years and Colin had been much younger. Josh took him on a little tour as he drove to the apartment.

"Do you like living here?" Colin asked.

Josh shrugged. "It's serving its purpose for now. I enjoy the work I do with Lance."

"And your music? Have you ever considered getting back into it?" Colin asked.

"I'm getting more involved in the music ministry at the church here. Playing the guitar."

"But you haven't thought about going back into performing?"

"I never wanted to be a solo act, and I don't know who I'd perform with now. The rest of the quartet has gone on to other groups."

"I'm sure if you put the word out, you'd have people interested in forming a group with you."

"Not likely if they have any memory of what went down before."

"You're scared," Colin observed.

"Scared?"

"You're scared to put yourself out there again. You're worried that people are going to judge you on your past actions, even though you've confessed it and been forgiven."

"It's kind of hard not to feel that way when the judgment handed to me by that community was pretty swift and harsh. Not saying I didn't deserve it, but it's hard to want to wade back into that." Josh knew his brother was right about his reluctance to return to the music he loved so much.

"I noticed you're not wearing your ring anymore," Colin commented. "Any particular reason for that?"

"I've just felt that maybe I needed to put the past where it belonged...in the past. And I couldn't move forward as long as I kept myself tied to it. I won't ever forget Emma and all that happened back then, though."

"I think you've been paying some sort of penance for that. Not just the affair, but everything that happened with Emma."

Josh shot his brother a look. "Those courses you're taking for your psychology degree are certainly paying off."

"Feeling a bit analyzed?" Colin asked, a thread of humor in his voice.

"Just a little. I realize I'm probably the most messed up person you know, but you keep this up, and I'll start charging you for practicing on me."

Colin laughed. "You're not the most messed up person I know. I'm actually really proud of you and how you've handled everything you've been through. I just want to see you doing what you love once again."

Josh shrugged. "I'm not sure how that would happen. I haven't had any clear direction from the Lord with regard to my music."

"And what about Cami?" Colin asked after they'd ridden in silence for a couple of minutes.

Josh frowned as he glanced at him. "You're no better than Amy."

"She's only fifteen. She didn't realize what she was doing."

"Well, you know better, so why are you asking?"

"You do realize, don't you, that the tension is very thick between you two."

"Tension? We get along pretty good. I don't think there's tension."

Colin slugged his arm. "Not that kind of tension."

Josh lifted a hand from the wheel to rub his arm. "There's no other kind of tension."

"Well, Cleopatra may have been Queen of the Nile, but you're the king. And if you want to keep Mom from suspecting more than she already does, you'd be wise to keep your distance from Cami. As in, not even being in the same room as her."

"That's kind of difficult," Josh said. "We're all going to be together for the next couple of weeks. I have no choice but to be around her."

"Then stop taking care of her, at least," Colin said.

Josh frowned. "Mom taught me to be a gentleman. I was

just helping her out."

"And would you have helped out just any woman the way you've helped Cami?"

Josh knew Colin was right. He found himself wanting to do anything and everything he could for Cami. He let out a long sigh. "Was Amy right? Is she your type?"

"Sure. She's gorgeous, funny and talented. What's not to like? However, if you're even remotely interested in her, she's off-limits for me." Colin paused. "I'm not telling you to distance yourself from her so that I can move in on her. That's not my style."

Josh was relieved to hear that, because he figured any woman in her right mind would choose Colin over him. Why would a woman go for the guy with all the baggage and who was totally unsettled in his life when she could have the younger, more focused guy who didn't come with a past? Not that it really mattered. Cami's overt interest in him had ended when she'd left six months ago. When she'd returned, she was more reserved and warier around him.

He swung into his parking space at the apartment block. "Grab your bag. We're on the second floor."

"What? You're not gonna carry it up for me?"

Catching a glimpse of his brother's cheeky grin, Josh returned the punch in the arm he'd received earlier.

Cami stood at the counter cutting the vegetables Jessa had brought in from her winterized greenhouse. Activity was going on all around her as Josh's mom and sisters had offered to help as well. She could sense Michelle's curiosity, but managed to keep her head bent over her work so as not to meet the woman's gaze. No doubt Amy had filled her mom in on all the information she'd managed to gather during the trip to Collingsworth. She wondered what, if anything, Josh had told his parents about her beyond her relation to Jessa.

"So, Cami, Amy tells me you're moving back to

Collingsworth," Michelle said.

Unable to ignore the woman without being rude, Cami looked up and smiled. "Yes. At least temporarily."

"Will you be looking for work here? Amy said you're a singer."

Cami nodded, not surprised that the girl had spilled it all to her mother. "Yes, I'm a singer, but I won't be looking for work right now. I might spend some time writing music. We were very fortunate to have inherited some money when our grandmother passed away. If I'm careful, I can live on that without having to get a job for a while."

Michelle nodded. "That certainly is a blessing. And it must be nice to have this place to come home to. It's beautiful."

"The renovations really turned out great," Cami agreed. "To be honest, I never thought I'd be happy to come back here, but Jessa has made it into a real home."

"Yes, I can see that. And Lance showed us the chapel, which is absolutely gorgeous and perfect for a wedding."

Jessa piped in then about the decorations for the wedding and thankfully took the focus off Cami. She finished one bowl of salad and started on another since there were so many people for dinner. As she continued to work, Cami heard the front door open, and male voices drifted down the hallway to the kitchen. Her stomach clenched as she recognized one of them as Josh's. Part of her wanted to escape, but a bigger part of her wanted to see him.

As he and Colin walked into the kitchen, she glanced up quickly. Just long enough to get a glimpse of him before looking back down at the chopping board and the vegetables there.

"Hi, Mama. How's my favorite woman in the whole wide world?" Cami looked up again to see Josh slide his arm around Michelle's shoulders and press a kiss to the top of her head. His affection for the woman was clear on his face.

"You say that now, but soon enough some woman is going to come along and take that title from me," Michelle said with a smile as she looked up at her son.

When Josh glanced her way, Cami looked down and continued to cut the vegetables. She was beginning to think it would have been better if she'd hung out in LA until a little closer to Christmas. It was one thing to have this *thing* between them when it was just her family and Lance around, but it was becoming downright awkward around his family. But at this point, if his family got the wrong idea about them, it would be his fault, not hers.

Things got a little more hectic when Dean and Violet arrived with Addy. They seemed unaware of all that had transpired during their weeklong honeymoon except for the birth of baby Benjamin. Violet couldn't seem to stop smiling, and Dean stuck close to her side. Cami was happy for her sister. Just like she was happy for Jessa with Lance and Matt and Laurel with Benjamin, but there was a slow growing ache in her heart for something like that for herself.

"And finally the man of the hour is here," Jessa said when Laurel and Matt showed up. She went immediately to take the car seat from Matt and set it on the counter so she could lift the blanket covering him. "Oh, he's awake!"

Cami knew it would be expected of her to look at the baby. She wasn't sure she had the strength just yet, but it wasn't Laurel's or baby Benjamin's fault that she was without her baby. They deserved their time in the spotlight. Wiping her hands on a cloth, she left the vegetables in order to go peer over Jessa's shoulder. The baby's blue eyes were open while his lips worked against an invisible nipple.

"Can I take him out?" Jessa asked.

Laurel nodded. "But let Cami and Violet have a turn with him. You've had lots of baby time already."

"Awww," Jessa said, but after she had unbuckled Benjamin from his car seat, she turned to Cami.

"Why don't you let Violet go first? I had the privilege of

meeting him already. I'll take my turn after she's done."

"You might never get a turn," Violet said as she took the little bundle from Jessa. She bent to press a kiss to his head. "Hey, little one. I'm your favorite aunt. If you ever need anything or if Mommy and Daddy are being mean, you just call Auntie Violet."

Laurel laughed. "This kid is going to be super spoiled. Already he's got Rose responding to his every cry and squawk."

"I bet she's a big help." Cami smiled at the girl who hovered next to Violet.

"Definitely. There's something to be said for an age gap," Laurel said.

"There are almost eight years between my two youngest, but I have to say that Colin wasn't nearly as interested in Amy as your daughter is in your son," Michelle commented.

Laurel smiled, and Cami could see the pure joy on her sister's face. "She was very excited about having a sibling. I think it helps that she's a girl."

"Well, if Amelia hadn't cried all the time and then spit up on me, I might have liked her better," Colin said from where he stood leaning against the fridge. "And she still talks all the time."

"You just keep talking smack about me," Amy warned. "I have so much ammunition should any woman ever decide to give you a second look."

Cami smiled at the girl's spunky reply. She definitely didn't let her brother run over her.

"I've already had a couple of women give me a second look," Colin said.

"Yeah, but they were smart enough to not stick around," Amy replied.

"Now, now, you two," Michelle reproved softly. "Don't give this nice family the impression that you don't love each other."

Colin walked to where Amy stood with her arms crossed. He looped his arm around her neck and brought her close enough to rub his knuckles on her hair. "Yeah, I do love this brat of a sister even if she drives me nuts sometimes."

Amy let out a long sigh and gave him an exasperated look.

Cami enjoyed seeing the camaraderie between Josh's siblings. She'd never really had anything like that with her sisters. They'd had their moments, but often the words spoken in teasing had held a tone of meanness. It was sobering to realize that too often those mean words had come from her. She was just so fortunate that her sisters hadn't given up on her, that even Jessa had come to the point where she'd just offered love without judgment. Cami knew she hadn't deserved even that much for all the trouble she'd caused.

"You ready for a turn?"

Cami's gaze came back into focus to find Violet standing next to her, an expectant look on her face. Though she wasn't sure she'd ever be ready, she nodded and held out her arms. As the soft weight settled against her, Cami wondered if her heart could break even more than it was already broken over her past. She stared down at the baby and found that his eyes were wide as he looked at her. Would hers have been a boy? She'd always thought of the baby as a girl since there had been only girls in the Collingsworth family, but maybe she would have had a little boy just like this one.

"Hello, little man," she whispered. "Welcome to the family."

A tear dropped onto his cheek, and Cami brushed it away with a fingertip, blinking to keep any more from falling. She swayed gently as she closed her eyes and lifted him to her cheek. His softness. His scent. It was almost more than she could bear, but he was the most precious thing she'd held in her life. Cami felt arms go around her, and soon found herself in the midst of a sister hug.

"Are you okay?" Laurel's words were spoken soft and low.

Cami nodded, because in a way she was. Even as this was the hardest thing she'd had to do in a long time, it felt right, and there was none of the guilt that had been there the last time she'd seen Benjamin. Somehow she knew that the acute pain she felt right now would begin the healing she needed.

She opened her eyes and through dampness looked at Laurel and smiled. "He's absolutely beautiful and precious. I have so much to tell you."

A smile spread across Laurel's face. "Jessa told me some of it. I'm so happy for you."

Cami nodded. "But there's so much more. Soon. Soon I'll share it with you all."

With more reluctance than she'd thought she'd have, Cami handed the baby back to Violet. "I'll let you snuggle with him a bit more while I finish up my job here."

Wiping her fingers across her cheeks to remove the last of the lingering moisture, Cami realized that Josh was no longer in the kitchen. Everyone else was still there except for the one person who knew her darkest secret, her deepest heartbreak.

Pushing aside the emotions stirred by that thought, Cami returned to her cutting board and was focused on the vegetables when a pair of denim-clad hips leaned back against the counter next to her. She looked up to see Colin standing there, arms crossed.

"He couldn't handle it," Colin said in a low voice. His blue eyes, so like his brother's, were intent on her.

"What?"

"Whatever just happened there with the baby. He knew what was going on with you but couldn't do anything about it. He had to leave."

"How do you know that?" Cami asked, wondering how much Josh might have told his brother.

Colin's lips lifted in a slight smile. "I know my brother. I know how to read people. You've got him tied up in knots."

Cami wasn't sure how she felt about that. "That was never my intention."

Or had it been? When they'd first met she'd definitely been trying to get a reaction out of him, but now, she didn't want to cause him any trouble. She didn't know what she wanted from him. Even now that her faith fell in line with his, she wasn't sure she was the best person for Josh. She came with so much baggage and, from what she knew of his first marriage, she was pretty sure that a relationship with another complicated woman was the last thing he needed. She turned her attention back to her task, but Colin didn't move.

"You know, I haven't seen Josh like this before. Granted I was only around thirteen or fourteen when he got together with Emma, and he was at boarding school most of that time. He was around the age I am now when they lost their baby, and she committed suicide."

Shock shot through Cami. She hadn't known about the baby he'd lost or the manner in which his wife had died. Setting the knife down, she looked up at Colin. "Why are you telling me this?"

Chapter Fifteen

So you know that Josh doesn't give his affections lightly. He's been through the wringer, and, while I'd like nothing more than to see him with a wonderful woman, I don't want him to get hurt in the process."

"I'm not planning to hurt him, but I don't know that we're right for each other. If you're thinking he could do better than me, then that makes two of us."

Colin arched a brow. "I don't know you well enough to be able to make that call."

"You're talking like you do," Cami remarked.

"A hazard of my chosen profession," Colin replied.

Cami resumed cutting the tomato on her board. "You a shrink?"

"Not yet, but working on it."

"So you're practicing on us?"

Colin chuckled. "Josh asked the same thing. I guess you could say I'm sort of using what I've learned, but more than anything I'm just trying to look out for my brother."

"I understand that, and will do my best not to make things more difficult for him." Cami kept her voice low, though with all the other conversation and commotion going on, it was unlikely that people would hear them clearly.

"I'm sure he'll make things difficult enough for himself. Just, if you notice him avoiding you, know that it's for his own sake, not because of anything you've done."

"Son, why don't you make yourself useful?" Michelle said as she approached them with a stack of plates.

"Will do, Ma." Colin took the plates and looked around.

"Through there," Cami said, pointing her knife in the direction of the dining room. As Colin moved from beside her, Cami saw Josh standing in the doorway to the hall. His expression was guarded as he watched Colin walk away from her. She turned her attention back to the salad, not wanting to know if he looked her way or not.

Dinner was a loud affair, with plenty of conversation going on around the table. Cami found herself seated between Violet and Amy and once again was peppered with questions from the teenager. As she looked around the table, Cami was grateful that she and Josh were on the same side so that she didn't find her gaze constantly drifting in his direction.

There was no more interaction between them throughout the evening, and he didn't even look her way when he, Colin, and Lance headed out for the apartment. She told herself it was just as well. Whatever there was between them seemed too intense for her to deal with right then. She'd never experienced such a connection with someone and yet, at the same time, such a fear of the intimacy it brought.

Since her return from California, she found herself experiencing a raw reaction to everything. It was like she'd had a buffer on her emotions that kept her from experiencing anything too deeply or fully. Now, that buffer seemed to have been stripped away, leaving her emotions much closer to the surface. The love she felt for her family. The sadness over her past. The joy of her newfound faith. The ups and downs with Josh. It was a rollercoaster like nothing she'd ever experienced before.

It had been such a long day that Cami didn't linger long before crawling into bed. She had yet to unpack her things, but there was time tomorrow. She didn't know how much she would be unpacking because she'd been serious about not staying at the manor if it would interfere with Jessa and Lance's newly married life.

Lance had taken longer to leave the manor, so Josh and Colin arrived at the apartment before him. The ride into town had been quiet, and once they got into the apartment, Josh got them each something to drink and they settled on the couch to watch the sports channel.

"Bet you'll be glad when you don't have to leave Jessa at the manor at the end of the day," Josh said when Lance walked in the door a few minutes later.

"Yep," Lance said with a grin. "It's getting harder and harder to say goodnight."

Lance got himself a drink and settled into the easy chair next to the couch. "Did you get much chance to talk to Cami on the ride home?"

Josh shook his head. "Amy had a million questions and then we sang Christmas carols. Why?"

"Guess she didn't share her news with you then?"

"What news?" Josh asked, frowning.

"She told Jessa and me earlier that she'd committed her life to God while she was in LA."

Josh was speechless. Of all the things he'd expected Lance to say, that hadn't been one of them. What had happened in California to bring about her change of heart? And why hadn't she let him know?

"I don't know all the details," Lance said. "Just that she

told Jess she was coming home to Collingsworth to wait and see where God might lead her next."

Josh stared at the television, trying to sort out how he felt about this revelation. From a purely Christian standpoint, he was happy for Cami. From his own perspective, he realized he'd been using the difference in their spiritual status as an excuse for not dealing with how he really felt about her. Now that was gone, and he had to face his fears head on.

"I thought you'd be happier about that news, cuz," Lance said. "I know it was a big reason why you never let yourself consider anything with her."

Josh nodded. "Yes, it was, but there's more. Most of it based on my own fears."

He saw Lance glance at Colin and then back at him. "Am I missing something?"

"Actually, everyone is missing quite a lot, but it's not my place to tell the story," Josh said. "Let's just say that Cami has issues, as do I, and I'm just not sure that I could be a good partner for her. She needs a stronger man than me. After I failed so miserably with Emma, I just don't want to risk that again with someone like Cami. She deserves better."

Lance lifted an eyebrow. "I never knew Emma that well, but I don't see Cami having any of the problems she had."

"Trust me. Between the two of us, we'd probably keep a shrink busy for a lifetime. I just don't know if I'm strong enough for her, and I don't want to fail her like I failed Emma."

"While I realize it's not your place to reveal anything, I really think you need to pray about all this. It's going to be mighty rough if you don't get this sorted out between the two of you. It's not like you're never going to see each other again."

"Maybe I'll look into moving back to Fargo in the new year," Josh said. "That would make it easier."

"Running won't solve anything," Colin commented. "And

you may feel that you're not strong enough, but God is. I think you need to be more concerned about whether or not this is what God wants. If it is, He'll be the strength you both need to grow your relationship into what He wants it to be."

Josh felt his stomach twist. "I prayed a lot for wisdom in dealing with Emma. I prayed that He would heal her mind and give her peace. He didn't answer either of those prayers. Why would He listen to me now?"

As soon as he said the words, Josh wished he could take them back. He had never voiced how deep the despair had been at not having God answer his prayers. But now that they were said, the hurt of feeling abandoned by God during that time of his life flooded him. He'd tried to live his life in a way that honored God since his affair, but in reality, he'd done it more so that no one would question his spiritual state. Meanwhile, he had come to expect nothing from God—especially when it came to himself. And he realized that it was the main reason he hadn't fully immersed himself in his music again. The Gospel music he had sung had always been so important to him, a reflection of his relationship with God. He just couldn't bring himself to stand in front of people and perform when his heart wasn't in it.

Maybe Cami hadn't been the only one in need of a change of heart.

He bent his head, the weight of the gazes of his brother and cousin heavy on him. So there he sat, an adulterer, a failed husband, and now a faltering Christian. He was so far from where he'd thought he'd be at this point in his life. The woman he'd loved. *Gone.* The baby they'd longed for. *Gone.* The career he'd enjoyed so much. *Gone.* In the end, God had left him with nothing. And maybe that was as it should be, given what he'd done. Did he dare try to reach for happiness once again? Or would that be taken from him as well? He didn't think he could stand any more loss.

Josh couldn't bring himself to look at Lance or Colin. He'd let them believe it had been Cami's lack of faith that had kept them apart when, in reality, his own faith had faltered so much that it didn't really exist except as a way to keep up appearances. That night on the beach with Cami had been the first time in a long time that he'd reached for the faith he'd once had in order to share it with her. And now she had found her way to God, and Josh felt more lost than ever.

"I think I'm going to call it a night," Josh said as he stood up. "I've got an air mattress set up for you in my room, Col, whenever you're ready for bed."

Knowing they'd probably talk about him once he left, Josh wearily went to his room to change. He was sitting on the side of the bed, checking his phone, when Colin walked in. He dropped his bag on the end of the air mattress and bent to unzip it.

"Bathroom's through there," Josh said with a nod of his head toward the closed door on the other side of the room.

Colin wasn't in the bathroom long, and though Josh wanted to feign sleep, he was pretty sure his brother wouldn't buy it. When Colin snapped off the lamp next to his bed, the room was plunged into darkness.

"You know you're not the first person to struggle with their faith," Colin said.

"I know," Josh replied. "I just felt that more was expected of me. That after all I'd done, I wasn't allowed to question God."

"He's still there for you, Joshie," Colin said, using the nickname he'd always used as a youngster trying to keep up with his older brother. "And you don't need to keep punishing yourself for what happened back then. You know the drill. Confess your sins and He is faithful and just to forgive you. And not just forgive but forget. You're beating yourself up over something that God doesn't even remember, let alone hold against you anymore."

Josh knew his brother was right, but fear held him back. He wanted to reach for the happiness he thought he could have with Cami. He wanted to reclaim the joy that his music career had given him. He wanted to live his life as unto God.

But last time, he'd failed so badly and then had everything ripped from him. How was it that his younger brother understood this so much better than he did? How was it that his faith was so much stronger? He didn't want to think about the disappointment his parents would feel if they found out how much his faith had faltered over the years, in spite of the act he'd put on for the world.

Saturday afternoon Josh made it through practice for the worship service the next day. He wasn't sure he should be playing, but didn't want to leave them in a lurch. And, using the excuse of giving Jessa a break from having to cook for a crowd, he managed to avoid the manor by having his family come to the apartment for supper.

Lance had still gone to the manor, so it was just him and his family. Even though Colin was aware of everything, he didn't say anything to their parents or siblings. Instead, they were able to enjoy a fun evening of food and some games before the rest headed back to the manor for the night.

Colin was blessedly silent when they crawled into bed that night. Josh was fighting both apprehension and anticipation for the next day. Seeing Cami was always bittersweet, and the next day would be no different. He knew he needed to figure out what was going on in his own heart. He just couldn't figure out how to do it without having to bare his soul to the world...or at the very least, his parents. And how did he reveal to Cami that, even though he'd known what to tell her for her own faith struggle, he wasn't the strong Christian she thought he was?

Cami was looking forward to church. It would be her first time attending without the attitude of just enduring the hour and getting out as quickly as possible. There was no Sunday school, so they were able to head for church together. Between them and Josh's family, they took up two rows.

As she followed the others into their pew, Cami spotted

Josh standing near the front with a handful of other people. The woman next to him said something, and he bent his head down toward her. When he straightened, he flashed the woman a quick smile and nodded. A knot gripped Cami's stomach. She was pretty sure Josh was avoiding her, which reinforced the fear that she'd had. He may have said it was her spiritual state that stood between them but, now that that was gone, it seemed it was just her and her past.

Cami let out a deep breath as she watched Josh and the others with him climb the stage. Josh picked up a guitar, and the worship team began to play. Clearly Josh wasn't just a talented singer. However, Cami couldn't help noticing that even though he appeared to be singing, he wasn't anywhere near a mic.

Trying to ignore the feelings seeing Josh stirred up, Cami reminded herself that her experience with God a few days ago had nothing to do with him. Her spiritual journey was between her and God. Whether it changed things with Josh or not, she had to keep her focus on God and seek His will for her life. She had hoped that that might include Josh, but now she wasn't so sure. It hurt to finally experience a connection with someone and have it go nowhere.

Instead of looking at Josh, Cami focused on the trio that led the singing, and when the worship team left the stage, she willed herself not to follow his progress up the side aisle to reach the pew where his family sat. As the pastor stood behind the pulpit, Cami pulled out her tablet to use the Bible app. She knew others might frown on her using it, but it was easier to find references if she could just tap the information into the search bar of the app. She still wasn't familiar enough with the Bible to be able to find the scriptures by herself.

It was poignant to listen to the pastor speak of Mary. Of how the young girl found herself unmarried and pregnant with a child who wasn't fathered by the man she was pledged to marry. Cami felt her thoughts going to that time in her own life. Though it hadn't been a Heavenly conception, she too had been unmarried and expecting a child. She recalled with more clarity than ever before the panic and fear that had overtaken her at the realization that she was repeating history. She realized now that this was when she'd begun to block out her emotions, to keep them from overwhelming her. It was the only way she could do what had to be done.

When the pastor ended his sermon a short time later, Cami bent her head with the others and prayed. *Please, God, take care of my little one. And let me see him or her again someday. Thank you for forgiving me for what I did. Give me peace. Give me guidance. Please help me to live my life to honor and glorify You from now on.*

Cami felt movement behind her as Josh left the pew to join the worship team on stage. She knew she wouldn't be able to avoid him for the rest of the day. A big dinner was planned back at the manor once again. But she knew she could do this. Her emotions may have been more fragile, but she was still strong. She'd gotten through worse.

Back at the manor, she changed out of her church outfit into a pair of fitted jeans and a loose sweater. She pulled on a pair of thick socks because she just couldn't seem to keep her feet warm otherwise. After changing, she joined the others downstairs. Once again, everyone had been assigned a task to prepare for the meal, and she found herself in the dining room setting the long table.

"Jessa said to bring you these plates."

Cami willed herself not to react to the sound of Josh's voice. With a smile, she turned to face him. "Thanks. You can set them on the end there."

"Are they for the other side?" Josh asked.

"Yep, she had to get the rest from the dishwasher."

"I'll give you a hand," Josh said as he moved to the other side of the table and began to set the plates in front of each chair.

Cami continued to set out the silverware, humming as she worked, determined not to let Josh's presence dim her spirits.

“Are the glasses here, or do I need to get them from the kitchen?” Josh asked.

Cami looked up, surprised to find him standing so close to her. His blue eyes regarded her without expression. “Uh, I think they’re probably in the kitchen.”

Josh nodded and turned to walk from the room. He was back in short order carrying a tray filled with glasses. Colin followed behind him with a second one. Cami thought he might set the tray down and leave, but he began to put them on the table.

“How’re you doing today, Cami?” Colin asked with a smile.

“I’m good. How are you?”

“Well, aside from trying to keep from turning into a popsicle, I’m good, too.”

“I hear ya.” Cami lifted a foot and pointed at it. “I’m wearing the thickest socks I can find to keep warm.”

“And you’re moving back here?” Colin asked with a lifted brow.

Cami laughed. “Yeah. Am I nuts or what? Actually, I’m not sure it’s going to be a long-term thing. At least right now I’m hoping it won’t be. I need God to lead me some place warm year-round.”

“Any ideas on where that might be?” Colin asked as he set the last glass on the table and picked up the tray.

“No, not really. But if it’s going to be music-related, there’s only one place I haven’t been yet to try to build my career.”

“New York?” Colin suggested.

“Been there, done that.” Cami straightened the silverware she’d just laid down. “Nashville.”

“That’s definitely the place to go if you’re into Country or

Gospel." Colin waved a hand to where Josh stood. "You should talk to Josh about Nashville. He lived there for a couple of years and might have some connections."

Ignoring the fluttering in her stomach, Cami smiled and looked in Josh's direction. "I just might do that if I feel that's where God seems to want me to go."

"Everything good to go in here?" Any further conversation on the subject was prevented by Lance's question as he joined them in the dining room. He carried a big platter that held the roast Jessa had put on earlier that day.

"Yep. You can set that right there," Cami said as she grabbed a couple of trivets and put them on the table for him to rest the platter on.

The rest of the group followed, some of whom carried the remainder of the food. Once drinks were poured, everyone settled down to eat. As usual, Cami made sure she was on the same side of the table as Josh and found herself seated with Amy once again. The girl seemed to have developed an attachment to her that Cami found amusing and endearing.

This time, Cami took the opportunity to ask more questions of the teen since they'd pretty much exhausted all the topics Cami was willing to discuss about herself.

"What grade are you in?" Cami asked.

"Eleventh," Amy said as she handed her a basket of rolls.

Cami tilted her head to look at her. "Aren't you just fifteen?"

Amy nodded. "But I skipped a couple of grades."

"Wow! You must be smart."

The teen shrugged. "I'm not the only one. All of us graduated early. Beth and Josh were both one year ahead, and Colin and I were two."

That certainly explained why Colin seemed further along in his chosen profession than she would have thought at his age. “Talented, smart, and beautiful. You’re a triple threat.”

Amy gave her a shy look. “You think I’m beautiful?”

“Definitely. Your hair has such nice curls, and your eyes are beautiful.”

“My mom says that Josh and I have the same eyes and hair. Does that mean you think he’s handsome?”

So much for avoiding certain subjects. “Well, sure he’s handsome. But to be fair, so is Colin. And so are Lance, Dean, Matt, and Will.”

Amy wrinkled her nose. “But don’t you think Josh is the most handsome?”

“Do you want to know who I think is the cutest guy in my life right now?” Cami leaned close when Amy’s eyes glowed with anticipation. When the teen nodded eagerly, Cami grinned and said, “Benjamin.”

Amy leaned back and shook her head. “That’s not fair. You can’t count babies.”

Cami laughed and realized that perhaps Josh wasn’t the only Moyer she was in jeopardy of losing her heart to. Amy seemed like the sort of teen she might have been, had she been in a different family. Asid from the smarts and beauty, of course.

After the dinner had wound down, Michelle commandeered her family into clean-up. Though Jessa protested, Josh’s mom wouldn’t take no for an answer. Later they all headed back to the church for the children’s Christmas program. As she sat in the pew with her family, at times cuddling baby Benjamin, Cami realized that this was what she wanted. This connection to family and friends, and a connection to a community and a church. It wasn’t something she’d ever had in New York or LA and, to be honest, she hadn’t been looking for it. But as her heart had softened to God, it also seemed to be softening to the world around her.

As the program ended, they all stood to sing with the

children. Out of all the other voices around her, Cami could clearly hear the rich tenor of Josh's. As they began the second verse of 'O Holy Night', she stopped singing just so that she could enjoy the sound of his voice. Then on the third verse she joined back in, closing her eyes as she sang.

Truly He taught us to love one another;

His law is love and His Gospel is peace.

Chains shall He break for the slave is our brother,

And in His Name all oppression shall cease.

Sweet hymns of joy in grateful chorus raise we,

Let all within us praise His holy Name!

Christ is the Lord! Oh, praise His name forever!

His pow'r and glory evermore proclaim!

She'd performed the song a few times and had memorized it, but singing it this time, with her whole heart in tune with the words, she held nothing back. Music had always been her method of communication. Whether people realized it or not, when she sang, she was sharing parts of herself with them. But where she'd once sung suggestive or shallow love songs, the music she wanted to sing now stirred a part of her heart that she'd never even known was there.

The pastor dismissed the evening with prayer and invited everyone to the basement of the church where there were goodies and drinks. It was a tradition she'd balked at as a teenager, but tonight she welcomed it and indulged in more than one sugar cookie with a heavy layer of icing and an abundance of sprinkles.

Before falling asleep that night, Cami spent some time reading her Bible. The pastor in California had given her a little booklet to give guidance on what to read as a new Christian. She wasn't sure why, but as she read, one thought kept coming to mind over and over. *Go visit your mother*. It was something she'd resisted since discovering where Elizabeth Collingsworth was, but suddenly it wasn't as objectionable anymore. As Cami lay curled up in her bed, she wondered if she would have even been able to make amends with Gran in her current state of heart.

Sleep tugged at her as thoughts of Josh filled her mind. Maybe nothing could happen with him until she had other things straightened out in her life. Tomorrow she would make a couple of phone calls and maybe take a short road trip.

"Can I borrow a car?" Cami asked at breakfast the next morning. "Just need to do a little running around."

"Yep," Jessa replied. "You can use Gran's. I'd let you have mine, but I've got to visit the caterer today and tie up a few other loose ends for the wedding. Don't forget about the fitting tomorrow at the bridal shop."

"I won't," Cami assured her. "But that fitting might be better after Christmas than before. The way I'm eating my dress might not fit in a few days."

Jessa laughed. "We'll tell them to leave it a tad loose."

Cami called Stan, their lawyer, and got the address for where Elizabeth was. She looked it up online, so she'd know where she was going and then shortly before noon she set out. She was glad the day was milder than other ones had been recently. It was cloudy, but she could handle that better than the frigid temperatures of late.

The hour and a half drive to the neighboring town where Elizabeth was went smoothly. It gave Cami plenty of time to think and sing along with the playlist of Christmas songs she'd loaded on her phone. She found it strange that Elizabeth was in a private home instead of a long-term care facility, but she figured it was the best way Gran knew to take care of her only daughter. The house was in a nice neighborhood, and as she pulled into the driveway, she could see the faint twinkle of Christmas lights.

She sat for a moment, suddenly nervous. After saying a quick prayer, Cami got out of the car. The wind had picked up on the drive, and a few light drifted around her as she walked to the front door. She rang the doorbell then pulled off her gloves as she waited for someone to answer. She'd called before leaving, and they'd assured her it would be a good day to visit.

The door was opened by a woman who appeared to be in her thirties. She wore a pair of jeans and a loose sweater and smiled when she saw Cami.

Chapter Sixteen

ARE you Cami?" she asked.

"Yes," Cami said as she extended her hand.

The woman shook it firmly. "I'm Marilyn. C'mon in." She stepped back to allow Cami into the foyer.

She showed Cami where to put her coat and boots and then led the way into the living room. The Christmas lights Cami had spotted from outside were wrapped around a large tree that stood in front of the window. There was a fire in the fireplace, and a Christmas program played on a large television. Her gaze finally settled on a woman lying in a reclined wheelchair near the fire. From that spot, it appeared that she had a good view of both the tree and the television.

"She loves the music and the lights," Marilyn said. "I hear from your sisters that you also love music."

Though Cami's attention was held by the woman in the wheelchair, she said, "Yes, I do."

"If you want to talk with her, I'll leave the two of you alone. She won't respond, and likely won't know who you are, but she likes the attention. I'll be in the kitchen if you need me."

Cami glanced at Marilyn and nodded. "Thanks."

Alone with the mother she had no real memory of, Cami approached her slowly. Her blue eyes were wide and her skin looked flawless. Her hair was graying, but appeared to be clean and styled. Though she was an invalid, it was clear that those who cared for Elizabeth were good to her. Standing next to the chair, Cami slid her hand into Elizabeth's. Surprisingly, her mother's gaze focused on her.

"Hi, Mom. I'm Cami." There was a stool next to the wheelchair. Cami pulled it over and sat down. The height of it kept her right at eye-level with Elizabeth. "I just wanted to come and see you. I know you probably don't know who I am, but I want to thank you for giving me life. I wish I had made that decision for my child."

Though Elizabeth didn't respond in any way, she kept looking at Cami. Not sure what else to say, Cami began to tell her about her life starting with her time in New York and then in LA. And because she'd never had a mother to share things with before, she shared her confusion and heartache over the situation with Josh.

"I think you'd like him, too," Cami said. "He loves music like I do. Maybe, if it works out, I'll be able to bring him to see you."

"Cami?"

Without letting go of her mom's hand, Cami swiveled on the stool to see Marilyn standing a few feet away. "There are reports on the radio that things are getting really bad on the roads. Do you need to head back?"

Cami released Elizabeth's hand and stood. She went to the large window and peered around the Christmas tree. The light wind and few flurries that had been kicking around when she'd arrived had morphed into something much more intense and scary. "Yes, I need to leave."

"Are you sure you can drive in this? You could stay here if

you want."

"I think it will be okay. I'll drive slowly."

Cami went and pressed a kiss to her mother's cheek. "I'll be back, Mama. Merry Christmas."

Marilyn walked to the door with her. "Are you sure you can't stay here?"

"My family is expecting me back. I have my cell phone if anything happens."

Within a few minutes, Cami was questioning her decision. However bad it had been in town, once out on the highway it was way worse. She slowed to a crawl, her hands gripping the wheel tightly. Gusts of snow totally obliterated her view of the road at times, and her heart pounded with fear. It took her almost an hour and a half to go what had taken her forty-five minutes on her trip earlier. She saw a blue sign indicating a rest area ahead, and though it wasn't the place she had been attacked, it took all her courage to make the turn that would take her off the highway. Now she was safe from vehicles on the highway, but did danger lie ahead?

She was surprised that there weren't more vehicles in the parking lot of the rest area. It was deserted. Perhaps people had been paying better attention to the weather than she had and decided not to drive on the highways. She wasn't used to checking the weather before she left to go somewhere, but clearly it was a habit she was going to need to develop if she lived here for any length of time. From her parking spot at the rest area, she could see that there was still some traffic on the highway. Obviously people who lived around here were also more confident driving in blizzard conditions, which was likely another reason for the lack of cars at the rest area.

Cami didn't turn the engine off, though she wasn't sure how long she could keep it running. She looked through the wet windshield toward the building that housed the restrooms for this rest area. Going into that building would be the wise choice. It would conserve her gas and offer her more warmth than sitting in the car. But who else might show up? She'd thought she'd been alone at that other rest area, too.

She picked up her phone and looked at the time on it. How long could she sit here before people would begin to wonder where she was? The phone showed she had service, though it wasn't a strong signal. She turned the phone over a few times in her hand. Maybe she'd wait a little bit longer. It was just past two o'clock in the afternoon. They wouldn't likely miss her until it got closer to dinner time. And maybe the storm wasn't as bad in Collingsworth. As soon as the blowing settled down a bit, she'd head back out.

"Anyone heard from Cami?"

Josh heard Jessa's question as he walked into the kitchen at the manor. He'd been in the living room with his dad, watching the reports on the weather channel. Last he'd heard, Cami had been in town running some errands.

"No," Violet replied, her brow furrowed. "Where did she say she was going?"

"I thought she was just going into town. She told me had some things to do," Jessa said as she picked up her phone. "I tried a little earlier, but it said the customer was out of range. Could the storm be affecting service?"

Josh tried to keep his concern about Cami from rising. If she was in Collingsworth, she should be able to make it out to the manor without any problems. When he'd come out with Colin twenty minutes ago, the wind had been blowing snow across the road, but there hadn't been any whiteouts. However, he knew how quickly that could change.

"I could phone Dean and have him look around there to see if he can spot the car," Violet offered.

"That would be great. I'm just a bit concerned with her driving in these conditions since she's not used to them," Jessa said. "But I don't want her to think I'm breathing down her neck."

Josh understood both of Jessa's concerns, but for him, knowing Cami's whereabouts was more important than anything else. She could be mad at them all later for trying to track her down.

Jessa's phone rang while Violet was still on with Dean, and she quickly answered it.

"Are you okay?" Jessa asked.

Josh wished he could hear both sides of the conversation since he was pretty sure it was Cami from Jessa's greeting.

"Where are you?" Jessa's brow furrowed as she listened. Josh hoped that Cami hadn't taken off again, but there would really be no reason for her to this time. "What were you doing out there? Cami? Cami?"

With a frustrated frown, Jessa lowered the phone from her ear. "Call dropped. She said she's at a rest area between here and Sanford."

"Sanford?" Violet asked, having ended her call with Dean. "What's she doing out there?"

"I was just asking her that when the call dropped. The only thing out that way is Mama."

Violet's eyes widened. "Do you think she went to see her?"

Jessa shrugged. "She hasn't talked about her at all. I don't know why she would have."

"With all the changes in her life lately, maybe she felt she had to make this connection, too," Lance pointed out.

Josh figured his cousin was right, but kept his opinion to himself. He was more focused on the fact that Cami was stranded at a rest area in the middle of a blizzard.

"I'm going to go get her," he said before he could stop himself.

All eyes turned toward him.

"Are you sure?" Violet asked. "I was going to have Dean send one of the guys out to check on her."

"I don't like the idea of her being at a rest area alone. They can be unsafe." Josh didn't want to spell out what everyone already knew. "My truck can handle the roads."

His mom laid a hand on his arm, her expression worried. At first he thought she was going to ask him not to go, but instead she said, "Don't go alone, sweetie. I would feel more comfortable if you had someone with you."

"I'll go along, Mom," Colin said.

"Call us as soon as you get there," Jessa requested. "Hopefully you can find a spot with service."

"And if necessary, wait out the storm there," Violet suggested. "I'll let Dean know you're heading out so he can tell his guys to let you by if they've blocked off any roads."

"Let me get some stuff together, just in case," Jessa said.

Within ten minutes, they were on the road with blankets, candles, matches, granola bars, and water. He doubted they'd need any of it, but better safe than sorry.

The road leading to Sanford was definitely in worse shape than the one from Collingsworth to the manor. Josh kept a firm grip on the wheel as he drove, slowing only when the wind caused a whiteout across the highway.

"Is she going to be upset with you coming to get her?" Colin asked after they'd driven a couple of miles.

"No idea," Josh replied. "Probably, but who cares. She needs to not be alone at that rest area."

"Why are you so worried about that? Are rest areas in this part of the state known for being dangerous?"

Josh glanced at his brother. "When Cami was attacked a couple of weeks ago, it was at a rest area."

"Didn't they catch the guy?"

Josh nodded. "I just don't like the idea of her being vulnerable to an attack again."

A sudden gust buffeted the truck, and Josh let up on the

accelerator when swirling snow blocked his view. They hadn't seen any other traffic on the road, but he didn't want to run into anyone...literally.

"Is there more than one rest area?" Colin asked after they'd been driving for about forty-five minutes. "Because I think I just saw a sign for one."

"Could you tell if it was on the side or the middle with access for both sides?"

"Think it said next right."

"Rats. We're going to have to find a place to turn around so we can get to the other side. I was hoping it was one that was shared by both sides."

Josh changed lanes and slowed down to make sure he didn't miss a spot where he could make a U-turn. He planned to do it even it was illegal, and he'd use Dean to pull strings if he got caught. Thankfully, that wasn't necessary as he came to a crossroads and was able to make the turn without breaking any laws.

He quickly found the exit for the rest area and pulled into the parking lot. It was empty except for one car parked near the building. He swung the truck into the spot next to it, and he and Colin jumped out and jogged through the swirling snow to the building. Warmth greeted them as he pulled the door open, but there was no one inside.

"Could she be in the restroom?" Colin asked.

Josh opened the door to the ladies' room and called out her name. There was no sound from within and no response to his query.

"Maybe she's still in the car," Colin suggested. "Could be she wasn't too keen on being in here by herself."

They exited the building and returned to where they had parked, going this time to the driver's side of the car. Colin stood behind him as he bent to knock on the glass. Josh realized it was running now, but was fairly certain it hadn't been when they'd arrived.

"Cami? It's me. Josh."

The windows of the car were smudged with moisture and condensation so Josh couldn't see clearly, and when he tried the door handle, it was locked.

"Cami!" He called more loudly and dropped to his haunches so that his face was level with her window. It could be she wasn't sure who it was banging on her window. He saw movement this time and heard the door unlock. Standing, he lifted the handle to open it.

"Josh?" Cami said as she got out of the car. "What are you doing here?"

"No one was really keen on you being here on your own," Josh told her as he moved to block her from the wind that whipped around them. "Let's go into the building. Save your gas, and it's warmer in there."

Cami seemed to hesitate, but then she leaned in to turn off the engine. She shut the door and shoved her hands into the pocket of her jacket.

"Let's go," Josh said. He slipped an arm around her shoulders and guided her toward the door of the building.

Once inside they stomped the snow from their feet.

"Colin?" Cami said as she noticed the man behind him. "I didn't know you were here, too."

"Yep, Mom wouldn't let Josh come alone."

Cami shot him a look, but he couldn't read her expression. "Guess everyone thinks I'm pretty dumb for not checking the weather before heading out."

Colin shrugged. "Not me. I probably wouldn't have thought about it, either. It didn't look bad this morning."

"Storms can come up quickly around these parts," Josh said. "What were you doing out here anyway?"

Cami's brows drew together, and it was a few seconds before she replied. "I went to see Elizabeth."

"Violet thought that's where you might have gone." Josh pulled off his gloves and put them in his jacket pocket. "How did it go?"

"It went fine," was her immediate response. She stared at him, her expression slowly darkening. He'd known she wouldn't be thrilled that he'd shown up, but Josh hadn't figured she'd be mad. Finally, she walked over to stand in front of him, her head tipped back so their gazes met. "Why are you here?"

Josh glanced at Colin then back down at Cami. "I told you. Your family was worried about you being out here alone."

"But, why you? I have two brothers-in-law, a soon-to-be one and a brother. And Dean could no doubt have conscripted a deputy or two to come rescue me. So, why you?"

Josh shoved his hands into the pockets of his jeans. "I volunteered."

"Why?"

Not being able to read her expression was making Josh very uneasy. He had a feeling that the answers he gave here were going to make or break things. "I was concerned—"

"Do you have some sort of savior complex or something?" Cami asked without allowing him to finish his explanation.

Josh saw Colin making some hand motions to him from behind Cami. Realizing his brother didn't want to be present for this, Josh tossed him the keys to the truck. Cami didn't move or look away from him during this exchange. Once Colin was gone, he looked back down at her and said, "What do you want from me, Cami?"

"I want to know why you're only there when you perceive me to be in need of rescuing or helping."

Josh frowned. "What do you mean?"

Cami stuck up her hand and raised one finger. "The bar." Two fingers. "Down at the beach." Three fingers. "After the attack." Four fingers. "The airport." And then her thumb. "Here."

"Well, in my defense, I didn't know you were going to be at the airport," Josh said, wishing almost immediately he could take the words back when her eyes flashed.

"You're confusing me, Josh, and I don't like that." Cami wrapped her arms across her front. "I felt a connection back in July, and I think you did, too, but you made it clear nothing could happen between us. I understand that now, because of you being a Christian, and I wasn't. But that's not an issue anymore, and I think you know that. Yet it seems to not have made any difference with you. Every time I turn around you're watching me from a distance. I can't deny that I'm drawn to you. I've never had these types of feelings about anyone before, but I don't know what's going on."

Josh stared at her. He knew he shouldn't have been surprised by her forthrightness, but it still took him aback. And he had absolutely no idea how to answer her. It was like every emotion he'd had was tangled up inside him. Guilt over Emma. Fear at the thought of trying to love again. Attraction to Cami. Being scared to let her down. Shame for not having a stronger faith. He wanted...needed time to sort it out. As many things as Cami had in her past, he had them, too. Could two such wounded people have a chance at finding happiness together?

He could see by Cami's expression that he was taking too long to answer. Emotion choked him, and all he wanted to do was to draw her into his arms and cradle her to his chest, to kiss away the confusion in her and in himself, too. But he could make no promises about anything. He didn't want to let her down like he had Emma. Not that he would cheat on her, but he hadn't been there for Emma when she'd needed him most. He hadn't been the strong husband she'd needed.

"Cami..." He barely got her name out, but no more words would work themselves past the tightness in his throat.

"Stay away from me. Don't look at me. Don't come near me. And whatever you do, don't ever rescue me again. I don't need it. I can take care of myself. I just thought maybe we could share the burdens we each carry from our past. But I'm not interested in being saved by you if there's nothing more." Cami spun on her heel and walked away from him, shoving open the door to the building when she got to it.

Josh hurried after her, a sick feeling filling his stomach. He tried to catch up to her, but she made it to his truck before he did. She jerked open the door and said something to Colin before unlocking her car and getting into the passenger side. As he approached the truck, Colin climbed out.

"What did she say to you?" Josh asked.

"She said she was sure you would prefer that I drive her car back to Collingsworth, but there was no way she was riding in the truck with you." Colin frowned. "What on earth happened?"

With the wind and snow swirling around them, it wasn't the time to discuss it. Josh wished she'd ride with him so they could talk about it, but something told him that his chance for talking was gone. "I'll tell you later. Just drive her home."

Josh decided that even though the weather hadn't improved markedly, it would be okay to attempt the drive back to the manor. "Let me go first so you'll know what's in front of you. Okay?"

Colin paused and then nodded. "Want me to tell her anything?"

Josh shook his head. "Feel free to agree with her that I'm a schmuck."

"I'll listen if she wants to talk, but otherwise, mum's the word," Colin said before he rounded the front of the car and slid behind the wheel.

Josh got into the cab of his truck and buckled up. Slowly he backed out and headed for the exit. He waited for Colin to fall in behind him before getting out onto the highway. Anger burned in him as he drove. Not at Cami. She'd had every right to call him out. But at himself. He had to get a grip on the mess he was in. He wasn't one given to pondering his emotions too much, but everything with Cami was forcing him to face them head-on. If he couldn't get over his past, there would be no future with her.

Josh knew that he'd had no right to take off his ring and allow himself to get emotionally tangled with Cami. Though he had been ready to put his past behind him, it hadn't been ready to let him go. That ring should have stayed firmly in place until he had worked through the mess of his past. Any woman would have deserved that, but especially Cami. Too bad he was realizing it a bit late in the game. Now he needed time, and she might not be waiting for him when he was finally able to commit himself fully to her.

And, once again, he had no one to blame but himself.

Chapter Seventeen

WANT to talk about it?" Colin asked.

Cami continued to stare out the passenger window. She still couldn't believe she'd confronted Josh that way, but it had been necessary. She hated the limbo she'd been in since returning from California. The mixed signals he was sending her made things too difficult. Now she knew where she stood. Whatever she'd thought he might feel for her was clearly a mistake. Tears burned her eyes, but she blinked rapidly to keep them at bay. Now was not the time, and it definitely was not the place.

"Cami?"

Realizing she hadn't answered his question, Cami looked over at him and said, "Not so much."

"Listen, don't give up on the guy. He's gone through a lot. Unfortunately, he hasn't worked through it like he should have and, now that he's finally thinking about the future, he has to face his past first."

"We both have stuff to work through. He knows that about me, too. I just don't understand the mixed signals."

Cami sighed. She really didn't want to talk about this with Josh's brother. Especially since she knew he was a budding shrink. "I'm not asking for a proposal from him. I just thought there was something between us."

"I think there is. I know even my mom has seen how he looks at you, how he treats you."

Cami turned back to look out the window. "There's more than any of you know about me. About the interactions between him and me. Believe me, not being a Christian was probably the least of my issues when it came to Josh. It's possible he just can't see past some of the other stuff."

"Given Josh's past, I have a hard time believing that," Colin said. "He knows all about those sins that people are quick to condemn."

The timing of all of this couldn't be worse, as far as Cami was concerned. They still had at least two more weeks of being forced into each other's company. Once Christmas and the wedding were over, it would be easier to keep her distance from him. In the meantime, she would pull herself together and not let anyone see how deeply this had hurt her.

"Do you have a girlfriend?" she asked Colin, hoping he'd be willing to change the subject.

There was a pause and then he said, "Well, maybe."

Cami turned in her seat to look at him. "Maybe?"

"I've only gone out on a couple of dates with her, so it's not like we're official or anything." He glanced quickly at her before returning his gaze to the road. "My family doesn't know about her yet, so no spilling that little secret."

"No worries. You keep your mouth shut about this, and I'll keep mine shut about your potential girlfriend."

"Deal. I'm hoping it turns into something a little more serious. I really like her."

"What's she like?" Cami asked, curious about what might attract Josh's brother to a woman.

"She's a lot of fun. When you're first around her, you think she's really quiet and reserved, but she comes out with these one-liners that just slay me. She's got a crazy sense of humor."

"Have you known her long?"

Colin didn't reply right away but then said. "Yeah. She's actually Beth's best friend."

"Oh. She's older than you?" Cami asked.

"Yes. Five years."

"That's not so bad," Cami told him. "Do you think your family would object?"

"I don't know. They all like her so I'm pretty sure they wouldn't, but we don't really want to create any awkwardness in the family until we know for sure if this is something we want to pursue. If it doesn't work, it's better if they don't know."

"Yeah, that makes sense." Cami smiled at him. "I hope it works out for you."

"Thanks. Me, too. She's a little more tentative about it, but I told her to take her time. She's worth the wait."

Worth the wait. Would Josh say that about her? And was he worth the wait? If he needed time, was she willing to take the chance of waiting for him, not knowing for sure if he'd agree to consider a relationship with her? It wasn't that like there was a line of guys waiting if she decided not to get involved with Josh, but she couldn't allow her feelings for him to continue to grow if heartache was going to be the end result.

Neither she nor Colin spoke much during the remainder of the drive. As they neared the manor, the roads began to clear, and the driving wasn't nearly as treacherous. Still, Cami breathed a sigh of relief when Colin brought the car to a stop in front of the garage. As she climbed out, she could see that Josh had also left the truck and was waiting for them to join him.

Inside the manor, she was greeted with enthusiasm and then a scolding from Jessa.

"Don't ever go off like that without telling someone," she admonished after giving her a hug. "Especially in winter. These storms can kick up without much warning."

"I didn't even think to look at the weather forecast before I left." She glanced at the mixture of her family and Josh's standing there. "I'm sorry for the trouble I caused."

"Did you go see Mama?" Violet asked.

"Yes. I knew it was time. In spite of the disaster of the trip, I'm glad I did."

"You were the last holdout." Violet beamed. "I'm so glad we've all been to see her now."

Cami glanced at Jessa. "You've been?"

Jessa nodded. "I knew that I needed to begin to face how I felt about that part of my past. The first step was to go see her."

Cami smiled. "Yes, I understand that."

Violet walked to where Josh stood. She gave him a hug and then said, "Once again, I owe you a hug for rescuing Cami."

Even from across the room, Cami could see Josh wince. Violet was so caught up in her own romantic newlywed fog that she had no idea what was going on between them.

"You're welcome. Just glad Mom had Colin come with me. He was a big help driving the car back."

"Well, I've got a huge pot of soup on the stove for anyone who's hungry," Jessa announced. "I figured it was a good meal for the stormy day. And there's fresh bread, thanks to Michelle. Help yourself and eat wherever is comfortable."

"I lit a fire in the living and dining rooms," Lance said. "It looks like the storm is hanging around for a while."

"I'm just going to go freshen up," Cami said after the

prayer for the meal. "Save me some."

Without a look at Josh, she left the kitchen and climbed the stairs to the sanctuary of her room.

Cami had actually thought that the days ahead would be difficult with Josh around, but he made it surprisingly easy. He didn't make himself scarce, because that was impossible with his family there, but he treated her just like he treated her sisters. She didn't catch him looking at her, and he didn't do any of the little things he'd been doing up till their discussion at the rest area. Cami hadn't realized just how much he'd done for her until he'd stopped. Doors held open. Heavy dishes carried to and from the dining room for her.

When their gazes did meet, Cami couldn't read anything in his eyes. Meanwhile, her heart broke a little more each day. He'd managed to switch off whatever might have been between them quite easily. Too easily? Maybe she had read far too much into their interactions and been presumptuous in her conversation with him.

They'd gone to a Christmas Eve service at the church, which had been beautiful with candles and carols. It had helped to get Cami in a better frame of mind. And then the next day, the manor had nearly exploded at the seams for Christmas dinner. In addition to Josh's family, Lance's dad had arrived with his brother and family in tow. Will's family, who had been staying with Sylvia, also showed up. It was all hands on deck for preparation, so it wasn't too overwhelming. And Cami was grateful for the new arrivals who took the attention off her. Of course, they came with their own drama.

Originally, Lance's family had planned to stay straight through until the wedding, but his sister-in-law made things very uncomfortable for all of them by fawning over Lance. Cami had found Jessa in tears the morning after Christmas. It had been all she could do to keep from seeking out the woman and giving her a piece of her mind. When Lance arrived, Cami told him what had happened, even though

Jessa hadn't wanted him to know. Cami didn't think it was right that Daphne got away with the snide remarks she'd made to Jessa. And Lance hadn't thought so, either. Within the hour, Dave, Daphne, and family were on their way back to Fargo with instructions to return for the wedding only if Daphne would behave.

The stress level in the manor dropped substantially once they left. Even Lance's father seemed more at ease, as plans shifted from Christmas to the wedding. Cami just wished she could get rid of the dark thoughts that kept dogging her. And the guilt. It popped up at the oddest of times and left her feeling sick. When she found that she was distancing herself again from the family and baby Benjamin in particular, Cami knew she needed to talk with someone. Not knowing who to call in Collingsworth, she put in a long-distance call to Pastor Miller.

She sat on the window seat in her room, staring out at the snow-topped chapel as she waited for him to answer.

"Hi, Pastor Miller. This is Cami Collingsworth."

"Cami! Merry Christmas. I hope you had a good holiday."

"I did. Thank you. I hope you did as well."

"It was very good. Grace got out of the hospital on Christmas Eve, so she was able to celebrate with us. She's doing much better."

"I'm so glad to hear that," Cami said. "I was very worried about her that day I found her."

"We all were, but God has blessed her with healing." He paused and then said, "Was there something in particular you needed?"

Cami took a deep breath. "I'm struggling with some things lately." At his encouragement, Cami told him the parts of her story she hadn't shared with him before. "I know you said that I might struggle still with the guilt, but I feel like I'm failing at this Christian thing. Shouldn't I be better able to handle it?"

"Satan loves to find our weak points and prey on them. Clearly, your guilt over your abortion is a weak point, so that's where he is going to hit you. It doesn't mean you're failing. God is there when we're feeling strong *and* when we're feeling weak. I don't know if you'd consider it, but I think you might do well with some counseling with regards to this. I have known women who made the same decision you did who are able, with counseling, to come to a place of peace about it. There are a lot of emotions tied to something like that, and there's no shame in getting help to sort them out."

"How do I find someone to help me?" Cami asked. "I've never been to counseling before."

"There are a few options, but if you'd like, I could phone the pastor of your church there to see what he might suggest."

"Would you do that? I don't really know him that well, though he knows our family."

"I know it's sometimes easier if someone else breaks the ice for you. If you give me his information, I'll give him a call and, with your permission share, confidentially, some of your story so he can tell me what resources might be available to you."

"Thank you. I appreciate that. This is all so new to me. I'm not even sure what I should be asking about."

"I'm glad you called. Too often people try to just muddle through things when we are here to help. God expects us to help others, so never worry about calling with questions or concerns."

Before hanging up, Cami promised to text him the information as soon as she got it. Leaving her room, she went in search of Jessa. She found all of her sisters together in the kitchen, Violet cradling a sleeping Benjamin.

"Where is everyone?" she asked as she joined them.

"Lance and his dad went out for lunch with Josh's

family," Jessa said. "I declined the invitation in hopes of a little down time."

"And we all showed up. I was beginning to wonder where you were," Laurel said with a smile.

"I had to make a phone call." Cami ran her fingers over Benjamin's soft hair before sitting down next to Violet. She looked around at her sisters, grateful that they were all together and for once, no other non-family members were around. "Do you guys have a few minutes?"

Jessa looked up from the list she was studying. "Sure. What's up?"

Nerves fluttered in her stomach, but Cami pressed forward, praying that her sisters would understand. "I'm sure you've wondered about my reaction to Benjamin when he was born." She looked at Laurel. "Some of it had to do with Rose's birth, but most of it had to do with the abortion I had."

There was stunned silence at her words. Then Laurel leaned forward and laid her hand on Cami's arm. "Why didn't you tell us?"

"I didn't think you'd understand. It wasn't until recently that I finally talked about it with someone. That person assured me that it wasn't the unforgivable sin I thought it was."

"Who did you tell?" Jessa asked.

Cami bit her lip then said. "Josh. He caught me in a weak moment down at the beach when I was drinking. All kinds of stuff comes out when I'm drunk."

"Josh? Really?" Violet said. "I guess that kind of explains the connection you two have."

Cami shrugged. "We each had our secrets, but it was his comments that started me on the journey to God." She shared what had happened in California and then about her continuing struggle with the guilt. "The pastor who helped me in offered to help me find someone to go to for counseling here. Jess, I was wondering if I could get the number for the pastor in Collingsworth."

"Definitely," Jessa said with a smile. "I know he'd be happy to help you or find someone who can. I think his wife is a counselor, as well."

Cami felt a weight ease from her shoulders. She'd been so sure she'd face judgment from her sisters, but as she told them more about what had transpired all those years ago, they offered love and support. At least this one area of her life was going better. Now if she could just get past Josh.

Josh tried to concentrate on the conversation going on around the table. Thankfully, Lance had reserved a small room at the Italian restaurant, so they didn't have to worry about disturbing other patrons. Though it was nowhere near as loud as the meals had become recently at the manor, there were still outbursts of laughter and loud voices as people made themselves heard.

"You okay, son?" Josh looked over to find his mom regarding him, concern on her face. "You don't seem like yourself."

Josh shrugged. "I'm okay. Just have a lot on my mind."

"Does it have to do with Cami?"

He shouldn't have been surprised that his mom had noticed, but he was. "Yes, partly."

"I thought when we first got here that there might be something brewing between you two, but since Christmas it's changed."

Josh nodded. "Yes, it has. Actually, it changed the day I went to pick her up from the rest area."

"Want to talk about it?"

Talk about it? With his mother? Josh wasn't sure he was ready to do that. How could he possibly share with his mom how badly his faith had been shaken after everything that happened with Emma? It had taken a lot of effort—and distance—to make sure that his family wasn't aware of his struggle. Hadn't he disappointed them enough?

"Maybe later. " He gave her what he hoped was a reassuring smile. "This is not really the place."

His mom patted his hand. "Just know that I'm willing to listen if you want to share."

A couple of days later, Josh found himself pulling into the church parking lot. After trying on his own for so long to get past what had happened, he'd finally accepted that he needed some help. If he wanted a chance for love in his future, he needed help to get beyond everything that still weighed him down and made him struggle in his faith.

He stepped into the foyer of the church and stomped his feet to shake the snow from his boots. Pulling off the cap he wore, he ran a hand through his hair to keep it from sticking to his scalp. He'd stopped by on the off-chance that he could chat with the pastor. Since joining the worship team, he'd talked with him a few times and had liked the man. He knew he should probably have made an appointment, but it had been too easy to put it off so far. As he'd driven by the church a few minutes earlier, he'd decided it was now or never.

Josh walked down the hallway that ran the length of the sanctuary to where the offices were. The pastor's secretary, who was also on the worship team with him, sat behind her desk. Alena Fraser looked up and smiled as he approached.

"Hey, Josh. What's up?"

"I just stopped by to see if I could talk to the pastor."

Alena wrinkled her nose. "Sorry. He and Susan are with someone at the moment. I can make an appointment for you, if you want."

Josh nodded. "That's probably better than just stopping in."

They talked for a few minutes as Alena looked through

the pastor's schedule to see what lined up with when Josh was available. As he leaned down to the desk to look at the calendar Alena had turned his direction, he heard a door open and he straightened when he recognized the voices. Glancing over, he saw the pastor and his wife step out of the office with Cami.

"Josh?" Cami said when her gaze landed on him. Her eyes were red and a bit swollen. "What are you doing here?"

Josh fingered the edge of his cap and cleared his throat. "I, uh, stopped by to talk with the pastor. I was just making an appointment with Alena."

"I have some time now, Josh, if you want," the pastor said.

Josh's gaze went back to Cami. He remembered seeing her for the first time. Her flirtatious looks and provocative outfits those first few weeks had both attracted and repelled him. He remembered listening to her share her deepest hurt. He remembered holding her as she cried. He remembered the way her eyes flashed with temper. He remembered, and he wanted.

He looked back at the pastor. "Yes, I'd like that."

When he looked back at Cami before following the pastor into his office, Josh couldn't read her expression, but he hoped that somehow she knew he was doing this for her. For them.

Shocked was the only word Cami could find to describe how she'd felt when she'd walked out of the pastor's office and seen Josh standing there. It had been an emotionally intense session with the pastor and his wife. This was the second time she'd met with them. She'd been a bit apprehensive the first session, not sure what to expect from the couple. She'd braced herself for judgment and condemnation, but instead found them to be very supportive and understanding. Even more encouraging had been finding out that Susan, the pastor's wife, had counseled others like herself, who had chosen abortion at some point in their past.

With her level of comfort rising, Cami had revealed more about her past to them this time around. It had left her feeling raw and vulnerable, so to walk out and see Josh had completely taken her off-guard. Was he there for counseling, too? Or was it just a quick chat with the pastor about something else? He'd been involved with the church for several months now, so it was entirely possible that it was just him stopping by for a chat. But the way he'd looked at her...

"Do you want to set up another appointment now?" Alena asked.

Cami turned her focus to the young woman sitting behind the desk. The same woman she'd seen Josh interacting with at the service the Sunday before Christmas. She had no reason—or right—to feel jealous, but it was there nonetheless. This young woman probably didn't come with a tenth of the baggage Cami did. What man wouldn't choose to be with a nice, uncomplicated woman who just happened to be attractive and talented?

She sighed as she nodded. "Any time after the first of the year. I think it's going to be busy the rest of the week with Jessa's wedding stuff."

After they settled on a date, Cami thanked Susan and left the church. The day was bright without a cloud in the sky, but the temperature had plunged overnight. She pulled her scarf tight around her neck and shoved her hands into her gloves. One of these days she'd remember to do stuff like that *before* she left whatever building she was in.

Back at the manor, Cami found Michelle in the kitchen with Amy and Bethany, but none of her sisters were around.

"Hey, Cami!" Amy said with a big smile when she spotted her. "We're making supper tonight. My mom told Jessa that she gets a break."

"That's great. What's on the menu?" Cami had tried to act

normal with Josh's family, even though she sensed their curiosity every time she was around them. "It smells delicious."

"Beef stew," Michelle said. "And fresh bread bowls."

"Sounds as good as it smells. Do you need help?"

Michelle shook her head. "With the girls' help I've got this under control. You get a break, too."

"Thank you," Cami said. "I think I'm going to practice for the wedding. Do you know where Jessa and the others are?"

"I haven't seen Laurel or Violet, but I think Jessa and Lance went into town. Lily's boyfriend picked her up a bit ago."

"Well, if anyone is looking for me, just point them in the direction of the chapel."

She went up to her room to change into something more comfortable. Not happy she had to bundle up to walk the few yards to the chapel, Cami knew she wouldn't be ready to practice if she didn't. A blast of wind greeted her as she stepped out onto the back porch. Thankfully, the path from the house to the chapel had been well shoveled, so she had no trouble getting to the building.

Lance had showed her earlier how to turn up the heat that was left at a low setting while the building wasn't being used. Wishing she had the nerve to try to start a fire, Cami made a couple of laps around the pews while listening to some of the songs she was considering. After the third time, the room felt sufficiently warm to take off her jacket and scarf.

She sat down at the piano and began to play and sing a couple of her favorite songs to warm up. With so much going on over the past week, she hadn't been able to get much music in, so instead of going right into practicing, Cami found herself singing some of the songs from her repertoire. No longer as comfortable with some of the suggestive lyrics of some of them, she moved into Christmas carols and then tried to pick out the melodies of the hymns and Gospel songs she'd been listening to lately.

Once again, the music soothed her and settled the emotions that had been brought to the surface by the session with the pastor and his wife. She knew that Violet hiked when she was in need of solace. Jessa turned to her plants, and Laurel had always found cooking or baking to help her. Lily didn't seem to have found that one thing yet like her older sisters had, but perhaps she hadn't needed it as much as Cami and the others. From what she'd heard, by the time Lily reached her teens, Gran was less involved in her life than she'd been with the older four. If that was the case, Cami was glad for her.

But for her, music was the one thing guaranteed to calm her down. As she ran her fingers up and down the keys, picking out an unknown melody, Cami wondered if one day she would no longer need that calming. Shouldn't God be the thing that now brought her peace? Just another unknown for her, but hopefully something she'd discover as she continued along. For now, she would begin to learn more of the songs that talked about God and the peace and joy He gave.

"Hey, Mom," Josh said as he shoved his gloves into the pockets of his jacket. "Smells good!"

"Beef stew for supper." His mom pulled him down to press a kiss to his cheek. "Hope you're hungry."

"Starving. How much longer?" He glanced around and saw that none of the Collingsworth sisters were present.

"I told everyone six, so just over an hour." She patted his stomach. "Think you can last that long?"

Josh grinned at her. "Maybe. But in the meantime, I have something else I need to do. That is, if you don't need my help."

"Everything is basically ready to go, and whatever's left Amy and Beth can help me with."

"Good. Now, can you tell me if Cami's around?"

Chapter Eighteen

HIS mom's eyes widened briefly. He thought for a moment she might ask what he wanted with her, but instead she said, "She went to the chapel to practice for the wedding."

"Thanks." This time Josh bent to press a quick kiss to the top of her head. "We'll be back for supper."

He went out the front door because it was where he'd left his boots and then circled around the house to the path leading to the chapel. When he reached the front doors, he opened them slowly, not wanting to interrupt her. He noticed as he stepped into the foyer that the doors to the sanctuary were closed, but he could hear muted piano playing from inside. He tapped the snow from his boots and shrugged out of his jacket before carefully opening the door and peering inside.

Josh felt a sense of déjà vu as he saw Cami seated at the piano, playing and singing, though this time he'd sought her out purposefully. He slipped into the sanctuary and let the door fall shut behind him. When she didn't turn around, he settled into the last row and rested his arms on the back of the pew in front of him. It felt right to be here with her. This place held both a spiritual and romantic atmosphere. It was a perfect blending that Josh wanted to be able to achieve with Cami.

If she would give him a chance.

It was then that he heard his own voice along with Cami's and the piano. Curious, he watched as she worked her way through the song that played from an electronic device resting on the piano and realized that this was how she learned new songs.

Hearing her work to learn one of the songs he'd sung so long ago grabbed at his heart. And the words and melody began to work themselves up from where he'd buried them so deeply. He bent his head until it rested on his arms. As he listened to himself sing, he mourned for the man he'd been then. He'd been so sure of his future, not even suspecting the fall that was to come. Though he'd thought himself a strong Christian, the true strength of his faith had been revealed when he'd given in to the temptation that had come his way.

A wonderful Savior is Jesus my Lord,

He taketh my burden away,

He holdeth me up and I shall not be moved,

He giveth me strength as my day.

For the first time in a very long time, Josh felt confident in the words of that hymn, humming along with Cami as she sang the chorus.

He hideth my soul in the cleft of the rock,

That shadows a dry, thirsty land;

He hideth my life in the depths of His love,

And covers me there with His hand.

As she began the last verse of the song, along with him and his quartet, Josh stood and walked down the center aisle of the sanctuary. He'd followed this path once before, but this time he hoped there would be a different outcome.

She still hadn't noticed him, so when she began to sing the chorus of the song once again, he joined her. Her head lifted as he came to stand beside the piano. She kept her eyes on him as they finished the song.

Josh smiled at her. "I wish you felt as comfortable singing with the real me as you do the recorded version."

Her cheeks flushed as she reached out to touch the screen of her phone and stop the song as it began again. "I figured I needed to start learning a new set of songs. Yours were a good place to start."

He stared at her for a long moment, drinking in the sight of her. For days now he'd been trying to avoid looking at her as she'd requested. But as she sat before him now, he couldn't look away. There was a deeper vulnerability than he'd seen in her before. He hoped that she saw something similar when she looked at him.

"Can we talk?"

Her eyes narrowed briefly but then she nodded. He wasn't sure it was the best move, but he wanted to get close to her, so she had to look at him and really see his heart. He approached the piano bench and, as he neared, Cami scooted to the other end of it. Thankfully, it was a bench that was big enough for two people. He straddled one end, and she tucked one leg up under her and turned toward him.

"First, let me ask you this. Have you given up on me? On us?"

She stared at him. "Was there ever an us?"

"Okay, let me rephrase that. Have you given up on the possibility of an us?" He saw her swallow and then bite her lower lip. Her hesitation concerned him, but he had prepared himself for this. "I know you told me to stay away from you. And if that's what you still want, I'll do it. But will you give me the chance to share some things with you first?"

This time she nodded, though he could still see wariness on her face.

"I was at the church today to get some help. I've come to realize that whatever I've been doing these past nine years, it hasn't been right or healthy. I could say all the right words like I did that night down at the beach with you, but I struggled to really believe them. I felt like God had abandoned me to the consequences of my sins.

"When you came back from California a Christian, it made me face how I'd been living my life spiritually. I was happy for you, but struggling with myself. As long as you weren't a Christian, nothing could happen between us. I'd been taught that from a young age, and I clung to it because I was determined I wouldn't make another mistake that so clearly went against what the Bible said. But then when that was no longer an issue, I didn't know what to do. Not because of you and your past, but because of mine."

Cami's brow furrowed, but she didn't say anything.

"I didn't feel worthy of you. I didn't want to fail you like I'd failed Emma. I knew that what you'd gone through had left deep scars, and I hadn't done so well in the past with a woman who had struggles like that. I wasn't sure I could be the man you deserved." Josh swallowed but kept his gaze tight on her beautiful face. "I went to the pastor today, to see if he could give me some guidance. The thought of not even getting a chance to see if God wanted something between us was more than I could bear. The pastor didn't tell me anything that I didn't already know, but he helped me see it in a new light."

When Cami didn't respond, Josh took a deep breath and pressed on. "I was trying to become the perfect man before allowing anything to develop between us. I wanted all of my past to be resolved, all of my struggles to be gone. Only, you weren't waiting around, and that scared me. The pastor told me that I was thinking like a person who was convinced they couldn't become a Christian until they were good enough. None of us can get past our failures and struggles on our own. God doesn't expect us to get through them by ourselves. He is there for each of us, but I also want to be there for you. And for you to be there for me. I want a chance to see if God has something planned for us. Together."

Cami blinked a couple of times. "I'm pretty messed up right now, and I have no idea what I'm doing with my life. Are you sure?"

"I'm sure. I want us to be there for each other as we trust God to help us through what we need to do in order to make peace with our pasts. I know it might not be easy at times, but I'm committed to doing what I must to get to that point. Today was just day one of my counseling with the pastor. I plan to continue on with it."

"I do too," Cami said. "I want to give us a chance. Being with you...you're not like any guy I've ever been around before."

"You're pretty unique yourself," Josh said, his heart lifting at her words. He held out his hand and waited for her to take it. When she did, he gave her hand a tug. "Come here."

Cami slid the short distance until her knees bumped his. Josh released her hand and leaned close, his hands resting on her hips. "Can I hold you?"

Her blue eyes widened as she reached for him. "I thought you'd never ask."

As he gathered her close, Josh knew he would do whatever he needed to in order to make this work with Cami. He just prayed that it really was God's will for them to be together. It felt so right, but he knew it wasn't always wise to trust his feelings. However, until God told him otherwise, he planned to look toward a future with Cami.

Cami watched as Lily preceded her down the aisle of the sanctuary. When her turn came she took slow, measured steps toward the front where Lance waited with his groomsmen. Josh, as best man, stood next to Lance. Both men had big smiles on their faces, but Cami had eyes only for Josh. With so much going on for the wedding, they'd hardly had any time to spend together. And when they were together, there had always been plenty of other people around too, so there was no chance to talk.

But after she crawled into bed, Josh had called her. The first night had been a bit awkward, but each night had gotten a little easier and now the conversation flowed unrestrained between them. She was learning what made him laugh and had been pleased to see his smile coming much more easily since their talk in the chapel. And knowing that the smile he wore now was only for her warmed Cami's heart.

Today, however, was for Lance and Jessa. So after giving him a wink and a smile, she turned her gaze to the back of the chapel where her sister appeared. Her long dress flowed softly around her tall, elegant frame. She'd chosen a dress in ivory that complimented her hair and skin. The tulle and organza of the dress gave Jessa an almost ethereal appearance. Her auburn curls hung free beneath the lace veil she wore.

Cami glanced at Lance and saw the dazed look on his face as he watched his bride move towards him. Once at the front, Jessa took Lance's hand, and they turned toward the pastor. Though she had loved Violet's wedding, this one moved her in ways that one hadn't. Cami knew it was because the state of her own heart had changed since then. Not just with regards to Josh, but she now understood the spiritual significance of the words the pastor spoke.

As they said their vows, Cami prayed that she might one day have a chance to exchange vows with Josh. When it was time for them to light the unity candle, Cami moved to the piano and then, surprising everyone there, Josh picked up another mic. Their first duet together was a love song that was as much for them as it was for Lance and Jessa.

Cami just hoped that in spite of the ups and downs that no doubt lay ahead of them, they would find themselves together forever.

Chapter Nineteen

ONE *year later*

Josh worked hard to curb his impatience even though he really did want to get on the road. Knowing how important this day was to Cami and her sisters though, he settled back in his chair with a smile. They still had time to get to the airport before their flight left. He was just really excited about this trip.

Benjamin sat in his high chair, a slightly bewildered expression on his face as he looked at the small bear shaped cake sitting in front of him. Everyone had a phone or camera pointed at the little boy.

"C'mon, baby," Laurel encouraged. "Taste the cake!"

Instead of touching it, the little guy just looked at the people surrounding him. When Rose approached his chair, he suddenly broke into a big grin and reached for the young girl.

"Benji, it's yummy," Rose told him. She dipped the tip of her finger in the icing and touched it to his lips. His little tongue darted out as he lifted a fist to press it against his mouth. It seemed he got a taste and realized it really was tasty as Rose had promised.

He lowered his hand leaving a smear of frosting across his face. This time he reached out and grabbed the ear of the bear. Everyone cheered as he got it into his mouth, smearing even more icing across his face. After that, it didn't take too long for Benji to completely demolish the cake with the help of his sister.

Once the cake was over, Laurel whisked the little boy off to clean him up. He'd already opened all his presents, so his aunts spent the time cleaning up wrapping paper and persuading his dad and uncles to help undo the securely fastened toys. Josh allowed himself to be talked into figuring out how to free a large truck from the cardboard packaging it was connected to.

By the time Benji toddled back with his mother, only one of them had been successful. The others were still muttering under their breath as they cut yet another piece of plastic strapping.

"I know you guys need to leave, Cami," Jessa said as she placed a hand on Lance's shoulder. "But we'd like to share some news before you go."

Josh waited for one of the sisters to blurt out the obvious announcement, but surprisingly, none of them said anything, just stared at their sister in anticipation.

Lance pulled Jessa down into his lap, both of them beaming. "We're excited to announce that in six months, Benji and Rose will have another cousin!"

Immediately all the sisters converged on Jessa and Lance. Violet moved a little more slowly because of the bulk of her own pregnant body. Last Josh had heard she was due sometime in the next month. It was a bit like an epidemic. Thankfully it wasn't something he and Cami had to worry about just yet. They had a few things to do before a baby could join their family.

As his gaze landed on the woman he loved, Josh couldn't

help smiling. This last year had been one of the best of his life, even though it had had some very low points as well. They had weathered a lot together as they'd worked through their own personal struggles. His smiled faded a bit at the memory of the break up they'd had just two months earlier.

She'd been focused on working on their relationship, and his focus had slipped to their music. He'd begun to arrange more performances, and more and more of their time together had revolved around the music they were now creating together. He tried to get her to see that it was necessary if they wanted to build a ministry out of their music. He'd been devastated when she'd told him that if all he wanted was a music partner, he could find someone else.

It had been a frustrating, heartbreaking week as he'd tried to get her to understand that he was trying to plan a future for them. She refused to talk to him beyond saying that their future was more than just music. Her refusal to consider his point of view had infuriated him at first, but after a couple of straight talks with Lance and the pastor, he'd realized that by neglecting their personal relationship, he was telling Cami that her importance to him was only in her talent.

He was grateful that she'd given him a second chance. It had taken a lot of talking, some groveling and the promise to cut back on the performances for a bit. He still itched to make bigger strides with their music, but he knew that Cami needed to move more slowly. Though he'd struggled with it during that week they were apart, the pastor had reinforced with him the importance of building a strong personal foundation for the two of them. The music would always be there, but nothing would succeed if they didn't keep God and each other at the forefront of their relationship. Faced with the prospect of losing Cami...again...Josh knew he really needed to start learning from his mistakes.

Once the women had moved from around Lance, Josh set the toy he'd finally freed onto the floor and stood. He gave his cousin a big hug. "Congrats, cuz. You're going to make a great dad."

"I sure hope so, but I'm more than a little scared."

Josh grinned. "Well, you have a couple of people you can go to for advice. Although Dean looks a little scared himself, whenever he talks about the coming baby."

"You just wait," Lance told him. "Your turn will come one day."

Josh hoped so, although it was something he didn't think too much about. He wasn't sure he'd be able to get excited about a pregnancy after what happened with Emma. He'd always thought once you made it past the first trimester that it should be smooth sailing, but that hadn't been the case. He wasn't going to be able to get excited about a baby until he held the little body in his arms and saw that it was alive and well.

"Guess we'd better be going," Cami said as she came up beside him.

Josh slipped his arm around her waist, drawing her against him. "Yep. You ready?"

She nodded. "My bags are by the front door."

"Okay. You can say your goodbyes while I load them up." Josh bent and gave her a quick kiss before heading for the door.

It didn't take long to put her bags into his truck. Cami came out onto the porch as he closed the back door. He had started it up so it would be a little warmer before they headed out.

"Give us a call when you get there," Jessa said as she hugged Cami. "I hope your concert goes wonderfully."

"Thanks. I appreciate any and all prayers."

After hugging her other sisters, Cami came down the steps to where Josh waited. He opened the door and helped her up into the cab of the truck. After she was settled, he shut the door and headed around the front of the truck to the driver's side, lifting a hand in farewell as he went.

As he headed around the driveway, Josh honked the horn once. They would only be gone a little over a week, but it felt like a much longer trip.

He glanced over at Cami as he turned onto the highway. "You okay?"

"Just nervous."

"You'll do great," he assured her with a smile. "But if you like, we can practice on our way to the airport."

Cami nodded and set up their music using the truck's stereo system. Of all the things they did together, singing was near the top of the list of favorites for Josh. To him, the way their voices blended was so reminiscent of how their lives had blended over the past year. And this trip was just the first, he hoped, of many to come.

Cami stood on the stage in front of the microphone, gnawing on her lower lip as she waited for the sound check to begin. She had never been so nervous about performing before, but this was different from the small churches they'd been in over the past few months. There had also been more publicity for this concert than for any of their others.

This was a huge church, the church Josh's family had been a part of for many years. There were no doubt people there who had known Emma, who knew everything that had happened with Josh.

She glanced over at Josh, frowning a little with irritation. He didn't seem nervous at all. In fact, he'd been a bundle of excitement since even before they'd left Collingsworth. Once on the ground in Dallas, they'd been going non-stop. Cami felt like she was one step away from falling apart, but Josh seemed totally unaware. All she wanted was an hour with just the two of them and some peace and quiet to calm things down.

These past couple of days had been reminiscent of the time right before their breakup. His focus had gone completely from her to their music. She didn't want that to happen again. She needed him to be able to see that she needed the focus on their relationship to stay strong. Without that, they had no music.

"Cami?"

Cami looked up at Josh's impatient tone. She just stared at him, willing him to see what she needed. When she didn't say anything, she saw his eyes narrow briefly then he crossed the stage to where she stood.

"I'm sorry," he said as he pulled her into his arms.

The tense breath Cami had been holding rushed out as she slid her arms around his waist. "I know we have to do this now, but can we have some time, just the two of us, later?"

Josh looked down and tilted her chin up with a finger. "Yes. I promise. Let's get through this, and we'll take some time for us before the performance tonight, okay?"

"I'm sorry. I just feel a bit overwhelmed."

"It's okay." Josh pressed a kiss to her lips. "I forget that you're not used to this like I am. Remind me of that if I forget again. Okay?"

Cami smiled at him. "I will."

"Ready?" he asked as he loosened his embrace.

Cami nodded and took her place once again behind the mic, her nerves calmed a bit.

The church was packed that night, and Cami's nerves returned in full force. As he'd promised, Josh had taken her out to eat, just the two of them, before they returned to the church for the concert. It had been what she'd needed, and she was glad he'd been willing to do it for her, for them.

This concert was a Christmas-themed one with a few Gospel songs thrown in, including one they'd written together. Part of their concerts had included short testimonies from each of them. Josh was definitely more comfortable than she was in front of a crowd. She never would have suspected it since he'd been so reserved when they first met. But he was in his element singing and talking with people. Cami was getting more used to it, but the testimony part was still something she struggled through. This was what she'd dreamed of for years, but now that it was finally a reality, she couldn't understand why it didn't come easier. She could perform in a bar full of patrons, but a church full of people was something altogether new for her.

One of the other difficult things about performing and meeting all these new people was that she found there were some of the fans who assumed that because they weren't married, Josh was fair game. Josh never encouraged them and always made it clear that he was with Cami, but lately she'd begun to wonder if he'd ever propose. They'd never discussed marriage much, though she knew they were both in it for the long haul. It just didn't make any sense for them to keep on this way, particularly if they were going to be traveling. This long distance trip had worked because they were staying with his family, but it wouldn't be practical if they were to go to places where they didn't know anyone.

Cami knew they'd needed this last year to strengthen themselves, their relationships with God, and with each other. Even the breakup had helped them. She knew Josh was the only one she wanted to be with, but if he didn't pop the question soon, she would be the one doing the proposing.

"Let's pray, babe."

Cami glanced over to see Josh standing beside her. He looked so handsome in his dark gray suit with dark green tie. She also wore a green silk blouse over her straight black skirt and heels. She slid her arm around his waist and rested her head on his chest while he prayed.

"Bless our performances here, Father," Josh said as he concluded the prayer. "In Jesus' name. Amen." He bent to give her a kiss. "This is gonna be great."

Cami wasn't one hundred percent sure she agreed with

him, but holding his hand, she followed him out onto the stage to loud applause.

Once they got past the first couple of songs, Cami found herself relaxing and enjoying it like Josh had said. The sharing of their testimonies was more emotional than usual because of Josh's history with the church, and Cami could see people wiping their eyes after he was done. She was very proud of him for sharing so openly with people, not making excuses for anything, just sharing about God's love and grace.

As he finished his testimony, the lights dimmed to just highlight them on the stage. Cami wondered if she'd forgotten this part of the program. She looked over to see Josh hold out his hand toward her. Without hesitation, she took it and allowed him to draw her to him to stand in front of the microphone.

"It was July last year that I met Cami for the first time. I'll be honest, the first couple of weeks of our acquaintance weren't exactly positive. When I said goodbye to her when she left for California a few weeks after meeting, I knew she had become very important to me even in that short time, but had no idea how God would work it out. As she shared earlier, she wasn't a Christian then, and I was definitely struggling.

"Somehow God saw fit to bring us back together after she gave her heart to Him. At that time, He also revealed to me that my heart wasn't as it should be. We've spent the past year not just working on our music, but on our relationships with God and each other." Josh glanced down at her, and Cami felt her breath catch in her lungs. "I never thought God would bless me with a second chance, but He has. I love this woman and am so thankful that God brought her into my life. Tonight, in front of so many of you who have prayed for and supported me over the years, I would like to ask her a question."

Cami lifted a hand to her mouth. Her heart pounded as she watched Josh go down on one knee. Tears blurred her eyes as she looked at him. And if she'd ever wondered about his love for her, there was no doubting it now. "Oh, Josh."

He released her hand long enough to pull a small box from his pocket. With a flick of his thumb, he opened it and pulled out a dainty ring. He slid the box back into his pocket and reached for her hand again. Cami was sure he could feel it trembling. Her whole body was.

"Camilla Rose Collingsworth, I love you and want to serve God with you by my side. Would you do me the honor of becoming my wife?"

There was no way Cami could talk past the tightness of her throat, but she managed to nod vigorously. Josh slipped the ring onto her finger and then stood to gather her into his arms.

"I love you, babe," he whispered in her ear.

"Oh, Josh," Cami said when her throat finally loosened. "I love you, too."

After the concert, there was a long line of well-wishers eager to offer their congratulations. Josh kept Cami close to his side as they greeted people. Once the crowd had thinned out a bit, Amy came scurrying to find them, a wide grin on her face.

"Were you surprised?" she asked.

"I don't think it's possible for me to have been more surprised." Cami laughed. "Did you know?"

Amy gave an enthusiastic nod. "But Josh threatened me with bodily harm if I said anything."

Michelle and Doug found them and also offered their congratulations along with hugs. "Welcome to the family, sweetheart," Michelle said. "I was beginning to wonder when Josh was going to come to his senses!"

Warmth flooded Cami's heart. Never in a million years had she imagined being part of a family like the one she had with her sisters and now with Josh.

They were among the last to leave the building, and as they walked out into the cool, but not frigid temperatures, Josh said, "Mom, we'll be home a little bit later. I think we need a little us time."

"Sure thing, son. You know where the spare key is."

Taking her hand, Josh led her to the car they'd rented. Once inside, he didn't start it right away. Both of them just sat there. Cami felt it was kind of a stunned silence, but then she reached out and took his hand. "Regrets already?"

Josh's head jerked around. "What? No. Never."

"Good, because there's no backing out now," Cami told him. She leaned forward, slipping her hand around his neck, and pressed her lips to his. As his hand cupped her cheek, their kiss deepened, and Cami moved to get closer to him.

They'd been careful to not let themselves get into a situation that would be hard to get out of, but, given that both had past physical relationships, it had sometimes been a challenge not to cross that line. But they'd resisted.

Josh ended the kiss and move back a little. "We're too close now to give in. I want us to start our marriage off right. I love you to death, babe, but you're too much of a temptation like this. Let's go get some ice cream."

Cami laughed, pressed one more quick kiss to his lips and settled back in her seat. "Okay. Ice cream it is. But just so you know, I think we've waited long enough. I'm not interested in a long engagement."

In the brightness from the streetlight above the car, Cami saw Josh look at her and wink. "Oh, I agree. One hundred percent."

The End

OTHER TITLES AVAILABLE BY

Kimberly Rae Jordan
(*Christian Romances*)

Marrying Kate

Faith, Hope & Love

Waiting for Rachel (*Those Karlsson Boys: 1*)
Worth the Wait (*Those Karlsson Boys: 2*)
The Waiting Heart (*Those Karlsson Boys: 3*)

Home Is Where the Heart Is (*Home to Collingsworth: 1*)
Home Away From Home (*Home to Collingsworth: 2*)
Love Makes a House a Home (*Home to Collingsworth: 3*)
The Long Road Home (*Home to Collingsworth: 4*)
Her Heart, His Home (*Home to Collingsworth: 5*)
Coming Home (*Home to Collingsworth: 6*)

A Little Bit of Love:
A Collection of Christian Romance Short Stories

For more details on the availability of these titles, please go to

www.KimberlyRaeJordan.com

Contact

Please visit Kimberly Rae Jordan on the web!
Website: www.kimberlyraejordan.com
Facebook: www.facebook.com/AuthorKimberlyRaeJordan
Twitter: twitter.com/Kimberly Jordan

Made in the USA
Monee, IL
01 December 2021